THE ACADEMY GAMES

AMBER PAIGE

*To my fellow perfectionists: you have fire in your veins, summon it,
and let chaos reign.*

TRIGGER WARNINGS

Bullying, mental abuse, parental abandonment, anxiety, violence, and blood.

PRONUNCIATION GUIDE

Ayra: Eye-ra

Ryne: Ri-ne

Cadie: Kay-dee

Machiis: Ma-kai-is

Traquore: Tray-core

CREATURE GUIDE

Adoring: Resembles a sparrow, loves compliments.

Astoria: Resemble shire horses, their manes, bodies, and hooves are four times the size compared to a regular stallion. Their coats are luminescent like stars.

Charming bird: Tiny, looks like a songbird.

Gifaray (gif-ar-a): Looks like a giraffe, medium-sized nose, two furry horns, and as tall as an oak tree.

Lapwrin: Has a mouse nose, long whiskers, and floppy ears.

Prowler: Panther-like creature with sharp fangs like a sabretooth.

Raspie: Very small, resembles a puff of fur.

AYRA'S PLAYLIST

Spells—Cannons
W.I.T.C.H—Devon Cole
. . . Ready For It?—Taylor Swift
Chronically Cautious—Braden Bales
How Villains Are Made—Madalen Duke
Daylight—Tayor Swift
I Don't Care—Katherine Li
The Man—Taylor Swift
Bad Guy—Billie Eilish
Panic Room—Au/Ra
Eat Your Young—Hozier
Mean (Taylor's Version)—Taylor Swift
DANCING ALL ALONE—Clinton Kane
Midnight Rain—Taylor Swift

RYNE'S PLAYLIST

Nice To Meet Ya—Niall Horan
Someone to You—BANNERS
Skin and Bones—David Kushner
Adore You—Harry Styles
This Is How You Fall In Love—Jeremy Zuker, Cutler
Wonder—Shawn Mendes
Lost In The Wild—WALK THE MOON
In The Stars—Benson Boone
She Looks So Perfect—5 Seconds of Summer
I'll Be Waiting—Cian Ducrot
Heaven—Niall Horan
Oh My Love—The Score
Black and White—Niall Horan
You Are The Reason—Calum Scott

SPOTIFY LINK

Some people define witches by their magic. Others define us as nothing more than chaos-wielding magicians. When in reality, only a few chosen souls can harness such power. Witches and wizards alike are gifted beyond any world's understanding. The masters say no one is perfect in understanding the elemental arts, crafting potions, or writing charms.

I say otherwise.

We are gifted for a reason. Perfection is the only way one can truly control one's power, and it's what witches and wizards should strive for. Anything less is an insult.

This is why I'm at the top of my class. Fraydora Academy for Witches is not for the faint of heart. Just because it looks pretty and grand on the outside doesn't mean the classes aren't brutal and grueling. Only the best of the best are accepted into this academy. Anyone who attends this institution should be proud of themselves. That doesn't mean you get to slack off though. Perfection is key, remember?

I'm walking along the cobblestone path adjacent to the West Wing. With each step I take, the grounds change from neatly trimmed shrubs and precariously placed seasonal flowers to untamed vines and overgrown greenery. The West Wing is where earth magic, herbology, and animal care are studied. Personally, I'm more of an East Wing kind of gal. There, the halls are crystalized and lit by an unknown fire source. The wind smells of calming eucalyptus, and the suns' light is so dim, you can see sparkles of sorcery in the air.

"What's she doing here?" Two feminine voices come from down the hall.

My azure robe whirls behind me as I stride farther down the pathway, my boots clack against the ground, and my shoulder-length chestnut hair that's tied back sways as I near the two younger witches.

"Shouldn't you be in class?" I ask them with a raised eyebrow.

I don't stop to ensure they scurry off. There's no need. They know who I am: someone not to be messed with.

I'm not a figure of authority. If a stranger looked at me, they would see an upperclassman witch. But those who roam these halls know otherwise.

I take my classes seriously. I don't talk unless spoken to, and friends were never my thing. Because of this, I was labeled a stickler, someone to be wary of. Which is fine. I'm not here to make friends. I'm here to master my craft and change the world itself.

Their footsteps fade as I round the bend, facing the door to the professor I'm aiming to see. I gently tap along the withered oak door and wait for a response.

"Come in."

The door creaks open as I turn the handle. Professor Floris

teaches potions and herbology. She has the vibes I would suspect a grandmother would have. She's gentle and soft-spoken, and she has this little ingredient and recipe book she carries around with her.

"Ayra, just the young lady I was hoping to see." Her ivy-green eyes flicker as a smile creeps along her expression.

"Is everything okay, Professor?"

Even though I'm a seventh-year student, I opted to take her advanced potions class, partly because doing so would help me prepare for the games this year. The other part is because I enjoy being around her. She emits a comforting aura that can make anyone feel safe. I would be lying if I said it didn't affect me just as much as the next person.

"Everything is fine, Ms. Brightheart. I was given the plea-sure of awarding you with some wonderful news." Her silver curls bounce as she walks toward me.

"Are you about to tell me what I hope you're about to tell me?" I can't fight my hopeful smile.

"Ms. Brightheart, congratulations. You were chosen out of sixty final-year witches to take part in the annual competition against Traquore Academy. Only twenty witches were chosen, and between you and me,"—she beckons me closer and lowers her tone—"You were the first name the headmistress declared."

My heart soars out of my chest, through the roof, and into the stars. This has been a day in the making since I was four-teen. Once I discovered what the games were, I knew it was my destiny.

Every year, final-year witches from Fraydora Academy face off against wizards from Traquore Academy. The games are different each year. They vary from potion crafting, spell writ-ing, scavenger hunts, broom riding, beast taming, and more.

The winning collegiate school is granted prestige and valor, and the witch or wizard, to claim such honor for their academy, is gifted a scholarship to whichever institution they wish to attend to pursue their mastery. Since my first year, I've worked hard, earning nothing but As or higher. I drove myself to the highest standard because magic deserves nothing less.

"Thank you, Professor Floris." I wrap my arms around her and squeal in delight.

"It'll be an absolute honor getting to watch you compete, Ayra." She pats my back and grins as I pull away. "Make sure you show those wizards who's boss."

No matter the world you reside in, one thing is always the same: men think they are superior to women. Even in magical realms, women are looked down upon. If you need a potion for mending a broken bone, ask a wizard first. If you need a spell written to rearrange the stars, the wizards are the way to go.

I call rubbish.

Magic coursed through the veins of women first. We were blessed by the moon herself. The tides flow in our favor, fire burns in our cells, the earth shudders under our feet, and the air bends to our will. The narrative changed the moment a male was gifted. Since then, witches have been second class to wizards. It doesn't matter that we've won more games. It doesn't matter if our test scores skyrocket beyond theirs or if our magic levels increase daily. Today's world only cares that wizards are men, plain and simple.

"I'll make you and this academy proud, Professor. I promise."

They've done so much for me. Winning is the least I can do for them. I'll show them it wasn't all for nothing.

The suns shine a little brighter back in the hallway. I stroll down the path with my head held high. Ignoring the lingering whispers and stares as classes are dismissed is easy. I just got the best news of my life, and no one can take that away from me.

"Brightheart!"

Okay, maybe one person can.

I turn on my heels and plaster a fake grin on my face. "Cadie, how are you?"

Cadie Blackwell, former best friend, current academic rival. We weren't always at war with one another, but years can change a person, and while I miss our friendship, I don't like the person she's become. Cadie is always either right behind or right ahead of me in terms of our studies. Her parents are one of the wealthiest couples this realm has ever known. They donated the entire North Wing to the academy a century ago.

Her ebony curls bounce with every step she takes. The overwhelming scent of lavender floods my nostrils when she stands before me, and I stare into her violet eyes.

"Looks like we both got some good news today," she says while flashing her unnaturally perfect teeth. Her white fluffy-tailed ferret familiar, Venus, is curled around her neck like a scarf.

"Congratulations." I meet her singsong tone with one of my own, putting on a strong front. "When did you find out? Professor Floris told me ten minutes ago."

Her lips drop into a scowl.

One for Ayra, zero for Cadie.

"Aw, too bad. Don't worry, I'm sure the news must have gotten to you late."

"You won't be so chipper when I wipe the floor with you. You'll be out on day one," she hisses.

The wind around us stills, muffled voices float in one ear and out the other.

"Maybe we should focus on beating the wizards. After that,

we can worry about who's wiping the floor with whom, okay?" I wink at her before spinning around to head to my next class.

"Day one, you hear me!?"

I raise my hand and wave my fingers. "See you in Extinction of Creatures class, Cadie," I call over my shoulder with a smug look on my face.

The witches chosen to participate in the games are excused from classes to prepare a week in advance. Even though I've been preparing since I was fourteen, I don't want to waste a second of time. With only one day before the wizards arrive at Fraydora, I need to take advantage of the quiet while I still can.

The corridor before the library expands with each step I take. The walls swell to make room for the vast space ahead. I admire the gray brick and the vines crawling up the stone, sprouting tiny crimson flowers. The lights that float above me dance and sway in the breeze. I'll never tire of witnessing magic at work. There are no words that can genuinely describe how beautiful the unknown is. And the smell? Magic smells differently for everyone. To me, it smells like burnt orange and cedar. I can always sense and smell magic, solely because it's always on my mind.

It's not a secret that I'm an orphan. My parents dropped me off at the academy doors when I was an hour old. The academy accepted me and helped raise me into who I am today. I lived here under the care of the professors for five years until I was of age to start my primary education. Then, I returned seven years ago to attend the academy. Still, someone within these corridors was always looking after me. Magic always protected me.

The grand, carved chestnut doors open on their own as I approach them. The room expands, swallowing me whole the second I walk across the threshold. With two steps forward, I place my hands on the balcony's rail and take a deep breath. Old books, yellowed pages, and parchment that hasn't been touched in centuries whirl my senses. My eyes lock onto the massive tree that grows in the center of the room. Along its branches and leaves are tiny speckles of light that bounce and twirl aimlessly. The amount of resource material this room holds is a mystery. No one has lived long enough to log everything. Which is saying a lot, given that witches and wizards tend to live past five hundred years old. The room itself documents history, spells, and new and updated potion crafting. There is no need for a librarian; simply ask the room what you're looking for, and it'll answer.

I descend the staircase that curves to the left and make my way to my secret cove. I'm feeling a little rusty on lunar phases and crystals. I need to ensure I'm in tip-top shape for this next week and a half.

"Library, may I please have resource material on lunar phases?" I ask while settling down in a chair by the window that overlooks the courtyard. A hard-bound copy of the lunar encyclopedia floats in on a breeze and lands softly in my palms. "Thank you," I whisper with a smile.

All right, let's do this.

The light that filtered through the window two hours ago is long gone. I close the book and rub my strained eyes. There's a reason I'm more proficient in elemental magic. The moon is too mysterious for me.

I place the book on the chair I was sitting in and stretch. Just as I'm about to leave, the floorboards creak in the distance. I scan the room around me, only to find dimly lit, empty chairs and silent, empty nooks.

"Hello?" I call out.

Silence fills my ears.

With one step forward, I stop. "Is someone there?"

Is Cadie messing with me? She and her cronies love scaring me.

"I know someone's there." With another step forward, my shoulders loosen as a gray and white tabby trots over to me. "Kikimara, where have you been? A familiar is supposed to stay by their witch's side, you know." I can't help but grin as Kiki closes the space between us. "Having adventures without me again?" I hold out my arms, letting her jump into my embrace.

Kiki found me, not the other way around, which I'm told is unusually rare. The day after I was dropped off at the academy's door, Kiki showed up. The professors love retelling this story, so I have it memorized.

To this day, the professors who were here when Kiki arrived are still baffled. Somehow, Kiki knocked on the door. Yes, she *knocked* on the larger-than-life door and waited for someone to answer. The very second the door creaked open, Kiki jolted down the hall and made all the right turns to my room. When she found me, she cuddled along my right side and refused to leave.

No one knows how old Kiki is. Familiars live as long as they have to. Some even roam the realms after their partner passes, moving on to the next witch or wizard in need. I scratch under her chin, releasing a mixture of white and storm-gray fur into the air.

"Ready for bed? We have a big day tomorrow."

Kiki meows in response.

While I don't plan on socializing with the wizards, I have to meet them. Every witch is to dress in their formal gowns and present an amicable front. It's tradition to have a little meet and greet over dinner. Because sure, let's make friends before we face off in a tireless battle of wit and skill.

"Let's go, silly girl. And no more journeys without me, I miss you when you're gone." I kiss the top of her head and make my way back to my room.

Even though Fraydora is spacious, we have to share a room with at least one other witch. Thankfully, my roommate doesn't get under my skin.

I step through the door and sigh in relief when Marley turns around with two cups of tea.

"Are you ready for tomorrow?"

Her familiar, Zachii, a lime green lizard, pops out of her straight silver hair that's pulled back in a messy bun.

"As I'll ever be."

Kiki leaps out of my arms and gets cozy on my bed.

We did a great job making our little room feel like home. We placed mismatched rugs along the cool stone floor. Plants and lit torches line the walls and ceiling. Any touch of free space is occupied by a book or empty potion bottle.

"You're going to do great, and I'll be in the crowd cheering you on."

They say every introvert has an extrovert soulmate; I'm starting to think Marley is that person. We met on boarding day when we discovered whom we were rooming with. Her cheery personality scared me at first because who enjoys waking up at the ass crack of dawn? She weaseled her way into my life any chance she got. She doesn't listen to the whispers or rumors about me. She knows the truth, and I'm glad I have her. I wouldn't have survived my teenage years without her. Who knows what kind of lunatic I would be if she weren't in my life.

Even a lonely witch needs a friend.

"Thank you. Just don't go flirting with all the wizards, okay?" I joke with her, and she offers me a half-smile.

"No promises, Ayra, no promises."

There's a reason the entire campus loves the games. If you're like me, you're excited to participate in the trials and prove yourself to the world. But if you're like Marley, you're excited to see all the guys and sneak around to find secret rooms to fool around in. No judgment from me. We all have our guilty pleasures. I never have, and I don't plan on partaking in that myself. My studies and magic require my utmost attention. No distractions, period.

"Just don't have too much fun," I say as she hands me a cup of tea.

"Without you? *Never*," she teases.

I snicker as my lips meet the rim of the porcelain teacup.

Orange blossom and fresh nectar lull my tension. I sigh as the perfectly warm liquid meets my tongue. "How are you so good at making tea?"

She wriggles her neatly trimmed silver eyebrows at me. "Now, that's a secret I cannot disclose."

I walk over to my bed and pull the curtain back before whispering, "*Changeisia.*"

My day clothes disappear and are replaced with flannel pants and a baggy T-shirt. I plop into bed and grin as my blankets cradle me. "Sleep well, Marley."

"You too, Ayra. Don't let those wizards get the best of you tomorrow."

Kiki snuggles against my right side and chirps in response.

"Yeah, yeah. Between you, Zachii, and Kiki, I don't think I have anything to worry about."

Besides, it's the wizards who need to worry, not me.

3

Traquore Academy is one of the finest magical schools in the realm. It's ranked right below Fraydora Academy for Witches. Magic glimmers off the volcanic black walls like a thousand glinting stars. The floors are ash gray, and torches line the halls, offering light in the naturally dark atmosphere. I thought it was normal, walking the gloomy halls day in and day out. I've never been more wrong.

Fraydora Academy is the definition of beauty. As I step out of the horse-drawn carriage, my jaw drops at the sight before me. The first difference between Traquore and Fraydora is the facade. The brick is light sandstone, and vines with multicolor roses crawl up towers and around the windows. Trimmed hedges and perfectly placed flower beds surround the entire structure. Tiny puff balls, also known as raspies, scurry across the lawn, and charming birds chirp in the trees.

"What are you gawking at?" my best friend, Machiis, asks while bumping into my arm.

Hayes, his familiar, is a hawk and charming bird hybrid. He's perched on his shoulder, scanning the surroundings. I'd be willing to bet Hayes will be soaring through the skies later today. He's itching to spread his shimmering brown-spotted wings.

"Have you *seen* this place?" I ask as I gape over our surroundings.

Machiis's brown eyes wrinkle as he scoffs. "You're impressed?"

"You're not?" I ask with a flabbergasted chuckle.

A group of smiling witches passes by, eyeing us like we're the next target for their bedroom exploits. He follows their movement with a devilish grin.

"I am now," he says with a click of his tongue, and I roll my eyes.

Machiis is a notorious mischief seeker—he always has been. We met one another during our first year of apprentice school. I was getting picked on by a group of wizards for my accent, and he stepped in front of me and threatened to break each and every one of their noses if he caught them talking to me again.

I wasn't born in this realm. I don't come from a typical magical family. Even though both my parents possess magic, I was born in the mortal realm, in England, to be precise. Hence, my accent confuses people. It's not thick, but it is noticeable, and people either love it or hate it.

Machiis and I were dubbed the dynamic duo in school, and it followed us all the way to Traquore. Over the years, though, our friendship has withered. Our likes and differences are becoming apparent. I'm more of a carefree, laidback, fun-seeking wizard. He strives to strengthen his connection to magic every day, and he loves trouble and girls.

"Do me a favor," I whisper as Headmaster Borrick's heavy

footsteps near us. "Leave me out of whatever your mind is calculating."

Machiis winks as Borrick strolls past us. "Let's go, gentlemen. We have an hour before the ceremony starts. I won't have you slacking off!"

After all these years, I've never gotten used to the power in Borrick's voice. I fall in line behind him, observing his broad shoulders and towering stature. The other wizards selected for this year's competition fall into formation, eyes straight ahead, shoulders back.

I can't help but admire the architecture when we pass under the archway as more charming birds fly overhead. I smile to myself as they soar through the halls right to an open courtyard. My familiar, Maren, a fuzzy lapwrin with a mouse-like nose, long whiskers, and big ears, pops out of my pocket and squeaks in excitement.

"I know, we'll explore, don't worry," I whisper.

He holds onto the hem of my jacket pocket with his paws, watching our surroundings in awe, just as I do. I thought the outside was mind-blowing, but somehow, the inside is even more astonishing. With each step we take, the corridors change. We started in a wing as bright as the two suns in the sky. The name Blackwell is engraved into a plaque above a large doorway.

Leaving that wing, we cross into one that slowly becomes overgrown. More animals appear, and wildflowers and snapping trees sway in a gentle breeze. The air smells like magic, with a hint of cinnamon and crisp apples.

"Pay attention, Mr. Gwydion!" Borrick calls without looking over his shoulder.

"I am," I whisper, as the smile grows wider.

Borrick shows us where we are to meet within the next hour, and then we're dismissed. Machiis grabs me along with two of his other friends and leads us to a courtyard with an overgrown oak tree in the center. Tilting my head back to admire the leaves, I have to shield my eyes from the two suns' rays. Miniature butterflies flutter around the tree, sprouting flowers where they land. This place is something out of a dream. That's the only explanation I can think of.

"Ryne!"

I turn around to meet Machiis's mischievous smile. He tosses a Disk of Unyielding up and down, catching it just in time before it hits the ground.

"How did you sneak that in?" I ask with my eyebrow arched.

"Don't worry about it."

We both grin, and with a gentle toss, he whirls the disk at me. I catch it before it rams straight into my chest. These disks weren't banned from Traquore, but many other institutions placed zero-tolerance policies against them. The thing with these disks is even if you toss them as gently as possible, they gain speed within milliseconds, and the longer they're in the air, the stronger they get.

"Hey, boys," a girl with black hair chimes as she approaches us.

I hide the disk behind my back and smile at her.

"Hello there," I greet, but her attention is glued on Machiis.

"Cadie Blackwell?" Machiis smirks, and a teasing sparkle emits from his eyes.

Her curls bounce as she nears us. I take a few steps forward, noticing a few other witches trailing behind her.

"The one and only." Her voice is smooth like velvet.

"How do you two know one another?" I ask.

"Our parents are on the same council. Met this trouble-maker at a ball a few years back," she teases and messes with his hair.

My nose itches from the sudden scent of pure lavender.

"Welcome to Fraydora. What do you think of our campus?" she asks.

"It's magnificent," I admit.

She meets my gaze and smiles, but something about it seems . . . off.

"While Ryne appreciates the architecture, I'm busy with something else," Machiis says in an attempt to flirt.

I have to hold back my groan. He's not the smoothest guy in the world, but somehow, it always works.

"Aren't you adorable?" Her tone is sickly sweet.

Machiis's eyes travel over Cadie's shoulder. I follow his gaze and catch what he's watching, or rather, whom.

"Who's that?" He nods toward the girl strolling down the hall, purpose evident in her light blue eyes and determined body language.

When Cadie notices who we're watching, she grunts in irritation.

"Ayra Brightheart. Stay away from her if you want to keep that disk of yours. You know what, just stay away from her period. She's got a stick up her ass."

I don't acknowledge Cadie. From here, I can see the girl's expression, how her head is held high, but her eyes are on the floor.

"Oh really?" Machiis says as he grabs the disk from my hand.

"What are you doing?" I move to snatch the disk back, but with a slight flick of his wrist, he launches it across the courtyard. "You're an idiot, Machiis."

Deep breaths. In through the nose for five seconds, then release slowly, allowing my shoulders to relax.

Today's the day. I move to stand in front of the floor-length, silver-gilded mirror and nod at myself.

"*Changesis.*"

My comfy clothes disappear, and a formal gown from my closet materializes, starting at the floor and forming all the way to my shoulders. The dress is ebony, but tiny specks of stars that flicker against any source of light line the bodice. I straighten the collar around my neck, letting the cape trail effortlessly down my back. Next, I tug on my sleeves, making sure they're free from creases and wrinkles. The other girls will opt to wear heels or boots, but not me. The flats I've chosen allow me to be ready to run or fight at any given notice, and who knows what will happen with the wizards on campus.

"*Draso.*"

As my whisper floats in the air, my dark, chestnut hair

weaves itself into a braided updo, and I mess with my bangs, making sure they're just right. I observe myself in the mirror, not recognizing the woman before me. My complexion is pale, but my cheeks are always a natural shade of pink. My blue, silver-flecked eyes sparkle in the sun.

With a brief nose wiggle, I sigh.

Here we go.

"Coming, Kiki?"

The lazy cat rolls on her back and yawns.

"Okay, maybe later." With a snicker, I step into the hallway, letting my determination lead the way.

As I stroll down the path on the outskirts of the courtyard, I hear unfamiliar voices. I glance to my right, where a group of witches and wizards intermingle. Another group sits under the oak tree that takes up at least half of the land. Farther down, four wizards, Cadie, and her friends, are dressed in their finest. It doesn't surprise me that Cadie is charming the wizards this early in the game. She always has a trick up her sleeve.

Snake.

I ignore the lot of them. The sooner I get to the Grand Hall, the better. I want to eat, get this meet and greet over with, and then go to bed. I'll get the interview out of the way tomorrow, and then the day after, the real fun begins, and I can't wait.

"Watch out!"

I snap to my right and hold my hands up defensively.

"*Vavido!*" I shout just in time to freeze the chaotic disk from ramming straight into my face.

I drop my hands, letting the toy shatter against the stone below my feet. There's a reason these things are called Disks of Unyielding.

"What were you thinking!?" I snap at the wizard jogging toward me.

His smile is the first thing I notice. It's kind and has a hint of worry. His golden hair is combed back, with one single loose strand resting above his brow. His uniform is refined: a pair of black trousers, a deep forest-green vest, and a cape with gold buttons and chains. His green, amber-speckled eyes wrinkle in the corners as he lets out an airy chuckle.

"Sorry, my friend doesn't know his own strength."

I glance over his shoulder and groan when I see the other three wizards attempting to hide their amused faces.

"I'm Ryne." He extends his hand, and I take it in hesitation.

"Ayra," I mumble.

His smile brightens, twirling a strange emotion deep in my stomach.

"Watch yourselves next time. There's a reason those things are banned here." I drop his hand and look down at the disk.

Raising my fingers and flicking my wrist, I cast a repair spell on the shattered toy. It lifts into the air, and when I drop my hand, the disk falls again, but Ryne catches it in time.

"If someone gets hurt by that thing, I will hear about it. Don't make that mistake twice," I state before carrying on down the tree-covered path.

"See you later!" he calls after me.

What a strange man.

Outside the Grand Hall, I wait for the doors to open. I rest my back against the cool gray stone and close my eyes. A few other witches and wizards arrive. I eavesdrop on their conversations, trying hard not to chuckle at their awkwardness. We don't get the opportunity to meet members of the opposite sex very often, unless we go off academy grounds or during the games. You can definitely tell too.

My lips curve into a cocky smile as I listen to them fumble over words, lose track of where they were going, and their blatant long pauses. Why are we making friends anyway? We'll be facing off against one another soon. What's the point?

"Hello, Ayra."

I squint open one eye and groan internally.

"My friend here wanted to apologize for, you know, almost hitting you in the face."

My eyes flicker to the wizard standing beside Ryne. His energy is askew and strange. Something about his aura is dark, but I can't pinpoint it.

"Sorry," he mutters, and I scoff at his lame attempt at an apology.

Ryne nudges his shoulder with an irritated look in his eyes. "Will you stop acting like such a child?"

"It's fine," I respond.

Ryne looks back at me with a kind smile, making my forehead wrinkle in confusion.

"We've heard about you, you know. I've gotta say, I'm not sure if that's a good thing," Ryne states.

A few witches across the hall giggle and point in our direction. Doesn't surprise me one bit. Of course, they started talking the second the wizards arrived. Women love to gossip, especially to someone they know hasn't heard the hottest news.

"And what have you heard?" I cock my head to the side, not caring but also just a tad bit curious.

"You're a stickler," the wizard with dark, unruly curls blurts out.

"I wouldn't say that." Ryne laughs off his friend's comment.

"No, he's right." I nod, knowing full well the image people hold of me in their minds. "Magic users don't take their gifts seriously enough; I think they should. If that makes me a *stickler*, then so be it."

His eyes find mine, and the faintest smile creeps across his face.

"That's an interesting take on things, don't you think?"

Just as I open my mouth to respond, the double doors open.

"Call it whatever you like," I whisper. "There's a reason I'm the most powerful witch here."

With my head held high, I walk away to join the line of witches that has formed before the entrance to the Grand Hall.

One by one, we file inside, and the moment I step through the doors, I admire the roof. The entire ceiling is canvased with an endless night sky. Shooting stars, meteors, and cluttered nebulas light up the atmosphere. Seating and dining tables are organized along either side of the room. At the end of the hall, the Headmistress of Fraydora, Illana, settles into her position right next to the Headmaster of Traquore.

The witches file into rows on the left side as the wizards follow suit on the right. When Illana sees me, she winks.

Illana always had some form of involvement in my life. I was told she was the one who cared for me the day I was abandoned on the academy's doorstep. She didn't sleep for weeks because she was worried I would pass away in the middle of the night. She helped me study until I reached my first year here. After that, she stepped to the side. She didn't want anyone to think I got in because of favoritism. I earned my way into this school. The Witches Council is in charge of the selection process. They look at behavior, academic standing, and attitude. I studied my way to this very spot. If anyone says I'm not deserving, they're full of it.

"Welcome, ladies and gentlemen." Her voice soars through the room effortlessly. "It's an honor to host another Academy Games here at Fraydora Academy. I am Headmistress Illana Solaris."

My eyes shift to the right as she discusses tradition and expectations. It doesn't take long for me to spot him. That smile can be seen light-years away. His jawline is sculpted to perfection, and his eyes hold a natural, curious twinkle as he watches the ceiling. He doesn't seem like the others.

Ryne tilts his head and catches me watching him. I snap back into position and pretend like I wasn't just observing him. *What's with me anyway? Focus, Ayra.*

"For those who don't know me, my name is Headmaster Borrick Sharpen. I have the pleasure of sharing the little change we've made this year." The man beside Illana crosses his arms over his chest while whispers circulate the room.

What are they talking about? Did I already miss some sort of key information?

"The strain between wizards and witches is known across the realms. So, we're taking a stance in hopes of changing the narrative."

Illana's lilac eyes meet mine as Borrick speaks.

"Instead of witches versus wizards, we will pair one wizard and one witch together."

My jaw drops before I can stop it. Heated hollering and shouts take over the room. What are they thinking?

"Silence!"

And just like that, the room falls still. Man, that guy has a powerful voice.

"Before anyone else protests. This decision was discussed by the council, and they approved it. So, I don't want to hear any nonsense about *tradition*. These games have taken place for nearly six centuries. It's time for change, just as the world changes." Illana beckons forth a mirror.

She unveils it, and I swear the glass breathes. "One by one, you will stand before the Glass of Prediction. The reflection will show you the name of the witch or wizard you will be paired with. Now, let's not waste any more time. Cadie Blackwell, please step forward."

Cadie exits the crowd and makes her way to the raised platform. Out in the crowd, someone whistles.

"Gentlemen!" Borrick shouts, and my hands fly to my ears.

I'm not sure how much longer I can withstand Borrick's voice.

Cadie stands before the mirror, her reflection showing her smug expression. Her opposite self disappears and is replaced with a name written in finely tuned cursive.

"Machiis Avium." Cadie whirls around just as the guy who lamely apologized to me steps forward. Cadie's curls bounce as she walks toward Machiis.

They seem like a match made from the deepest abyss of the underworld if you ask me.

"Perfect, please take a seat, you two." Illana gestures to the right side of the room.

I guess we're not sitting with our own kind this year either.

One by one, witches and wizards alternate standing before the mirror. There's only a handful of us left by the time a familiar name is called.

"Ryne Gwydion."

I force my gaze forward, not letting myself glance at the wizard who elicits these odd feelings within me. Borrick pats him on the back as he passes to stand before his reflection.

I drop my attention to Ryne's feet. *How does someone get their shoes to be so shiny?*

"Ayra Brightheart."

Slowly, I drag my gaze from the floor to Ryne, meeting that rather annoyingly gorgeous smile of his.

You've got to be kidding me.

I think I know this feeling he stirs within my veins. It's not intrigue or giddiness. No, not at all. It's pure irritation.

Ryne

5

Ayra scrunches her face when I approach her. It reminds me of the look my mom used to throw at me whenever I would break a crystal glass or track mud on the carpet. She makes it look way more adorable though.

When her name appeared in the mirror, I smiled at my reflection, and I still can't wipe it off my face. I'm not sure why, but I feel a tether attempting to pull us together. Curiosity is tugging on my muscles, and I want to discover why I feel this way toward a witch who doesn't seem to give a flying fuck about me.

Maybe that's why I want to explore this strange connection. Who doesn't enjoy a challenge?

I'm used to being able to charm people, especially with my accent. Yet when I first spoke with Ayra, nothing fazed her. I want to dig into her essence and find out what makes her tick.

Approaching her, I quickly learn I'm something that makes her tick.

"Gwydion," she greets me while crossing her arms over her chest.

"Brightheart." I match her gesture, and she presses her lips together.

"What's with the smile?" she asks, her tone suspicious.

I shrug my shoulders and soften my expression. "I like smiling at you. I can't help it."

She rakes her eyes over me like she's trying to figure out the sequence of my DNA. I take the opportunity to do the same, and color rushes to my cheeks. Her body is breathtaking, with dips and curves I've never seen before on a woman my age. Her hair is twisted in braids, with an intricate crescent moon hair clip holding them together. Blush covers her cheeks, and her eyes subtly glisten as she examines me.

When we meet each other's gazes again, her expression hardens, and I offer her a sincere smile.

"You don't have to look at me like that," I chuckle.

"Like what?" she asks while tilting her head.

"Like I'm a thorn in your side. Like I'm going to hinder your chances at winning."

Pushing back her shoulders, she squints as if she's in deep thought. "I never said that."

"No, you didn't. But it's written all over your face."

"I know people like you. You think your charm will get you wherever you want to be. I deal with people like you every day. I won't fall prey." Her tone is stiff and unshakable.

"What do you mean?"

With another sigh, she looks away, and her eyes gloss over. "Nothing. Forget I even said anything."

"Ayra, I don't think my smile gets me places. And I don't know what kind of people you're talking about, but I can guarantee I'm not like them."

"You were with the group that threw that disk at my face."

I open my mouth but end up closing it because she's right. I was with Machiis and the other guys when he threw that disk. Who knows what she was thinking when she saw me running toward her. Cadie mentioned that Ayra has a "stick up her ass," and I also got the sense that they don't get along.

I'm willing to bet gold coins that Cadie and other witches tease Ayra simply because of who she is. It would make sense. Why else would she say that to me?

"Machiis is an asshole, but he's my friend. I'm not going to make your life a living hell. I want us to be friends—"

Her scoff cuts me off.

"I don't have time for friends, especially not with a wizard."

"Isn't that the whole point of the change this year? To show the world that the younger generation is ready to break the stigma?"

She tilts her head before dropping her arms and clasping them behind her back.

"I made a good point, didn't I?" I tease with a broad smile, and it only grows when her mouth turns upright.

"I bet you think you're charming, don't you?" she chimes, and my body sings in response.

"Maybe," I reply with a wink. "Is it working? Am I breaking that shell of yours?"

She steps forward, and I'm swept up in her natural scent. Ayra smells like a crisp autumn breeze and subtle hints of green apples. When she closes the space between us, I gulp as my heart stutters.

"Absolutely not." She smirks at me, sending a thousand tiny, winged wisps into a frenzy in my stomach.

"Oh really?"

"Really," she reaffirms, but I can see past her act.

"I'll ask you again, Brightheart. Just wait. I'll win you over."

When she steps back, the heat that washed over me fades away. Ayra smiles at me before she spins around, and I'm left with an amused grin.

Something tells me my charm is already working on her because Ayra Brightheart, the supposed stickler, just smiled at me.

Ayra

6

I can't wipe the look of annoyance off my face. My nose flares out, and my lips scrunch together as the crowd around me starts to talk and laugh. I glance down at the silver crystalized fork in my hand, pushing around bite-sized pieces of filet mignon, and then trail my gaze along the table. The cloth is dark amethyst, with specks of floating stars dancing along the fabric. I move my eyes up to where burning candles float just above an iron-clad candelabra.

"Why don't we introduce ourselves?" Ryne says while clasping his hands together. "I'm Ryne Gwydion. I'm twenty-one, and I enjoy movies from the human realm."

I tune everyone out as I play with a random piece of broccoli. Ryne is sweet, I'll give him that. But what's the point of getting to know one another? We'll be at odds soon enough . . .

"How about you, Ayra?" Ryne asks, sounding genuine.

I grimace as Cadie chuckles across from me. My eyes gloss over her before meeting Ryne's sparkling green irises.

"Is this necessary?"

He nods in response.

With a sigh, I give in. "I'm Ayra Brightheart. I'm twenty-one, and I enjoy—"

"Rules," Cadie says before bursting out into laughter.

I lean back in my chair and drop my fork. "Sure, let's go with that."

The tension between the two of us grows. Ryne shifts in his seat uncomfortably.

"You're not going to eat, Ayra?" Ryne asks with a hint of concern.

"She's too pissed off to eat," Cadie chimes in.

"I'm sorry, was he talking to you?" I ask while fixing my attention on her.

"Are you okay? You do look angry." Ryne lowers his voice, but Cadie still hears him.

"She's surrounded by guys, that's why," she snickers.

I drag my hands in over my face. "Again, I'm pretty sure he wasn't talking to you."

Of course, I had to sit directly across from Cadie. The realms are getting a kick out of torturing me today . . .

"I'm not mad." I turn to face Ryne. "This is just my face." Sarcasm soaks my tone.

His eyes flick between Cadie and me, and the slightest smile forms along the corners of his mouth.

"Why do I get the feeling you guys have a past?" Ryne has the tiniest bit of an accent.

I'm just now noticing it. It sounds formal and ancient. Must be from an outside realm.

"That's putting it lightly." I force a grin before going back to playing with my food.

"Let me guess. You two were friends but then stopped because she's a stickler, right, Cadie?"

What is this guy's name again? Machi—something or whatever.

"Do you think that hurts my feelings? Because it doesn't." My teeth meet the side of my cheek. *Hold it together, Ayra.*

"Let's just say Ayra and I don't see eye to eye," Cadie scoffs.

"Again, it's because of the whole stick up her a—"

My chair screeches against the floor as I stand abruptly. Flames overtake my hands against my will. The fire doesn't burn me. It's more of a comforting aura of undying warmth. It does, however, scorch the beautiful tablecloth I was just admiring.

"Ms. Brightheart." Illana's voice echoes down the hall. "Is there a problem?"

Mach—whatever his name is—smirks. I'd give anything to wipe that stupid look off his face.

"No, there's no problem." With a single release of air, my flames extinguish. "Excuse me." I push the chair out of my way and storm out of the room.

I don't pay attention to the muffled whispers; people are always talking about me one way or another. Once I'm far enough down the Grand Hall, I rest my hands on my knees and force myself to breathe.

Out of nowhere, Kiki throws herself at my legs.

"Oh, thank Hecate herself." She must have felt my mixture of chaotic emotions. "Come here, girl."

I pick her up and cuddle her. Running my hands through her long, velvet fur, I release a pent-up sigh.

She's always working her magic on me. Old texts say that familiars are like soulmates. They know when they're needed most, and when they find you, they attach a part of their essence to yours. Maybe that's why Kikimara sought me out when I was one day old. She knew I needed her. Ever since then, she's offered me nothing but never-ending love and support. Marley gets me, but Kiki understands me.

"Thank you," I whisper, placing a kiss on the top of her head. "Let's go to bed, I've had enough of today."

Night falls, and the two moons canvas the blanketed sky. I can't help but soak in my surroundings. The hallways aren't usually quiet, but tonight they are. With the wizards here, a curfew has been set for the nonparticipating witches. One by one, candles ignite above my head. They float along the ceiling as if they're in the current of a river. I pass the same tree as earlier. Tiny glowing insects roam the tree's trunk and fly through the air like fairies from another world. We don't have fairies in this realm, I've only read about them in books.

There are a total of fifty-seven known realms. This realm is Hecatium Valora. Some realms consider us magic wielders, blessed by Hecate herself. Others call us evil, cursed, and horrid. I don't care what the other worlds think about us though. I know we're gifted because magic is nothing but beauty.

Fairies, vampires, and monsters of legends don't roam these lands. They have their own world and troubles. I hope one day I get to see a mythical creature in real life, and I don't mean something as simple as a prowler or a gifaray, I see those every day. I mean the kind of creatures I only read about in books. Fire-breathing dragons, the hairy man-ape that lives in the mountains, the mysterious lizard that lives at the bottom of a great lake in the mortal realm. Those are the mysteries I want to witness.

Two furry raspies play at my feet, making me stumble. These creatures are nothing short of adorable. They're like two puffs of brown fur with tiny paws and big black eyes. It must be nice having a friend to roll around with. Someone who helps you forget about simple things like looking before you cross the pathway.

"Hey, wait up."

Oh, there's that feeling I completely forgot about, the one that now lives rent-free in my stomach. I ignore that accent that I can't seem to pinpoint. It must be somewhere from the mortal realm, old English, maybe?

"Ayra, hey." Ryne catches up to me, running his fingers through his golden hair. "Where are you going?"

"Why does that concern you?"

Kiki tilts her head to look in his direction.

"We're partners, remember?" His eyes float down to the furry mess in my arms. "Who's this?" He reaches out to scratch the top of her head.

"No, don't."

Before I can warn him, he makes contact with her. And you know what she does? She purrs. Kiki never lets anyone but myself touch her. Why in all the eleven hell fires is she letting *him* touch her?

"Is this your familiar?"

All I can do is nod. "Yeah . . ." I draw my answer out as she leaps from my arms to his.

Okay, now I'm utterly shocked.

"What's her name?"

The smile that spreads along his cheeks somehow lightens the darkness that surrounds us. Must be some kind of illumination spell.

"Kikimara."

"Hi, lovely," he whispers as she rubs her nose against his, and my eyes nearly pop straight out of my skull. "Listen, about Machiis—"

Oh, that's his name.

"—he's a bit of a jerk, I'm sorry."

The ember specks in Ryne's eyes sparkle as I meet his gaze. There has to be magic in there too . . . strange.

"It's fine." My voice doesn't come out like it usually does. What's going on with me?

His expression softens as I accept the apology he's making on behalf of his friend. Wonder how many times he's had to apologize for Machiis.

"Can I walk you to your room?" he asks.

"Uhh . . ."

Kiki presses her face against his cheek, not sure she's willing to leave him yet.

"Sure." I start back down the path, our footsteps in time with one another.

I observe him from the corner of my eye. The way he scans his surroundings reminds me of a child in complete fascination.

"Traquore looks nothing like this." He gestures to the river of candles that dance along the ceiling.

"What does it look like?" I've never been to Traquore, so I don't know much about it.

"Every wing looks the same. Every hall is built from the same volcanic black brick. Torches line the walls, hand-lit, not by magic. I've only seen a few rooms here, but I can tell you that this place is like stepping straight into a fairytale." His eyes glimmer as he takes in the two full moons that hang low in the sky, one azure blue, the other dark amethyst. "I never knew magic was so—"

"Beautiful?" I don't mean to cut him off, but I don't think I insulted him either.

He turns to meet my eyes, giving me a warm smile. "Yes, very beautiful."

My breath catches in my throat, and my blood turns about two degrees hotter. *He wasn't talking about me. Stop it.*

"Are you ready for tomorrow?" I drop my gaze and change the subject.

"It's going to be interesting. That's a definite."

With a total of forty magic users entering this year's competition, they had to split us up. Twenty of us will attend one game. The other twenty will attend another. Ten winners will emerge from each set, then the next day, we'll do it again. Just when things weren't complicated enough, they placed us into a bracket system.

"I get the feeling I was paired with a pretty smart witch though."

I scoff as my feet carry us toward my room.

"Top of your class, right?"

At least he knows some authentic pieces of information, not all rumors and speculation.

"That's right, and you?"

He shrugs. "Don't really care about academics or standings. Not sure why I'm here. I'm failing all my classes."

I stop dead in my tracks.

"You're what?" There's the tone that was missing a few moments ago. "How did you get selected then? Did you *charm* your way in?"

His nose scrunches as he thinks.

"No," he chuckles. "I'm not sure why I was selected. I have a feeling the headmaster played his hand."

I can't pick my jaw up off the floor.

"You're joking. Please tell me you're joking." A pleading laugh spills past my lips.

"No, not joking. It should be fun though; I love a good competition." His tone is so carefree it hurts.

"I can't believe this," I mutter. "I'm going to lose everything I've worked for, and it's all because of a careless wizard."

I don't stop the words that leave my mouth. There's no

point. It's nothing but the truth. All the sleepless nights, extra reading, all my handwritten notes. They're all for nothing.

"I wouldn't say I'm careless. Nor did I say that I wasn't smart."

"But you're failing all your classes."

"Classes bore me. I'm more of a hands-on learner."

I squeeze my eyes closed and press my palms into my eye sockets.

"Let's just have fun."

"*Fun?*" I drop my hands back to my sides.

What does that word even mean? It feels weird leaving my mouth.

"You're funny, Ayra." Ryne nudges my arm, that smile still beaming across his face.

Kiki leaps out of his arms and strolls down the hallway right back to my room.

"Guess that means the party's over."

"Party?" Why can't I stop repeating what he's saying? What are these words anyway?

He lets out a deep chuckle, one that bounces off the walls.

"See you tomorrow, new best friend."

"Good night, and I'm not your best friend," I call after him as his cape twists around his legs.

"Yes, you are!" He spins around to face me, grinning that grin of his.

"No, I'm not!"

With a wink, he turns around and heads back down the path. "See you tomorrow for the group introductions, Ayra!"

"The what!?"

What in the underworld is going on? And what have I gotten myself into?

Ryne

7

If the games weren't flipped upside down this year, the first match would have started tomorrow, after the introduction interviews. Instead, the headmasters arranged a group meet and greet, and tomorrow, we get to spend one-on-one time with our partners and then race the realms for the first time.

I run my hand through my hair, tousling it. A few lingering witches whisper as we pass by, their gazes fixated on me, but I'm too busy admiring the details along the archway.

The magic here is unbelievable. Between the intricate carvings along the stone and the flickers of light in the wood, everything here seems to glow. I don't know how I'm supposed to return to Traquore Academy after this. I'm not sure I *want* to.

The wooden floors don't creak when I step across the threshold into a common area. The room isn't too spacious, but it isn't crowded either. Small mahogany tables are flanked by lounge chairs covered in deep violet velvet. A large hearth is at the back of the room, made of hand-placed brick, perfectly cemented in place. Flames hungrily lick the timber inside the fireplace, and the light from the fire creates a cozy aura.

I get the feeling we're going to need a comfortable atmosphere for this meet and greet.

Personally, I don't understand why witches and wizards hate one another. I've met witches in the past and dated a few. They would tell me stories about how their friends despise wizards, mostly because of the flack they get for not being born a man. I'm not dumb, I know that society seeks wizards over witches. I just wish I understood why. I wonder what would happen if we got along, how much the world would change.

Borrick hands me a pamphlet as I stroll into the room.

I flip through the identical sheets of paper and snort. "You don't trust us to ask our own questions?" I ask as he continues passing out the bland questionnaires.

"Absolutely not," he responds without looking at me.

"What are you afraid of, Headmaster?" Machiis asks with a grin.

A sharp whistle from one of the wizards echoes around the room as the witches start to trickle in.

"Gentlemen!" Silence falls when Borrick raises his voice. "I'm afraid of you embarrassing yourselves," he hisses before he goes back to handing out the pamphlets.

I observe the ladies as they file in, their headmistress handing them similar questionnaire packets.

Witches and wizards really aren't that different. Our eyes hold the same flicker of curiosity and hope. Like us, witches want to see the world change. Granted, not all of us are ready for such a feat, but most of us are.

Machiis doesn't waste a second when Cadie walks into the room. I peer over my shoulder to watch their interaction. Machiis neatly slicked his black hair back, and his dark brown eyes reflect the hearth's fire. He smiles at Cadie as he approaches her, and his smile widens when she returns the favor.

If I didn't know Cadie, I would think she was gorgeous. While I don't know her well, I know she has no problem tearing other people down. Her amethyst eyes, curly black hair, cunning smile, and glowing skin aren't as appealing when you know the kind of person she is on the inside.

It doesn't surprise me that Machiis has fallen head over heels already.

I turn around in time to see Kiki in the corridor. I walk across the room and kneel as she enters the room.

"Hey, girl," I whisper while scratching the top of her head, unleashing a few strands of her storm-gray fur into the air. "Where's your witch?"

I feel her before I see her. Looking up, I witness the exact moment she turns the bend, a heavy sigh escaping her chest when she sees where Kiki ran off to.

"Why do I get the feeling you enjoy making Ayra chase after you?" I ask Kiki with a smirk.

She responds with a chirp and nudges against my ankle.

"This cat is going to be the death of me," Ayra exclaims as she closes the distance between us.

"But she's so cute." I scoop Kiki up in my arms and cradle her against my chest.

Ayra furrows her brows. "You can keep her; she likes you more than me anyway," she says as her shoulders drop, with the smallest smile.

Maren pops out of my pocket and squeaks.

"Who's this?" Ayra tilts her head and squints.

He crawls down my arm and sniffs her finger.

"Maren, meet Ayra."

Maren takes her finger in his paws, and my brow arches. "I think he likes you," I say with a soft chuckle.

"He's very sweet," she whispers, her smile growing.

I have to stop myself from saying "wow" because *wow*, her smile is otherworldly. Her irises shimmer with a mix of silver and blue. I'm not often at a loss for words, but I am now.

"Are you okay, Ryne?"

Man, I love how she says my name.

I blink myself back into the moment and force myself to nod. "You have a lovely smile—"

"Brightheart!" Cadie interrupts me, quickly ruining the moment between Ayra and me. "Sit your orphan ass down."

Ayra's smile disappears, her eyes gloss over, and the shield surrounding her heart goes back up.

I'm not the best in academics, but that doesn't mean I'm a fool. Ayra likes to pretend that Cadie's words don't get to her, but they absolutely do.

"Ms. Blackwell!" Headmistress Illana shouts. She rushes over to Cadie and lowers her voice, reprimanding her.

Ayra brushes past me and takes a seat at an empty table.

I take a step toward her, but Borrick grips my shoulder. "This way, Mr. Gwydion."

I don't tear my gaze off her until I have to. Kiki leaps out of my arms and runs across the room. At least I know Ayra has some support.

Borrick escorts me to a table with a witch I haven't met.

Headmistress Illana and Borrick start to go over the rules. Ask the questions on the card. The wizards will shift down a chair when the chime goes off. Behave, *blah blah blah*.

Honestly, I'm not focusing. I'm too busy trying to catch a glimpse of Ayra. I need to be sure she's okay, but I'm so far across the room that other witches and wizards are blocking my view.

With a sigh, I slump in my chair, offering a tight smile to the witch across from me.

Looks like I don't have a choice; I have to wait until it's my turn to sit across from her.

"Hi, I'm Ryne Gwydion." I offer her my hand, my leg jostling under the table.

I've lost track of how many witches I've met. My mind went blank after the first conversation. The good news is that Ayra is in my sights. The bad news is that she looks frustrated, like she's ready to fly out of the room without a moment's notice. What makes it worse? She's currently talking to Machiis.

The witch across from me clears her throat, but I barely register it. Machiis just said something that clearly got under Ayra's skin.

The pamphlet in my hand crumples as I ball my hand into a fist.

"Am I boring you, darling?" Her singsong voice makes me cringe.

I bring my attention across the table to Cadie, not able to force a smile.

"Hi, Cadie," I mutter before I go back to watching Ayra and Machiis.

"I'm starting to take this personally," she says with an obnoxious chuckle.

"Why is that?" I ask without looking at her.

"Well, I'm far more interesting than Brightheart."

I scoff.

"What's so funny?"

I meet her gaze, noticing her neatly trimmed eyebrow is arched. "You're interesting, Cadie, but not in a good way."

"Please elaborate." Her faux innocent tone dissipates, quickly showing her true colors.

"For one, you're a bully—"

Her snort cuts me off, but I don't waste a second in continuing.

"You're cruel and fake, someone who belittles others so that you can feel better about yourself. Shall I go on?"

The bell rings, but I don't move, even though I desperately want to sit across from Ayra.

"No need," she bites out, squinting her eyes.

I stand from my seat and force a smile her way. "Have a lovely day."

Out of all the years to change the games, they had to pick this year. I'm sitting across from a wizard who won't stop talking about the anatomy of the newly discovered cat-ape hybrid. I don't need a mirror to know the expression on my face is a lovely mix of confusion and disgust. I was trying to follow the guidelines for this meet and greet, and I'm pretty sure I asked him what his favorite book was. So we're already off to a lovely start.

When the bell chimes, I release a heavy sigh. Only four more wizards left before I can head back to the library and study.

"It was nice to meet you," the wizard says with a smile.

I already forgot his name, the cat-ape hybrid took all the empty space in my mind.

"You too." I plaster a fake grin on my face. *Just kill me now.*

"Well isn't this a nice surprise," Machiis says as he settles in the chair across from me.

You know, I take it back. *Now* you can kill me.

"Let's just get this over with." I don't bother covering the irritation in my tone. "What's your name?" I ask while scanning the checklist the professors handed us before we started this damn thing.

"Machiis Avium, but you already know that."

I roll my eyes. "Unfortunately . . ." I mutter.

"What's your favorite subject?" he asks while jotting my name on his card.

"Elemental Arts, you?"

Four minutes and counting.

"Potions."

His answer makes my eyebrow raise. "Seriously?"

"Absolutely, I love making things explode."

Ah, that makes perfect sense. "Of course you do," I whisper, feeling more than unamused.

His lips form a sly smile. "Who's your best friend?"

"Why is that any of your business?" I bite back at him.

"I'm just curious." He shrugs, but I know where he's going with this.

"You want to know if someone like me is capable of having friends, correct?" I lean back in my chair, crossing my arms over my chest.

"Smart girl." His sickly confident tone has me rolling my eyes.

I don't tear my eyes away from his, not even when the bell rings.

When another wizard comes up to my table to inform Machiis of the switch, he stands and bows. "Have a lovely day."

When he turns around, I flip him the middle finger.

"I don't blame you. I often flip him off when he's not looking."

My entire body freezes when I hear his voice. Slowly, I drop my finger and meet Ryne's gaze. A mischievous grin graces his lips.

"You didn't see that." I stumble over my words, which only makes Ryne chuckle, and damn, I thought his voice was mesmerizing.

"Oh, I didn't see anything, Brightheart," he says with a wink.

I clear my throat and sit against the velvet backing in my chair. "Shall we?" I gesture toward the cards in our hands.

"I think we already have the name part down. What's your favorite color?"

I glance at the cards, knowing for certain that question isn't on the list.

"That's not—"

"I know." He cuts me off. "I just want to know what your favorite color is."

My socialization gauge depleted thirty minutes ago, so I give in. "Midnight blue, you?"

"Dark forest green."

I open my mouth but close it immediately. My dumb ass almost just said, "Like your eyes?" *What in the underworld is wrong with me?*

"Since we're straying from the cards, can I ask you a question?"

"Is Ms. Brightheart breaking the rules?" Ryne clicks his tongue in amusement.

"I take it back—"

"No! Please, ask me. I have to know what's on your beautiful mind."

I ignore his compliment and give in to my curiosity. "Where's your accent from? I've never heard anything like it."

Ryne leans forward, resting on his elbows while offering me a conspiratorial smile. "Do I fascinate you, Ayra?"

My cheeks burn, and I huff. "No."

"You really are something else. I will tell you, but only because I like you."

I like you. Three words I don't hear often, and it makes my heart kick up a notch.

"My parents are Realm Hoppers. When my mom was pregnant, she and my father were in England, a country in the mortal realm. They took leave when I was born, and they fell in love with being settled down. Naturally, I picked up the accent."

I rest my chin in my hand and hang on to his every word, mesmerized. He's a natural storyteller.

"That's wonderful," I mumble.

"I'm glad you think so because not a lot of people feel that way."

"What? Why?" I ask, shaking my head and sitting up straighter.

"My parents and I returned to this realm so I could start the first year at the lower-level wizard academy. I was teased relentlessly for having such a strange accent. It wasn't until Machiis stepped in that the bullying stopped."

"They're fools," I say without thinking. "Your accent doesn't make you who you are. If anyone still gives you a hard time about it, they're idiots."

Ryne offers me a sweet smile. "Did Kiki find you?" he asks as Maren pops out of his black sweater pocket.

"She did." I gesture to her napping on my lap.

Just then, his tiny pocket-sized lapwrin, also known as a mouse with two oversized ears, scurries down his arm. Cautiously, he walks over to me. I offer him my finger again, and I smile against my will.

"He doesn't normally do that," Ryne offers as Maren takes

hold of my pointer finger. "He's rather skittish. Maybe he senses you're not as intimidating as others say you are."

I glance up at Ryne, soaking in his carefree, genuine nature.

"I could say the same about Kiki. When she jumped into your arms last night, I was afraid she was going to claw your eyes out." We both chuckle, something I can say I haven't done in a while.

"Are you ready for the games?" He raises his left brow, and my eyes skim over his ruffled golden hair, admiring how the color glows when light hits him.

"I've been working toward this for years."

He nods. "You're not nervous?"

I shake my head.

"What will you do if we fail?"

"That's not an option," I say without a second thought.

"Why is that?" Any amusement in his expression disappears, leaving nothing but concern in its wake.

"I can't fail. Everything I've done has led up to this point. I won't even give the thought any consideration." This is why I spend all my free time studying, why I'm a social recluse, why I prefer my familiar's company over that of anyone else. I can't let anyone distract me.

"Failure doesn't mean *you're* a failure. You understand that, right?"

The bell chimes, but Ryne stays in his seat, refusing to budge until I answer him.

"If I fail, I'll not only let myself down, I'll let this academy down. I have too much to prove."

He scans my features one last time. "If you ask me—" He stands and walks over to me, leaning down to whisper in my ear.

My stomach tightens from his proximity, and the scent of burnt orange overwhelms me.

"—the aim for perfection is never-ending. Don't push yourself until you reach a breaking point. You've already proven yourself, Brightheart."

When he steps away, I gasp for air because I didn't realize I was holding my breath.

He offers me a gentle wave before moving down the line. "See you tomorrow, partner."

"Why do you look like you're about to walk to the gallows?" Marley asks with a hint of laughter.

Normally, I would retort and defend myself, but she's right. My forehead is wrinkled and my lips are turned downward—my resting bitch face is fierce.

"I have to get quality time with my partner today," I say through gritted teeth.

"I'm not sure that's worthy of the face you're making," she snickers as she peers through the reflection of the mirror I'm standing in front of.

An idea sparks in my head, and I meet her gaze in excitement. "Remember that spell you asked me to cast on you during our first year? The one that would make me look like you?"

"The one you said you would get me expelled for?" she says while placing her hands on her hips.

"Yeah, that one. I think we should trade places today."

"Sorry, girly, maybe if you took that midterm for me, I would have agreed," she teases. "He can't be that bad."

Oh, but he is. The thought of spending my entire day with him is exhausting. I'm not sure how long I'll be able to survive his lopsided grin or his ridiculously charming accent.

With a shake of my head, I clear him of my thoughts. If I can survive almost seven years in this academy, I can accomplish anything. Ryne Gwydion is no one special. I just have to get today over with, and everything will be okay.

"So, when can I meet this infuriating wizard?" she asks as I button the final clasp of my midnight-blue cowl neck hoodie.

I'm not sure what our plans entail today, so I opted for a more casual look. I don't wear leggings often since the school uniform consists of gowns or formfitting broom-riding pants.

"Tomorrow, I presume." Releasing a shaky breath, I feather my bangs and tighten my high ponytail.

"What am I supposed to do while you're gone?" Marley asks with a hint of sadness.

"Something tells me you'll figure something out," I say with a laugh. "Keep Kiki out of trouble for me?"

I glance over at the furball stretched at the foot of my bed. Yeah, she's definitely not moving an inch today.

"Always. Zachii and I will be the best company."

The tiny green lizard blinks one eye at a time at me. He and Marley are so alike it's uncanny. She told me how when they united, it felt like the hole in her heart stitched itself together, and she felt complete.

I'm sure I would have felt the same way when I met Kiki. Not every witch is blessed to meet their familiar at such a young age like myself. I know Kiki is my life partner because I don't feel complete without her.

"I'll be back soon, hopefully," I say while turning around.

"Have fun!" Marley calls as I close the door behind me.

Why does everyone keep using that word? I feel like I'm hearing it more and more now that the wizards are here. It's peculiar...

Ryne and I agreed to meet outside the main doors of Fraydora. As I walk outside, the suns are warm, but the air is crisp. The seasons in this realm are similar to the ones in the mortal realm, but ours are harsher and more consistent. It snows every winter, and the temperature always drops below freezing. Each summer, the air is sweltering, but with no humidity, it's tolerable. Fall and spring are my favorite, mainly because the air is cool and the suns don't make you sweat. Thankfully, we're in the middle of spring, so I can get away with wearing a sweater.

I perch myself on the railing of the stone staircase and wait for Ryne. He's not late; I'm just early. My nerves always get the best of me, and I hate being late for anything. If I'm a minute behind, my stomach twirls and flips. Breathing exercises often help with my nerves, but it doesn't seem to be cutting it lately. I've always had anxiety. The pressure to succeed is a heavy burden, but it's one I have to live up to. I won't accept failure of any sort, ever.

"Good morning, partner," Ryne greets.

He walks down the path that runs through the academy grounds. He didn't exit through the main doors like I expected him to.

"Morning," I say with a tiny smile.

I push myself off the railing and meet him in the middle of the cobblestone path. His smile grows when the distance between us closes. He's also dressed more casually today, wearing a simple pine-green sweater and a pair of black jeans. His hair is neatly combed back, and his eyes sparkle from the rays of the two suns.

"So, what did you want to do today?" I speak up with a shake of my head.

"I was hoping for a tour of the academy." He sways back and forth in excitement.

"A tour? Oh . . ." I was expecting something more from him, but I can manage a tour. "Well, we can start here—"

"I was thinking we could start a bit higher up." His expression turns mischievous when a broom materializes in his hands.

"I don't have my broom with me." My nose wrinkles.

I love riding as much as the next person, but I get the feeling that keeping up with him would be a challenge.

"That's okay. We only need one." He settles on the seat of his wicker broom and gestures for me to sit behind him.

"Is going to make me sick?" I ask, and he chuckles.

"I'm an excellent driver. Come on; we have places to be."

"Shouldn't I be the one navigating?" I ask with a raised brow.

"Now, Brightheart. Where's the fun in that?"

Ryne

10

I want to freeze time. I could if I knew she wouldn't berate me for it. The expression on her face is priceless. Anytime I say the word fun or hint at something that may put her out of her comfort zone, her face scrunches, and it's fucking adorable. I know once I mouth the spell, any chance at friendship with Ayra would be over, and that's not in my deck of cards.

"Let me get this straight. You want me to give you a tour, but you're driving the broom?"

Damn, I know she's irritated right now, but I can't help but smirk.

"Absolutely." I pat the seat behind me.

Her eyes scan over it, then back over me. With a shrug and a sigh, she relents and settles in the seat.

My broom is hovering, itching to go. It has the same spirit as I do.

But before I kick my feet off the ground, I glance over my shoulder. "You might want to hold on."

The scowl she offers me is one that needs to be documented in history books.

I turn back around, and she's oblivious to the grin on my face. Wrapping her arms around my waist, she inches closer.

My heart stutters, and my eyes close against my will.

She is the definition of magic. There's no other way to describe the feeling she stirs in my chest.

"Ryne, are you okay?" she whispers, all prior annoyance seemingly gone.

"I'm great. Ready?" I ask, trying to hide the fact that her proximity has left me breathless.

"As I'll ever b—"

She squeals as I press my feet into the ground, and we soar straight into the air. Her grip around me tightens, and she presses her face in between my shoulder blades. As we gain altitude, my hair blows back with the wind current.

Once the temperature drops and the view of the entire academy becomes clear, I stop the broom so we can enjoy the view.

"Why did we stop moving?" she asks, but it's muffled.

"I forgot to ask, are you afraid of heights?" I question while placing my right hand over her intertwined fingers.

"No, I just didn't expect you to go so fast," she admits as her left hand weaves into my right.

"I just want to enjoy the sight for a moment. I'll warn you before we take off again," I say in an attempt to comfort her.

She nods, and her nose stops pressing into my back as she pulls away.

"Wow." Her tone is full of awe, and wow is an accurate representation of how I'm feeling.

The grounds never seem to end. Sprawling hills of vivid green grass, and fields of wildflowers where honeybees live like royalty, you can hear the distinct *buzz* from here. The architecture of the academy is unbelievably gorgeous. The building reminds me of a castle, like they plucked it right out of a fairy-tale. Each corner of the academy has a tower with multiple astronomy decks. I'm willing to bet you can see every nebula from there.

"Do you see that?" Ayra asks before pointing to the center of the courtyard.

Vibrant lavender and deep blue portals whoosh open and closed, professors and students alike taking advantage of the free day ahead of them.

"This is amazing . . ." Her voice falters in wonder.

She scoots closer to me, resting her chin on my shoulder as she observes the view.

"You've never seen Fraydora from above?" I ask, noticing her hand is still wrapped in mine.

"No, never."

It doesn't surprise me. Ayra has said more than once that she's serious about her studies. I get the feeling that most of her free time is spent in the library, her head buried in a book. The thought of her alone, spending all her time reading text-books, makes my heart ache. She deserves to see and experi-ence everything the realms have to offer, but her need for perfection blinds her.

I wish she knew that no matter how hard she tries, she'll never reach the goal she's working toward. Not because she's not brilliant or motivated enough, but because with each win she obtains, her standards get higher. At a certain point, the air becomes thin, and she won't be able to breathe anymore. The weight of perfection will crush her.

"Can we fly over the courtyard in the West Wing?" Her tone is eager, and I grin.

"The one with the giant tree, where all the animals gath-er?" I peer over my shoulder. She's nodding, and her eyes shimmer with excitement. "I think we can fit that in on our tour. Ready to go?"

"Just don't drive like a maniac," she states with a sigh.

"Sorry, I don't make promises I can't keep." I smile mischievously before urging the broom to go top speed.

Her shrill laugh widens my grin. I'm starting to think that becoming Ayra Brightheart's friend won't be such a difficult task after all.

If we didn't have our first interview tonight, we would have flown throughout the evening. There were places on the grounds of Fraydora that Ayra had never seen from the skies, and she wanted to see it all. But when the clock tower struck and the suns started to set, it was time to bring our little adventure to a close.

Once we land, her hair is mussed from the wind, and her cheeks are red from smiling and the slight nip in the air.

"Ready for tonight?" I ask as we get off the broom.

My question wipes the smile off her face, leaving her with a strange, breathless, blank expression.

Her shoulders drop as she releases a long sigh. "Yes and no."

"That's an interesting response." I smirk but soften my expression when I catch her hands fidgeting. "Why yes and no?"

"Yes, because I'm ready to get it over with. No, because I don't do well in front of people. Public speaking is my weakness."

"The only one, I presume?"

She lets out a tiny laugh.

I offer her a gentle smile and take her hand in mine. "We're a team, remember? If it brings you any comfort, I'll be right next to you. Feel free to use me for support. Squeeze my arm, lean against me, punch me."

Ayra snorts, and her entire posture relaxes. A wave of relief washes over me.

"You would let me punch you in front of millions?" Her brows raise, and her lips turn upward.

"I'd let you do more than that, Brightheart."

I smile as Ayra laughs, pushing my forearm. "You're trouble, Ryne Gwydion."

With a step forward, I grab her wrist before she can back away. "Oh, darling, I'm that and so much more."

'm not sure how the interviews slipped my mind. I was
so excited to participate in the actual games that I forgot
about the media coverage. Crowds have always bothered
me, but over the years, my skin hardened. Whispers and
constant taunting will do that to you. A trait I can thank
Cadie for.

I keep my gaze on the floor as I walk toward the main foyer
of the academy. The heels of my shoes clack against the floor
while I try to control my nerves. *I'm just a face in a crowd. Raise
your head. You can do this.*

When I reach the last turn, I raise my head and adjust my
posture. My expression stills, and my muscles tense as I
prepare myself for what's to come.

Stepping through the door, I scan the room for familiar
faces. Or rather, the one person I'm discovering is more than I
bargained for.

Earlier today, I was ready to throw myself off a tower. The

idea of spending most of the day with Ryne irritated me. But somehow, it was the exact opposite. During all of my years here, I never explored Fraydora from the skies. I didn't know there was a grand garden on the east grounds or a scriptorium pushed into the mountains in the west. I wanted to see it all, and Ryne was eager to continue our adventure.

Now, all I want is to rewind time and go back to that moment. I want to feel the wind in my hair and the suns' rays on my skin. Instead, I'm in a room full of both familiar and unfamiliar faces. I'm pretending to be strong, but deep down, I want to crawl into bed and sleep until the games begin. At least there, I know I can handle what's to come.

As I walk deeper into the foyer, eyes land on me. I feel them crawling over my exposed skin and casting judgments. Marley begged me to let her dress me for tonight. I gave in because she swore that I would like what she picked. And I do like it. I'm just not used to dressing like this. I'm used to long sleeves and fabric that covers every inch of my skin. I tend to stick with dark colors and modesty, but Marley decided I should go all out.

The gown is sleeveless. The cobalt-blue bodice hugs my curves and pushes up my breasts. The color changes as the dress reaches my hips, changing from blue to sunset orange with hints of dancing embers. The fabric is soft to the touch, reminding me of a combination of silk and tulle. The dress changes back to cobalt blue near my feet, and I have to hold the gown in my hands as I walk because of the impressive length.

I reach up and make sure the golden hair clip keeping my curls half up is locked in place. When I drop my hand, a strong gravitational pull averts my gaze to my left, and when my eyes meet his, my heart hammers in my chest.

My feet are frozen in place even though my body is urging me to close the distance between us.

His eyes widen, and his cheeks turn pink as he examines me from afar.

My heart and my head are at war, and it's leaving me with feelings I'm not accustomed to.

For instance, I shouldn't be admiring him or how his black corset hugs his figure. Or how his sleeves are so tight that you can see his muscles straining against the fabric. I shouldn't feel wobbly or like my body is going to give. And I definitely shouldn't be smiling right now.

Forcing my expression to stiffen, I lift my right foot to take a step forward and use all my willpower to raise my left. My conscience is screaming at my heart to stop racing, but it's as if it has a mind of its own, ignoring every signal my brain is firing at it.

When I reach him, I open my mouth to greet him, but words fail me. I don't know what I was going to say. I just know I want to speak so he could respond. So I could hear his voice and soak in his attention.

His green eyes shimmer when they trail up from my waist back to my eyes, and I groan when my stomach starts to tickle.

Cut it out, Brightheart. Now is not the time.

"Don't you clean up nice," he flirts with a smirk.

"You're not too bad yourself." It takes everything I have to keep my voice steady.

This is beyond frustrating. I can't let him get to me like this. I've waited for this moment for years. I won't let a man distract me. Not now, not ever.

"Ready to get this show on the road?" He offers me his arm as the other contestants start to file through the main doors.

I want to give in. I want to accept his gesture and let him

try to ease my bubbling anxiety. But if I do, I'm showing him that I need him. That I'm weak. And that's far from who I am.

So, I stand up straight and pretend to ignore his offer. "Let's go."

Ryne

12

The woman from earlier today is gone. Her smile is different, and her eyes no longer shimmer. This witch is putting on a face, and she thinks she's fooling me. When she stands next to me, I can feel the tension that settles in her bones. One touch . . . that's all I crave. And I can't help but wonder, does she crave it too? Would my touch ease her nerves? I may never get the answer to that question. Not if she keeps avoiding my support.

The suns are setting when we step outside. I would admire the sight, how they cast amber and marigold on the horizon, but I'm too busy staring at the woman next to me. The hue of the setting suns wraps around her, giving her hair red highlights, reminding me of the fire that overtook her hands during our first dinner. Her skin sparkles, almost like glitter is kissing her shoulders and chest. I could look at her all day if I knew she wouldn't be insulted by my lingering gaze. And the last thing I want to do is disrespect her.

"Ryne, look." Ayra tugs on my sleeve and directs my attention toward the creatures drawing the carriages.

"No way . . ." I mutter as the breath leaves my lungs.

"I've only ever read about them in books." Her astonishment matches mine.

It brings a smile to my face knowing the woman from this morning is still within her.

"They're stunning." I want to tell her how gorgeous she looks, but again, I don't want to make her uncomfortable. So, I keep my gaze on the mythical star grazers and watch as pairs start to fill each carriage.

To see them is a privilege, and I'm not going to waste a moment. Astorias resemble shire horses. Their manes are full and long, but their bodies and hooves are four times the size compared to a regular stallion. They're commanding and magnificent, and their coats are luminescent like stars. And when they stomp their hooves, the sound can be heard from miles away. When they're in flight, to the naked eye, they look like comets in the sky, flying through galaxies across the realms.

Each carriage fits one team, and by the time ours arrives, the suns have set, and the two moons start to rise. Both Ayra's and my gaze settle on the astoria before us. With a cautious step forward, the pebbles under my feet crunch, but the steed doesn't startle. I don't look back when I extend my hand to Ayra, hoping she'll take it.

"Aren't you glorious?" I ask in awe while my hand lands on its mane, brushing through its silky locks with my fingers. Running my hand up to his neck, I give him a firm pat. His dark blue eyes meet mine as I pet him. "I'm sure you know this already, but you are a wonder."

"They really went all out for a simple ride down to the

Colosseum." Ayra ignores my hand and moves to stand beside me.

"They did, but can you blame them? The Academy Games is a beloved event. It's the only time the realms join together. I think some grandeur is necessary."

With a small step forward, Ayra extends her hand and places it on the astoria's muzzle. When he bumps against it, she takes a step back from the force, and her smile is as beautiful as the stars above.

I don't want this moment to end, but with a few other teams waiting for their carriage, I open the door.

"Ready, Ms. Brightheart?"

When she steps in front of me, I offer my right hand and secure my left over my stomach as I bow.

"Now, this grandeur is not necessary," she sighs.

Tilting my head up, I look at her and smile softly. "You're worth all the grandeur. Anyone who doesn't treat you like a queen isn't worthy of you."

Her cheeks blush and her eyes widen.

I went too far. Classic Ryne move. I freeze while the air stiffens between us. She's contemplating how to react, and I'm preparing myself for a lashing.

"That's very kind of you. Thank you." Her response is sweet and to the point.

Her hand then meets mine, accepting my offer to help her into the carriage.

When she sits down, she looks at me and nods toward the seat beside her. "Are you coming?"

The delay in my response makes her chuckle.

"Yes, sorry." I climb into the carriage and sit on the velvet cushion next to her.

The door closes by itself, and not a second later, we jostle forward.

A few minutes of silence pass between us. The grounds of Fraydora Academy are vast, and I don't recall seeing a Colosseum during our adventure today.

As time passes, Ayra's leg starts to jostle more and more, indicating that we must be getting closer.

"What's your favorite kind of tea?" My random question makes her leg stop, and she arches her eyebrow as she looks at me.

"My favorite tea?" she repeats.

I nod while holding back my smile. My mom taught me this trick when I was younger. If you ever want to comfort someone or try to ease their anxiety, ask them a random question. Not only will it interrupt their current thought process, it will force them to think of something entirely different.

"Well, Marley makes little tea bags with orange blossom, dried honey beads, rose petals, and small sprigs of jasmine. I don't know how she does it, but I can never replicate her recipe. She makes it for me every evening, and it's something I look forward to."

Her leg isn't shaking, and her chest isn't heaving. I don't think she's noticed, but I definitely do. So, I keep the conversation going.

"Do you prefer cookies or scones with your tea?"

"Chocolate chip cookies, one hundred percent."

I meet her wide smile with one of my own. "We have a lot in common, Brightheart."

Maren pops out of my pocket and squeaks in agreement.

Ayra offers him a sweet smile.

"Who would have thought," she says in a low whisper, making me wonder if the comment was more to herself than to me.

I open my mouth to continue but close it when the carriage

comes to a halt. The door opens by itself, and a hum of excitement fills the atmosphere.

I look over at Ayra and notice her pupils have dilated and her chest is rising and falling rapidly once again. Consequences be damned, I grab her hand and squeeze it in reassurance.

"Look at me," I urge her.

Her cheeks flush when her gaze meets mine, and our knees touch, but the contact makes her leg stop jostling.

"I haven't known you for long, and you have no reason to trust me. But believe me when I say you are the fiercest witch I've ever met. Crowd anxiety is real, and it can be debilitating. It's nothing to be ashamed of. I'm *here* for you."

I take a deep breath, and she follows my action. Holding it for a moment, we let the breath out slowly while maintaining eye contact.

"You and me, okay?" I ask with a steady tone, and she nods while taking another deep breath.

Not letting go of her hand, I step out of the carriage and offer her my strength while she exits. When her feet meet the pavement, I make sure her balance is stable before releasing my grip.

Ayra starts down the path, but I move without a second thought. I grab her wrist to stop her and lean in close to her ear to whisper, "Show them what you're made of."

An explosion of cold chills erupts over my body. When Ryne steps away, he smirks before nodding toward the Colosseum. He doesn't offer me his hand. Even if he did, I wouldn't accept it. I can't. Because if I did, it would show him and everyone else that I'm weak. Like I need a man to stand beside me and provide strength, and that's the last thing I need.

I can do this.

With one foot in front of the other, I focus on the sensation of my heels hitting the ground rather than my pounding heart. Ryne walks next to me, and when I glance over at him, my heartbeat increases twofold, making me groan internally. This entire day, Ryne has worked his magic on me. It was nice while it lasted, but it can't continue.

So, I ignore how his green eyes widen in wonder when he takes in the grand sight of the outdoor Colosseum. I haven't been here myself more than once. I remember the first time I saw it, and I'm willing to bet my expression matched Ryne's.

The structure hasn't aged a day since my first year, and I highly doubt it will.

The amphitheater is twenty stories high. Pristine stone columns tower in front of us, and vibrant vines with multicolored flowers sprout meticulously along them. Fireflies soar in the air, illuminating the path where light from the lamp posts doesn't reach.

Looking up, I focus on the shooting stars and crescent moons. If I weren't walking into what could very well be my doom, I would consider this to be an enchanting evening. But the buzz of excitement is in the air, and applause from the audience in the Colosseum reminds me that the beauty of this night is a facade.

When the first team walks under the archway, the noise is raucous, and it only grows when more teams file through.

My spine straightens, and my joints stiffen. A feeling I've become accustomed to. I let it fuel me. My body knows what I need, and right now, I need poise and confidence. Ryne and I walk under the entryway. With a slow yet shaky outtake of air, I hold my head high and block out the noise around me.

I scan the crowd, curious to see what kind of audience the games attract. Beings I've only read about in books now stand in the same space as me, and I don't know how to process these thoughts and feelings. Orcs, trolls, elves with sharp ears, and stunning fae clap as I pass them. A strange fluttering sensation brews in my chest, and it only worsens when my arm brushes against Ryne's. Turning my head, I look at him for a moment, curious at how his magic is working when he's not looking at me or casting a spell.

A strand of hair has fallen on his forehead, and I have an undeniable urge to brush it away. If my joints weren't stiff, I would give in. I would trace his jawline with my fingertips just to see how my body would react to the sensation. But with the cameras and eyes of millions, I don't allow myself to give in to curiosity. Instead, I raise my dress with my right hand and take the few stairs up onto the stage.

Ryne and I sit in a set of chairs near the back, and when the final teams take their spots, the lights go out, and all noise ceases. My left leg starts to shake while we wait for something to happen, but it stops when Ryne rests his thigh against mine. I look over at him, relieved that he can't see me in the dark.

Why does his touch ease my nerves? How can a simple look or smile from him make my body relax? How does Ryne affect me like this? I've known him for two days now. None of this makes sense. And now is not the time for puzzles of the heart.

"Stop looking at me," I whisper to Ryne.

"Who said I was looking at you?" I can hear the smile in his voice.

One by one, the lights start to turn back on, and out of the corner of my eye, I see Illana and Borrick waiting to make their appearance.

"I think you were looking at me, Ayra," Ryne whispers as he scoots his chair closer to mine.

"I don't know what you're talking about," I bite back and roll my eyes.

The lights hit us, and with a slight chuckle, his eyes glimmer as he looks at me. "Sure you don't. Whatever you say, Ms. Brightheart."

"Now, isn't this a lovely crowd!" Borrick booms as he steps onto the stage, standing front and center.

The audience clamors, clapping and hollering.

Headmistress Illana walks in next, and her gleaming smile and neatly pinned-back dark hair are as perfect as she is.

"Lovely indeed. It is the utmost honor to be the first to say this to everyone." She lets a few moments of silence pass by to build the anticipation. "Welcome to The Academy Games!"

Thunderous applause follows suit. There must be a charm in place because my eardrums don't rupture from the noise.

"Can we give our contestants a welcome they won't forget!?" Illana's voice surrounds the stadium effortlessly.

Cheering and praise reverberate from the crowd. I look around, happy that the cameras aren't visible. If they were, my anxiety might be worse than it currently is.

"You may have noticed our witches and wizards are sitting next to one another rather than on opposite ends of the stage like in previous years. The council decided it was time for a change, and no better time than the present if you ask me!"

"Now, we have a lot of names and faces to introduce everyone to. This interview will be the only one in this manner. We'll meet our teams, but you'll only learn more about them if they progress in the games. Our next interview is more personal. So, you'll have to stay tuned for that and hope your favorite moves on," Borrick states as a hue of light emits from behind us.

"Shall we meet our contestants?" The crowd roars in approval, and Illana beams. "Let's get started."

The teams of witches from Fraydora and wizards from Traquore are introduced. When their names are called, their portraits and stats are displayed behind us.

Participating in the games was never a goal of mine. My academics aren't the greatest, and my magic isn't honed in on one specialty. I'm not sure what my stats will say, but I'm curious nonetheless.

Cadie and Machiis are called, and when they stand, Ayra lets out a tiny groan. She doesn't bother to look at their statistics. She keeps her eyes straight ahead, pretending to look at the crowd when she's really looking up at the night sky.

I, on the other hand, am full of wonder. Pivoting my head, I look at the screen and nod with a small yet impressed grin. Cadie is second in her class. She specializes in light magic as well as charms, broom riding, alchemy, and dueling. Machiis is in the top ten of our class. His specialty is fire and blast magic.

His top skills are in potions, dueling, and casting battle charms.

No surprise there.

Cadie smiles at the crowd, not a drop of sweat to be seen. Her posture is straight, and her curls are free of imperfections. She's wearing a formfitting red gown with gold detailing and gems. Machiis matched his corset with her dress. His hair is ruffled, and his expression matches Cadie's. They're a power dynamic, and they know it.

"Ms. Blackwell and Mr. Avium. I get the feeling you two will be a fierce team to defeat. Tell me, how do you plan on winning The Academy Games?" Borrick asks.

Cadie steps forward, and she offers the crowd a sweet smile. "My partner and I may be powerful, but we are more than that. We want to show the realms that witches and wizards can work as a team. We'll win by working together, and once we win, we'll change the world."

She raises both her and Machii's hands, and the crowd cheers in approval as Ayra scoffs.

The pair sit back in their seats. Meanwhile, Ayra's attention is locked on Cadie. Her fist is balling her dress, twisting and wrinkling the fabric. My arm grazes her bare skin, just enough to try and earn her focus.

"Ayra," I whisper under Borrick's booming voice.

"Our next contestants are an unlikely pair—"

"Ayra," I mumble louder as Borrick prepares to announce the next team.

Her jaw is clenched, and the tiny muscles in her brow are twitching.

"Please, look at me," I urge her.

"Ayra Brightheart and Ryne Gwydion!"

The spotlight lands on us. Ayra stands and smiles at the

crowd. This expression isn't one I've seen from her before. This one is full of cocky confidence. This kind of look screams "I'm here to win. And *no one* will stand in my way."

I stand a few seconds after Ayra. After buttoning my jacket, I secure my hands behind my back. Putting on a fake grin, I look at Ayra in my periphery, only to find her oozing faux confidence.

And I may not have known her long, but even I know that's not a good sign.

I don't have to look over my shoulder to know that Ayra is at the top of her class, but I would be lying if I said I didn't want to learn more. Also, I want to know what was said about me ...

My eyes widen at Ayra's stats. She's not just brilliant, she's a fucking genius. They couldn't narrow down her top skills because she's highly skilled in *everything*. This woman is the embodiment of perfection. It doesn't come as a surprise when fire is listed as her strongest form of magic. I witnessed it during dinner on the day we first met. When I look at her, I see the cracks she pretends aren't there. I wonder how long she thinks she can carry on like this.

My scores appear next, and I let out an airy chuckle. Unlike the other contestants, I'm nowhere near the top of my class. Hells, I'm not even in the top fifty percent. I do find it rather entertaining that they listed charisma and charm as skills. And my most powerful form of magic is alchemy and flying? The flying I get, but alchemy? Really?

My eyes dart over to Headmaster Borrick, only to discover he's already observing me. The headmaster and I have an *interesting* relationship. During my first day at Traquore, I shattered a historical stained glass window with a Disk of Unyielding. Machiis was with me, but he's a faster runner. Borrick grabbed me by the back of my collar, and I fell flat on my ass. Two months of detention and multiple meticulous repair charms later, I was free.

I was in and out of his office for five years. He would scold me one day and then praise me the next. To this day, I don't have an answer as to why his mood is hot and cold around me, but it's fun getting under his skin.

The crowd may be wondering why I'm in the games. Honestly, I am too, though part of me has an inkling. I may not be smart or magically inclined like the others. There is one thing that I have that no one else has, and that's intuition.

I listen to my gut. I can attune to my surroundings and adapt in less than a blink of an eye. The professors at Traquore didn't encourage this because they praised books and knowledge. I scoffed every time. Borrick sees this in me, and he knows I'm capable of more than I let on. Maybe, just maybe, he sees something in me that I don't. And perhaps participating in these games will help me discover that part of myself as well.

Ayra and I are different. Everyone can see it. But we have more in common than everyone thinks. We share the same desire for adventure, love for animals, and the need to understand the world around us. And I can't wait to bring her to this realization as well.

"Mr. Gwydion."

I give my attention to Headmistress Illana, flashing her a broad smile.

"Tell us, are you excited about the changes that were made this year?"

"Absolutely," I respond without another thought, and the crowd chuckles.

"Please, elaborate," Illana insists, and who am I to deny a chance in the spotlight?

"Well, my partner is magnificent. She's wise beyond her years and powerful. I'm excited to get to know her more and see what we can do as a team. It's time witches and wizards work together. We're finally taking a step in the right direction."

"Do you feel the same way, Ms. Brightheart?" Illana redirects the question.

Ayra's shoulders drop as she releases a wisp of air. "Yes, it's been a pleasure getting to know Ryne. He's kind, charming, funny—"

"But how do you feel about the change?" Borrick cuts Ayra off midsentence.

"It was bound to happen. It's about time the world acknowledges the rift between witches and wizards. I agree with Ryne. This is a step in the right direction." Ayra's mouth hangs open for a second before she closes it, piquing Borrick's curiosity.

"I sense a 'but' coming."

Ayra smiles before looking down at her feet. A brief moment passes before she catches herself. She raises her eyes and meets Borrick's gaze dead on.

"But we should also be wary of our own kind. Witches can be just as cruel as wizards or other beings, especially to one another."

If I could, I would slap my hand across my forehead. Either Ayra has no idea what she's doing, or she knows exactly what she's doing. Either prospect has a worrisome outcome.

I glance over at Cadie. Her perfect poise is cracking bit by bit. Her pale skin now has a blush of pink. Her eyes are locked on Ayra, and Machiis is trying his best to earn her attention, just as I was doing with Ayra mere minutes ago.

"Are you saying that witches are cruel?" Borrick arches his brow as Illana's cheeks drain of their color.

"I think my partner means that—" I start, but Ayra chimes in.

"Most witches aren't, but there are some who are cold and calculating. Not every witch is like that, just as not every wizard is pompous and hardheaded. All I'm saying is that we are taking a step in the right direction, but let's not forget to keep an eye on our own kind. If we want change, if we want to better the realms, we have to fix ourselves first."

"That is very good advice, Ms. Brightheart. Thank you." Illana steps forward to stop the conversation from continuing.

The spotlight dims before moving to another pair. Ayra and I take our seats, and I watch her closely. She and Cadie are in a stare off, and it can go either one of two ways.

One, Ayra and Cadie brawl it out center stage, right here, right now. The spectacle will get them disqualified, and Ayra will spiral.

Second, Ayra and Cadie continue to let the tension grow. It will pull, and the tether will begin to fray. Something will snap the cord, and they'll face the inevitable. A battle between them would be a sight to see. They're both powerful and ready to unleash their anger toward the other. I don't want to see Ayra hurt or worse. I won't let Ayra stoop to Cadie's level, and won't let her become the type of witch she loathes. I'll do everything I can to ensure she stays true to herself, whether she wants me to or not.

"Look at me," I whisper into the shell of her ear.

When she doesn't look, I tilt her chin toward me using my hand. As she looks at me, the ice in her eyes begins to thaw, and her breathing starts to slow.

"I don't know you well, just as you don't know me well. There's history there, between you and Cadie. Everyone can see it, but I won't let you give in to the anger. You're better than that. It's you and me. We're a team, and I have your back, trust me."

Ayra's body stiffens, and she looks into my eyes before saying, "Trust is a game for fools."

"Y ou have some explaining to do, missy," Marley chastises me when I walk into our room.

I rub my throbbing temples.

Ryne and I just got back. We didn't discuss the interview, but I could tell he wanted to. I wasn't in the mood. I didn't want to take my aggression out on him so I stayed silent.

"Shall I start?" she asks.

"I don't want to talk about it," I groan before casting the spell to change into a comfy pair of pajamas.

"The good news is that you were the most stunning witch on that stage."

I side-eye her while pulling down the blankets on my bed.

"The bad news is that your answer may have riled up the entire witching community."

"I didn't say anything that isn't already a fact." I climb into bed and sigh as the cool blankets weigh down on my body.

"Yes, but you said that witches are cruel to their own kind."

"I said to keep an eye on your kind because they can be cruel just as everyone else," I sigh.

"I know what you meant, but not everyone knows you like I do."

I hear Marley get comfortable in her bed. The lights dim, and Kiki cuddles close to my stomach.

"I don't regret anything I said," I offer back.

"I know you don't, and you shouldn't. It was a small moment, and the buzz will simmer down. But now you have to be more careful because Cadie may think you called her out on stage, in front of millions. You didn't name her, but the entire school will know who you were addressing. I just don't want to see you get hurt or, worse, disqualified from your dream."

She's looking out for me, just like Ryne. Marley has always had my back. I can't fault her for caring and wanting to protect me. I close my eyes and release a heavy exhale.

"You're right. I'll be more careful with my words. It might be best to find me some media coaching."

Marley snickers. "I'll add it to my resume, right next to personal fashion consultant."

I chuckle in return. "Thank you, Marley, for everything."

"Just don't forget me when you make it big. Now, get some sleep. You have another big day tomorrow."

I smile and run my fingers through Kiki's fur. She starts to purr and arches her back against me. It's not long before my body relaxes and submits to my exhaustion. I wish I could say that nothing is on my mind, but I would be lying.

His smile, the glimmer in his eyes, and his words echo in my mind.

"I have your back, trust me."

Trust doesn't come easy to me. It takes time for someone to earn it. Marley has my trust, and she does everything she can to ensure she doesn't lose it. We were friends for years before I fully believed she wasn't talking behind my back or out to get me. Now I know that was never the case, but when you grow up surrounded by peers who do nothing but tease and whisper about you, the ability to trust fades away.

Ryne wants me to trust him, and I've only known him for a couple of days. The curious thing is, I feel myself wanting to trust him, and no matter how hard I try, the sensation won't go away. He's done nothing to earn my trust. Sure, he says things that reassure me. He's kind and caring, and he worries about me. But that doesn't equate to trust . . . right?

My stomach flips and warms at the thought of him. I don't have time to concern myself over this, so why am I?

With a disgruntled sigh, I give in to my fatigue.

His face is the last thing I see before I fall asleep.

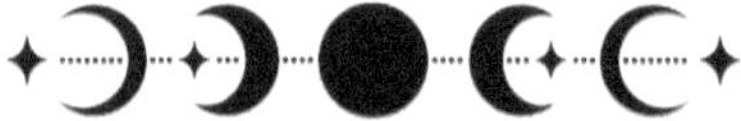

"Rise and shine!"

I shield my eyes from the overpowering glare of the suns' rays.

"Get up, sleepy head," Marley chimes in her singsong tone.

I flop over on my side and hide under my pillow. "What time is it?" I call out, still groggy from the abrupt alarm.

"Well, the suns have been out for three hours now."

"Three hours!?"

My pillow flies across the room, landing on the floor with a muffled *thud.* I roll out of bed and whisper, *"Changesis."* Fumbling over my feet, I straighten my star-light-blue tunic with a matching waist-length cape.

Through the mirror, I catch Marley's reflection as she whispers a spell, fixing my hair just how I like it. The hair clip materializes out of thin air and pulls my hair into a half-up style. I feather my fingers through my bangs, getting ready in record time.

"How do I look?"

Marley gives me a thumbs-up along with a wide grin. "Like you're ready to kick some butt."

I notice Marley is dressed when I turn on my heels. "You look like you're ready to kick some butt too."

Marley pinned her sleek silver hair back with two tiny black moonstones clipped above her left ear. She paired her ankle boots with formfitting black trousers and a royal crimson tunic with silver crest buttons.

"I have a very important job today, you know." She pulls on invisible suspenders and winks. "Cheering on my best friend, that is, right, Zachii?"

On cue, Zachii pops out of her collar and weaves his way into her hair. His scales fade from lime green to the exact same shade as Marley's lunar-kissed hair.

Speaking of familiars. . .

"Have you seen Kiki?" I scan the room, unable to locate her.

"Uhh—" Marley spins around the very moment a rhythmic tapping bounces off our door.

I crease my brow and tilt my head. Pretty sure we weren't expecting anyone this morning. My boots clack against the floor as I make my way across the room.

I crack the door open and peek my head out. "Hello—oh."

"Morning, partner."

I think Ryne needs a name for this grin of his. I need a better word than *chipper*. However, after yesterday, I feel my walls starting to break down around him, and it worries me. I didn't expect to spend the entire day with him, but our time together flew by. Before we knew it, the moons rose, and it was time to return to the academy grounds. I can't believe we spent our day flying together. I wasn't sure what I was walking into yesterday, but it was surprisingly nice.

A familiar meow averts my attention. Kiki strolls into the room without a care in the world.

"And where have you been?" I ask her with my hands on my hips.

"She was outside my door this morning."

I turn my attention back to Ryne.

"She was outside . . . your room?" What should have come out as a complete sentence doesn't. Instead, it comes out in unequal halves.

"Yeah, thought I'd walk her back. Does she run off on you a lot? Maren doesn't run away from me, can't imagine what would happen if he did." He rakes her fingers through his hair as he looks at me.

"She let you escort her back?" I ask, still completely dumbfounded.

"I think we may need to swap familiars." Ryne laughs as Maren's pink nose wiggles up and down, moving his short, paper-thin whiskers along with it.

"Hi again." I reach out with my finger to let him get familiar with my scent.

I've always had a soft spot for creatures and monsters. It started with Kiki and then moved on to animals that I would run into around campus. I could watch them do even the most mundane tasks. I think I'm drawn to mystical creatures because they're kind. They don't talk behind your back or whisper when you pass them in the halls. They're often soft and fluffy, which is a plus.

"He's growing very fond of you," Ryne says with a soft chuckle.

A smile creeps on my lips when I meet Ryne's eyes.

"He's very sweet," I whisper.

Marley clears her throat behind me, settling into the empty space between me and the door.

"Hi there, I'm Marley," she greets while extending her hand toward Ryne.

"Ryne Gwydion, I'm Ayra's partner."

I pull my hand back to my chest, letting Maren pop back into Ryne's pocket.

"Oh, I know. I've heard *so* much about you." Marley winks.

"Is that a good or bad thing?" Ryne laughs, sounding nervous.

"Both," she laughs.

Ryne and Marley start to chit-chat.

I turn around and point at a now lounging Kiki. "*Traitor*," I mouth, knowing full well she understands me.

"Ready, Ayra?"

I whirl back around at the sound of Ryne's voice, my eyebrows arching. I don't know what today holds, but Ryne failing all his classes worries me. I can pick up his slack though. I'm more prepared than anyone else.

"Let's have fun, shall we?" He offers me the crook of his arm, but I don't take it.

I move past him and stroll down the hallway. When I look back, I see Marley's arm linked through Ryne's, and a different kind of warmth fills my core. One I've never felt before. It's teetering on jealousy. What's with all these unfamiliar feelings?

I ignore the shared glances between Marley and Ryne. It's the same kind of "chipper" grin.

Fun.

We don't have time for *fun.* Now is the time for diligence. The games are no joke. The games are for winning valor and notoriety, nothing else. *Fun* doesn't fit the mold here. I don't need Ryne and his *fun.* I can win this competition on my own.

I don't need a man to save the day.

Never have, never will.

The three of us arrive in time. We weave through the ever-growing crowd to get closer to the Grand Hall entryway. Once we're close enough, I release a puff of air, and Marley heads toward the stands for the audience. The sooner we find out which bracket we're in, the better.

With a sharp snap, the room's lights are extinguished. Mummers and hushed tones fill the space. Creaking comes from the front of the hall. The taller-than-life doors open, letting a forceful blast of wind spill out and rush past us. One by one, small flecks of burning white light float back into the room, creating a miniature galaxy above our heads.

"Welcome, everyone!" I know it's Illana without even looking. Her voice echoes across the room naturally, her tone smooth like a lullaby. "For five centuries, the annual games between Fraydora and Traquore have stood tall. I'm sure you've all heard by now that the council has decided to switch things up this year. On your left, the first game will take place, and on your right, the second. If you listen closely, you will hear your destination. Before we continue, I would like to introduce you to the winner of last year's games, Mera Zelds."

As Mera steps forward, I can't help but admire her. I remember watching her last year, excited for the chance to join the games myself. Mera was at the top of last year's class. She excelled in earth and flora magic. Watching her toss wizards to the side like they were nothing more than a speck of dust was impressive. I'm surprised she's here. Most previous winners don't attend the games after they graduate, solely because they're busy and required elsewhere.

"It's an honor to be welcomed back to Fraydora Academy. I can safely say I've missed these halls. I'm sure you want to know how I managed to win the games, but if I tell you, you won't discover yourself or what you're capable of. What I can share is that you should expect to be blindsided. Be ready and willing to go with the flow. You already have a massive change to accept, so don't think for one second that this will be the only shocking factor these games have to offer. I wish you the best of luck, and I'm excited to see what each of you are made of." With a grin, Mera steps back, and Illana takes her place.

"With that being said, I'm asking the room to silence. Listen, and your path will speak to you."

I side-eye Ryne, whose arm is now brushing against mine. The cuff of his jacket feathers along my bare wrist, a combination of velvet and silk. Black suits him, must be the golden-brown hair.

Oh my gosh, Ayra! Stop and focus!

If a pin were to drop, we would hear it. Feet begin scuffing to the right and left. I close my eyes and let out a sigh of tense air.

Listen.

Ignore your surroundings. Nothing exists right now, just silence and secrets.

"*Ayra.*" A mixture of different voices floats in my ear.

"*Ayra Brightheart.*"

My head tilts ever so slightly. The voices grow louder with each word they offer me.

"*What an interesting sorceress you turned out to be.*"

"*Yes, very interesting.*" The voices split in two, yet they still hold a strange echo.

"*Which way should we send her?*"

"*Yes, which way?*"

"*To the right, my dear.*"

"*Yes, follow the right path.*"

"*And remember.*"

"*Ah, yes, remember . . .*"

I wait for the voices to finish their sentence, but I'm met with nothingness.

What am I supposed to remember? I don't think I'm forgetting anything. *What a strange set of voices.* I must have gotten the rejects or something.

My eyes open as Ryne opens his. With a firm nod, we head off to the right, making sure not to bump into any lingering witches and wizards.

"That was strange, right?"

I nod as we turn the bend. "You have no idea."

Farther down the hall, we meet a group of eighteen other witches and wizards. With Ryne and I, that makes twenty. We have our full bracket now. The door opens on its own, and as we file in, Kiki runs up to my side.

"Hi, lovely," I whisper down at her.

When I drag my eyes straight ahead, I can't help but gawk. With each step we take, the room swells, and cheering sounds from all over. Above us, the crowd grows by hundreds. It's true when they say these games draw all the realms together. You'd have to be here to believe it though. Straight ahead, ten stations are spread out, and when I see Professor Floris, I smile confidently.

I don't need Ryne or his *fun.*

This is something I can manage myself.

No doubt about it.

Ryne

16

"*Aren't you a bubble of light?*" A feminine voice giggles in my ear.

"*He's handsome, too.*" Another voice crawls into my mind.

"*He's not very complex though, is he?*"

I can't help but scoff in amusement.

"*Oh, he found that funny,*" the second voice chimes.

If I could talk back, I would tell them that no matter what they say, they can't hurt my feelings. I learned to rise above the teasing of others. The voices are trying to get under my skin, but it won't work. No matter how hard they try.

"*He thinks he can be her friend.*"

My forehead wrinkles, and my lips purse in annoyance.

"*He didn't think that was funny.*" The second voice cackles, eliciting a deep sigh from me.

"*He has no idea what he's getting himself into.*" They both chuckle.

"*Ayra is power,*" they say as one.

"She is perfection."

"She is more than you'll ever hope to be."

"What makes you deserving of her friendship?"

"Who are you, Ryne Gwydion?"

"Let's find out . . . go to the right."

And then they're gone.

Before I open my eyes, I take a moment to compose myself.

Those voices were wrong about me, but they hit a nerve. I'm fully aware of how smart and powerful Ayra is. I haven't seen her full potential yet, but I saw her ignite a tablecloth without blinking.

I've never been proficient in battle magic. I'm more of a lover, not a fighter. That doesn't mean I won't fight or stand up for what I believe in, even if that means I have to throw a fireball at someone.

Headmaster Borrick put me in the games for a reason. I'm failing my classes, but it's not because I'm unintelligent. I just don't care enough to focus. I want to be outside, exploring mountains and admiring mythical creatures in other realms. Sure, I should focus on my studies because, ultimately, they'll help me after I graduate. But I have a one-track mind, and right now, it craves adventure.

And I want nothing more than to be Ayra Brightheart's friend.

Do I deserve to be her friend? Probably not. Ayra is my exact opposite, yet I get the feeling she's more than she's letting on. When we went on the broom ride yesterday, she lit up and let herself enjoy our time together.

Something tells me that she doesn't allow herself to enjoy the little things. And when I gave her the opportunity? She shined.

I may not deserve her friendship, but I'm a pro at breaking the rules.

My eyes flutter open, and I turn my attention to Ayra the second she looks over at me.

We nod at one another before heading to our right. Our footsteps echo down the hall, both of us silent. I'm still shaken by the voices that irked me deeply.

"That was strange, right?" I ask her before we reach the end of the hall.

"You have no idea," she mumbles, sounding a bit dazed.

Ayra and I stand side by side near the other witches and wizards gathered in front of the main doors.

Within a matter of seconds, the doors open and my attention is pulled into the room. I smile as Maren pops out of my pocket and crawls onto my shoulder. Together with our familiars, we walk into the room, and I glance over at Ayra.

Her gaze is hard while she takes in the crowd. I smile wide at the sight of so many people and creatures.

I nudge Ayra's arm, but she doesn't acknowledge me. With her eyes on the stations at the front, she's in game mode.

I only hope I can keep up with her. Show her that I'm not a thorn in her side. Prove to myself, and her, that I am worthy of her friendship and perhaps more.

Ryne and I are placed at a table in the middle of the stadium. His eyes scan the room in awe. I join him because who knows when all of these realm travelers will next be in the same room together. I mean, how often do you see a fanged immortal sitting next to a horned green giant? And just when you think you've gotten the lay of the audience, the room grows, housing more and more spectators.

I suck in as much air as I can through my nose. *Just focus on the task, nothing else.*

"Welcome, competitors!"

Roars and cheers circulate the room. My fingers tap the cherrywood workbench anxiously.

"It is an utmost pleasure to host one of the first sets of games this year." Professor Floris's normal gentle tone is replaced with one that booms and echoes around the stadium.

"Are you okay?" Ryne leans down to whisper in my ear.

"I'm fine."

When did I lose my breath? I don't remember holding it in.

Ryne arches his brow at me.

"Tell me, Ayra. We're partners, remember?"

With a sigh, I give in. "I didn't expect so many people."

He places his hand over mine, gently squeezing it in support.

"Focus on the professor and the table, okay?"

I stare down at our hands and nod.

"Pretty sure Kiki will step in if you need her to."

Kiki nudges against my ankle, backing Ryne up.

"You're right, thank you." I let out a sigh of relief. *Breathe and focus. It's that easy.*

With another squeeze, he lets go of my hand.

"Fellow magic users, are you ready to receive your first task?"

As the room cheers, an assortment of herbs, flowers, flasks, and mysterious jars of liquid materialize in a haze before us.

"You see, I need a potion for my ailing night terrors, but I can only afford these resources. Your task is to create a tonic using what's in front of you. Not every item needs to be used. I'm granting you two hours. Your time starts now!" Professor Floris releases a spark into the air.

I glance down at the table, picking up each item to examine herb after herb. I only recognize one plant here, a sprig of peppermint. Everything else is foreign to me.

"Does any of this look familiar to you?" I turn to face Ryne just as he slides a white flower behind my ear.

"Isn't that lovely?" He grins that grin of his, irking my soul but melting my heart.

"We don't have time for games, Ryne."

"But isn't that what this is, a *game*?"

I squint my eyes condescendingly. *Great, so he's a smart-ass too.*

"Ha, ha, very funny." I pick up the crimson-red flower and

hold it up to my nose. *It smells sweet and kind of reminds me of a love spell ingredient.*

"You don't recognize any of this?" I ask, feeling frustrated.

"That's Monarda fistulosa," he says like he knows it like the back of his hand.

I raise my eyebrow in shock.

When he catches my puzzled expression, he chuckles. "Bergamont, from the Land of the Night."

"How do you know that?" I ask, and he shrugs his shoulders.

"Read about it in a comic book."

Of course you did.

"Okay, can you heat some water in the flask for me? Set it to a constant ninety-eight-degree bubble."

"Why ninety-eight?"

"Just do it." I hold back the snap that threatens my tone.

Everyone knows ninety-eight is the standard temperature for extracting vital components from herbs and flowers. The fact that he doesn't know that worries me.

I work on identifying the rest of the herbs, but with no resource material, I'm at a loss. Why did they provide herbs we never learned about? To mess with us, I'm willing to bet. To weed out the best of the best in one fell swoop.

I pick up a spring of something. Its leaves are green like pine. It smells earthy, and as its scent takes over my nose, I feel a surge of power shudder over my spine.

"That's Artemisis vularis, also known as mugwort. Be careful smelling it, that herb enhances magical abilities. After your emotional flame hands the other day, I worry you may set the entire room ablaze." Ryne smirks before he whispers a spell to ignite embers beneath the flask with his pointer finger.

"And you get this information from comic books?" I ask.

"Well, yeah, how else would I know? They don't teach us this stuff in class."

I huff out an irritated breath. "What is this then?" I hold up the dark ocean-blue star-shaped flower.

"Borago officinalis, a.k.a. borage. Grows in the mortal realm."

"And this?" I gesture to the flower he placed behind my ear.

"Lpomoea alba, a moonflower." He points to the peppermint sprig next. "Mentha piperita, peppermint. The mortal realms make hard candies that taste just as it smells."

How many fun facts does this guy have?

"What do these herbs all have in common?" I remove the moonflower from my ear to examine all the herbs at once.

"They all enhance different kinds of dreams," Ryne whispers, not wanting anyone else to hear him.

"Do you know which one does which?"

Professor Floris specified she's having night terrors. We need to find the right mixture to ward off the shadow dancers.

"Of course I do."

"How do we extract the components?" I ask him, feeling hopeful.

"That I don't know." He clasps his hands together and smiles ear to ear. "Should be fun though. Let's get started."

According to Ryne, bergamot is used for sleep restoration. Borage is a stimulant, so we opt out of adding that to the mix. Moonflower is mainly used for lunar spells, and it's poisonous. Given that we don't know how to properly extract its properties, we decide against it. The peppermint eases troubling thoughts and can relieve headaches. Lastly, mugwort. Ryne says it drives away demons, adding it could amplify the bergamot and peppermint.

Ryne starts grinding down the bergamot with a mortar and

pestle as I stare at the sprig of peppermint, thankful there's one herb here I know how to extract. Quickly, I set up another beaker. Without a spell, water flows from my two fingers, filling the glass half full. With a snap of my fingers, I boil the water instantly. We only have thirty minutes left; we can't waste any more time.

"Did you just do that without a spell?" Ryne asks in disbelief.

It's only then that I hear the mumbles around the room.

"Elemental magic is like second nature to me. I've never needed spells for it."

This time, his eyebrows furrow. "That's super impressive, Ayra."

I hold onto his gaze longer than I should. His attention on me disrupts those darn feathered creatures in my stomach again.

"You really are something else, aren't you?"

I tear my eyes away from his and drop the minty sprig into the boiling water. How can I be *something else* when I couldn't even identify the resources in front of me? I didn't prepare properly; I should be ashamed of myself.

"How do you think everyone else is doing?" Ryne asks.

I turn to face where he's looking. As I open my mouth, a fire-cracking explosion erupts across the room. The heat blasts our way, but I block it using a cooling protection aura.

"I take it back," Ryne mumbles.

Looks like we aren't the only ones stumped.

"Can you add the bergamot powder to the flask when you're done?" I ask.

With a firm nod, he gets back to work.

"Oh, but first." His fingers feather just above my ear, securing the moonflower back where it was. "It looks better there."

Don't look at him, Ayra. Focus.

I shut my mouth and start grinding the mugwort. Ryne sprinkles the crimson powder into the flask. The clear liquid transforms into a light pink.

"How much do we add?"

Ryne shrugs again at my question. "The more, the merrier, I guess."

I really hope we don't cause another explosion. Or, worse, a blast so powerful we wipe out the entire room. I take half a teaspoon of the mugwort and watch it dissolve.

"What do you think?" I ask him with an arched brow.

The liquid boils in the glass beaker, and the light crimson layers itself just above a deep forest green.

"A tad more mugwort," he offers.

"Twenty seconds!" Professor Floris calls out.

"Are you sure?" I ask Ryne, unsure what to do next.

"Yes, we should ward off as many demons as possible."

Placing my trust in his comic book knowledge, I sprinkle another half teaspoon in the flask. The deep-forest-green color flows from the bottom of the liquid all the way to the top.

"Ten." The audience shouts into the room.

I side-eye Ryne, concern and doubt filling my expression.

"Are we good?" I ask.

"Eight," the room chimes.

"More," he responds with a confident nod.

"Are you sure?"

"Five."

"Another teaspoon. Trust me," he reassures.

"Four."

I freeze, unsure of what to do.

"Three."

"Trust me, Ayra," he urges while locking eyes with me.

"Two."

I dump another teaspoon into the mixture and watch it swirl, mixing in. A puff of smoke escapes the beaker.

The smell hits me first. It's a strange, minty, yet sweet scent, kind of like the syrup you would take for a cough.

"Time!" Professor Floris shouts as another spark of light explodes in the air.

Professor Floris, Illana, and Borrick stop by each station around the room. One by one, they go over the tonics, listening to explanations and step-by-step procedures. No one moves after their judging, indicating that we won't know who makes it to the next round until the very end.

When Professor Floris and the two headmasters face Ryne and me, I hold my breath. The first thing they do is take a whiff of the concoction.

I'll have to remember never to play cards with them because their faces remain still and expressionless.

"Tell me what you used, Mr. Gwydion," Borrick states.

"Bergamont, peppermint, and mugwort."

All their eyebrows wrinkle at the same time.

"Mugwort?" Borrick asks as he tilts his head.

Ryne nods firmly.

"How much mugwort?" Illana asks while trying to shield the shock in her voice.

"Two teaspoons."

Professor Floris nods, but I think she forgot to lower her furrowed brow. "Thank you, Ms. Brightheart and Mr. Gwydion."

We're left in silence after that, neither of us knowing what to say or feel.

Never in my life have I felt so helpless. I knew nothing about the herbs and flowers that were placed before us. I had to rely on outside help. I can't remember the last time I had to do that. Placing blind faith in a complete stranger is against my internal code. Not only did I place my faith in a stranger. I placed it with a wizard I know very little about, other than his annoying chipper smile and the fact that he's failing all his classes.

"What do you think?" Ryne leans into my ear.

The three judges return to their platform.

"I don't know." My voice trails off as Illana steps forward.

"We placed a tremendously difficult task before you. Some of you prevailed, while others failed." And I swear her eyes land directly on me. "When I call your names, please step forward."

I shift my weight from one leg to the other, waiting impatiently as she calls out the names of other teams. I tilt my head, catching Ryne meeting my gaze at the exact moment. He grins softly, but it's not the kind of grin I got this morning. This one comforts me, dissolving my anxiety in seconds.

Six teams are called forward, and none of them include us. All hope vanishes. We really messed this one up, didn't we?

"If I called your name you—"

"I'm sorry, Ayra."

This is what I get for trusting a wizard . . .

"—did not make it to the next round."

My shoulders slump forward, the weight that was there moments ago disappearing. Ryne scoops me up in his arms and spins around.

"We did it!" He beams, and I smile widely in return.

"Mr. Gwydion."

Ryne drops me the second Borrick clears his throat.

"Sorry, sir."

Illana smiles as the entire room chuckles. I fidget with the flower in my hair, making sure it's still in place.

"If you did not surpass this challenge, please exit the room. Please don't belittle yourselves. You should be proud you made it this far. Thank you for your knowledge and continued loyalty." Illana smiles at the group that files out of the room.

"I didn't expect anyone to pass this test. Honestly, I'm surprised we only had one explosion." Laughter circulates the room as Professor Floris speaks. "Two teams made the perfect tonic. The first team is Cadie Blackwell and Machiis Avium."

How did I not notice Cadie was in the room? Normally the stench of overpowering lavender is a dead giveaway.

"The second team not only perfected the tonic; they got the extract measurements and extraction methods."

Kiki leaps on the table and collides with my hand.

"We did it, girl," I whisper and smile at the furry mess she leaves behind.

"Ayra Brightheart and Ryne Gwydion."

My attention is pulled to the front of the room. Disbelief runs rampant through my veins.

"We what?" I can't help my jaw from dropping as Ryne picks me up and spins me around again.

"I knew comic books and trivia weren't a waste of time."

The room explodes in laughter again as I'm settled back on the ground.

This man needs to stop messing with my balance.

"Great job, you two." Professor Floris beams at the two of us in that grandmotherly way.

"The next round will take place tomorrow. There are eight teams left, so we will split you up again for four teams against four. I suggest you prepare for the unknown and take today as a learning opportunity. Not everything you learn will be within these challenges. Mysteries do await you." With Illana's final words, the room erupts in applause.

Ryne's smile is contagious, and one of my own wrinkles along my cheeks.

"That was fun, wasn't it?" he asks me as Kiki rams her head against his palm.

Was that fun? Is that what *fun* is?

"Yeah, I guess it was."

We filter out of the room in pairs. The crowd cheers as we pass by, growing louder when Ryne raises his hand to address them. Of course he can win the hearts of thousands with a simple, charming gesture. This man oozes main character energy.

Kiki trails at my feet, but I take her in my arms when we pass the threshold into the hallway. Lingering witches and wizards roam and chat with one another. Some meet up with friends who were sitting in the crowd cheering them on.

I wonder where—

"Ayra!"

There she is.

Marley charges toward us, wearing a large, sparkling smile. "You guys were amazing!"

She wraps her arms around me, ignoring Kiki, who cuddles against my chest. She pulls away to give Ryne the same treatment.

I curl my fingers in Kiki's velvet gray fur, seeking comfort.

"So." She clasps her hands together. "What are we going to do to celebrate?"

Ryne's eyes flick my way for a brief moment.

"Brightheart." Cadie's heels clack against the hardwood floor as she makes a beeline for me.

"Yes, Blackwell?" I chime, unamused.

Machiis trails behind her with confusion etched in his expression, his familiar flying overhead.

"For years, we've attended the same classes and studied the same materials. How in the great underworld were you able to make a *perfect* tonic?"

Kiki growls and the vibrations rattle my bones.

I side-eye Ryne, but it was a stupid move because she saw it. "Ah, of course. You rode on the back of your teammate."

"What in the hells is that supposed to mean, Cadie?" I bite out.

She takes a step forward, her overpowering lavender scent making my nose twitch and my eyes water.

"It means you use what you can to your advantage. Just like you used Illana to get into this academy in the first place."

Oh, now that's a new one.

"That's ridiculous," I spit out.

"Back off, Cadie." Marley butts in, growing more defensive by the millisecond.

"They pity you; you know that? The poor witch who was dropped off at the academy's front door. You're only here because they feel bad. You only got in the games because the headmistress has a soft spot for you."

Kiki's fangs protrude as her growl grows louder; her claws dig into my skin. Venus, Cadie's familiar, is notably absent, which most likely has to do with Cadie's declining attitude.

Dark magic isn't abundant in this realm, but that doesn't negate its existence. While I've never seen Cadie cast a spell from the dark arts, her demeanor is changing, and her familiar is noticing it. When a witch or wizard starts to teeter toward the dark side of magic, their familiars are the first to notice, and they begin to detach from their partner. There was a moment when I worried that's what was happening with Kiki and me, but she's a cat, it's in her DNA to adventure off without me. My heart pounds against my rib cage, and the heat in my hands grows hotter and hotter.

Breathe, Ayra.

"Let's just all relax." Ryne steps forward, placing his hand on my shoulder. "We were just about to go celebrate moving forward in the games. Why don't you join us?"

Cadie's eyes never leave mine.

An internal duel is waging, ready to spark at any given moment.

"I'd rather suck on a goblin's crusty toenail," I hiss before spinning around.

It's easy to ignore the scoffing and last-minute remarks. They can celebrate on their own. I won't participate. Why would I? All I would hear are cutting remarks and false justifications. I need to prepare for tomorrow.

Nothing else matters.

Ryne

19

"That's right, run away, Brightheart!" Cadie calls out as Ayra walks away.

Marley doesn't chase after her like I expected her to, so I start down the hall, but Marley wraps her hand around my wrist and pulls me back.

"Don't," she whispers, ignoring Cadie as she continues on about how Ayra is a waste of space. "She needs time to cool off, trust me."

I nod, and Marley drops my wrist. She doesn't make a move until she knows for sure I won't chase after Ayra.

"I'm getting real sick of your shit, Blackwell." Marley's normal cheery tone is replaced with one that snaps like a grumpy dragon turtle.

"I don't recall talking to you." Cadie brushes Marley off as she tosses her long hair over her shoulder.

"You think you can stroll through these halls and wreak havoc? Let me tell you something." Marley stands toe to toe with Cadie. A tiny lizard reveals itself on her shoulder. "You're not better than any of us. You're a witch who comes from money. That's it. I'm tired of you treating my friend like she's the dirt under your shoe. Karma's a bitch, more so than you."

Before she can respond, Marley turns around and storms down the hall, leaving me, Cadie, and Machiis speechless.

"Are you going to let her talk to you like that?" Machiis asks.

I make eye contact with the witch, and her rage attempts to pierce right through me, but I refuse to bow to her will.

"No, I won't waste my time on scum like them." Cadie turns around and struts down the hall.

Machiis offers me a nonchalant look and shrugs his shoulders.

"See you later, Ryne," he says before he chases after her like she's suddenly his master.

It doesn't surprise me that Machiis fell under whatever spell she's casting. He loves to think he has everything under control, that he's the puppet master, but he's not.

Machiis is more of a follower than a leader and always has been. When we were kids, he was quick with his words, but the action never followed unless someone else took the lead, and most of the time, it was me. I've been replaced, though, with a lavender-smelling devil. I don't consider myself a leader, but Machiis was safe with me. Now, he's following the wrong path, and nothing I can do will guide him back.

I head down the corridor in the direction Ayra and Marley stormed off to. I look to my left and right, unsure which path to follow. Maren chirps before crawling out of my pocket. His nose wiggles up and down as he sniffs the air.

"Do you know where she went?" I whisper, hoping Maren will lead me to Ayra and not Marley.

Maren leaps off my shoulder, landing on the floor with ease, and scurries down the hall. I jog after him, not caring about the confused looks and muffled laughter from passing witches and wizards. I know Marley said Ayra needed time to cool off, but I need to make sure she's okay.

I want her to know she's not alone.

Not anymore.

I hunker down in my usual spot in the library. Portals open as I peer out the window, and both witches and wizards pass through them, ready to celebrate moving forward in the games. I wonder what it's like to have a group of friends you don't have to worry about. What is it like to have someone who cares about you? I have Marley and Kiki, but why doesn't that feel like it's enough?

I forcefully shake my head. *Now isn't the time.* I need to focus on tomorrow. Illana said to expect the unexpected, so, I ask the library for something completely out of my wheelhouse.

"Can I have a stack of fantasy fiction books, particularly those that include magic?"

If the library had eyebrows, I'm sure they would have raised right through the endless ceiling.

One by one, books stack before me. I take the first one from the tower and flip to the last page. This book has about two hundred fifty pages, roughly an hour's time for me. I wasn't always a fast reader. That was a skill I had to work on and refine.

I'm taking a risk here, but I can pull an all-nighter and get through this stack. Hopefully, the knowledge within these texts will provide me with some much-needed wisdom.

I open the book to the first page and breathe in the smell of old paper. Nostalgia washes over me as my fingers dance along the page, comforting me like a long-lost friend. I'm brought back to when I first discovered this cove. Cadie and I were still friends, and I hadn't been beaten down by my peers yet. I was looking for a quiet place to read, and when I say I stumbled upon this place, I mean it.

Kiki decided to join me that day. Mistake number one. She bolted through the main doors and scampered past witches and their familiars. I apologized profusely as I trailed behind her. I was ready to scold her when she skidded to a stop, but the moment I saw the floor-length window and cozy chairs, I told her she was a brilliant adventurer.

Just like animals, books are near and dear to my heart. If I want to see a different world, I could always portal jump, but there's something different about living a second life, even if it's only in your head. In stories, I could live the life of a queen, rule a kingdom, or tame dragons. I could be an herbalist and craft potions, a rogue who does nothing but collect bounties. I could live a thousand lifetimes in one, and not everyone can say that.

Kiki stretches awake from her nap as I finish the first book for the evening. She trots off without a care in the world, leaving me in silence. I can't blame her for her natural instincts. She'll come back when I need her. She always does.

"Hello?"

My eyes shoot across the rows of overstocked bookshelves.

"Ayra?"

The way he says my name still doesn't sound right. His voice is effortlessly smooth yet deep. I guess I'm just not used to a guy saying my name.

Ryne turns the bend with Kiki leading the way.

Oh, you went to fetch my *new best friend*. Thanks for that . . .

"There you are," Ryne says like he's been looking for me for hours. "What are you—wait a second." His eyes light up as he recognizes the book in my hands. "Ms. Brightheart, are you reading fiction?" A teasing smirk spreads along his lips.

"What do you want, Ryne?" I try to hide the sigh from my voice, but I fail. *Just like how I failed today's challenge . . .*

"Marley and I have been looking for you."

I roll my eyes. "Don't lie to me."

I know Marley isn't looking for me. She knows better than that. Whenever I get in these *moods*, she knows I need time to cool off. I would only lash out at her otherwise.

"Okay, fine. *I* was looking for you."

I raise my eyes from my book and meet the concerned glint in his ember-speckled eyes.

"Why?" I ask as he takes the chair across from me.

It screeches across the floor as he drags it closer to me.

"I was worried."

"Why?"

His smile spreads wider, laugh lines crinkling in the corners of his eyes. "Is that all you can say?" he asks with a hint of a chuckle.

He reaches for me and brushes his fingers along my cheekbone to remove the moonflower I forgot about. "I'm worried because Cadie said some pretty awful things, and I saw the look on your face when you walked away." He twirls the white flower in his hand as he speaks. "Does she always talk to you like that?"

"Her and everyone else," I admit.

"Really?" He softens his voice. "That's not okay, Ayra."

I shrug my shoulders. "It's fine. I'm used to it."

"I know you don't like it, don't lie to me."

I meet his gaze again. What is he talking about? I don't care what anyone says about me. None of it matters in the long run.

"In the Grand Hall, when Machiis called you a stickler, your hands set ablaze. Just now, when Cadie said those hurtful things, I saw the flames dancing in the veins along your hand. You don't like it, Ayra, and you shouldn't. It's not kind, nor is it acceptable."

I can't formulate a response. His words sink in one by one.

Not kind.

Not acceptable.

Don't lie to me.

What an interesting witch you turned out to be.

Yes, very interesting . . .

All the whispers and rumors that float around about me are ruthless. I let them hurt me until the pain became nothing but numbness. Does this mean I'm not as strong as I think I am? Or does it mean something else entirely?

"That doesn't mean you're not strong, Ayra." Ryne pulls the thought right out of my head, voicing it out loud and giving it life. "It makes you a witch with flesh and bones. Words aren't supposed to hurt, but when they do, they sting, and they can leave you feeling exposed. I know you can put Cadie in her place; I've seen you do it before. Just be careful. Don't let her turn you into a villain." He offers me the flower back.

I take it gingerly, letting it rest on the pages of my newly opened book. I glance over at him again. My eyes dance around his, and a soft smile tugs on the corner of his mouth.

"Now." He stands and extends his hand out. "Why don't we go celebrate."

"I should really study—"

He takes my hand and pulls me forward. "Nope, we're going to go have some fun. You and me, how does that sound?"

My hand sings against his palm, a comforting, scorching sensation feathering along my skin. My heart skips a beat, which sounds like a medical concern . . .

"Did I lose you, Ayra?"

My hand tightens around his like it has a mind of its own. "No."

Ryne notices and his expression mirrors mine. His golden hair shrouds him in a natural aura of light. He is the definition of a carefree, ray-of-sunshine wizard.

I shouldn't let myself get wrapped up in his unpredictability. But right now, I *want* to be around him. I like the smile that threatens my usual blank expression. I like how he makes me feel. So, I ignore the rational part of my brain and decide to trust him.

"What did you have in mind?" As the question leaves my mouth, he winks at me.

"Now, that's a surprise, Ms. Brightheart."

"Where are you taking me?" Ayra asks with a hint of laughter.

I knew I had to cheer her up. She was an amazing team player in today's challenge, and now, she deserves to have a good time. While I believe she considers hanging out in the library to be a *good time*, she deserves more. I couldn't waste another second; the idea flooded the forefront of my brain, and excitement took over.

"I told you, it's a surprise," I say while peering over my shoulder. "And don't even say it. I get the feeling you hate surprises."

She chuckles, and color rushes to her cheeks. As we turn the corner, she opens her mouth to respond but quickly snaps it shut at the sight of the deep multicolored portal.

"Ready, Brightheart?" I tighten my grip around her hand. Her eyes are fixed on the portal ahead. "Brightheart?"

Her jaw clenches, and perspiration shines across her brow. "Um—" Ayra's voice drops as she struggles to find words. "It's just—" She lets out a heavy sigh and closes her eyes. "I've never portal-hopped before."

With her eyes closed, she doesn't see the small smile on my face. I let a few moments of silence pass. When I don't say anything, she squints her eyes open. I feather my thumb along the back side of her hand.

"Why aren't you saying anything?"

My grin spreads, which causes her to respond with a smile of her own.

"This is going to be so much fun." I tug on her hand as we draw closer to the portal.

A rush of air surrounds us. The fact that I get to be the first person Ayra portal hops with is exhilarating, and I know she's going to enjoy where I'm taking her. I can't wait to see the look on her face.

"Wait!" She pulls on my hand.

I turn around to face her. Not thinking, I weave my hand through her hair. "Trust me."

I take a deep breath in through my nose and drop my shoulders from my ears as I release it. With a slight nod, I let Ryne take the lead. One step at a time, we near the portal.

A smell I'm not familiar with surrounds me. It's cold and smells like fresh snow.

Ryne steps through the portal halfway, making sure to keep his eyes locked on mine.

"Just follow me and breathe, okay?" He reassures me while stroking his thumb along the back of my hand.

"Okay," I mumble.

With another step, Ryne is gone. The only part of him that remains is his hand that's intertwined with mine. *Breathe.* One step forward. *Close your eyes.* Then one more step. I grip onto Ryne's hand, too afraid to let go. A harsh, cool breeze whips around me, almost knocking me over.

"Open your eyes, Ayra," Ryne whispers in my ear.

When did he get so close? With a few blinks, I adjust my vision and take in the new surroundings. I can't help but gasp.

Snow dances around us, landing at our feet and covering the ground. The night sky here is pitch black, with tiny specks of stars. The moon is crescent-shaped, but there's only one, so I know we're in a different realm.

What makes me stagger back a step is the building that looms ahead. A staircase with too many steps to count leads up to what looks like a coliseum. The building looks like it belongs to Fraydora Academy. Tan pillars make up the castle-like structure. Windows and covered paths line the outside, and the building hugs a courtyard on both the left and right sides.

"Where are we?" I say under my breath as I step closer.

"The mortal realm," Ryne tells me.

"But *where* in the mortal realm?" I look up at him, discovering he's watching me intently.

"I believe the humans call it Center City, Philadelphia," he says, and I repeat his words under my breath. "This is the art museum."

My eyes widen in amazement. "An art museum?" I ask with a grin.

He nods, and a loose strand of his golden hair drapes across his forehead. "Figured if you like libraries, this would be right up your alley."

I've never been to an art museum. I've seen art around the academy, in the library, but an art *museum?*

"And . . ." He tugs on my hand, and we start our climb up the never-ending staircase. "We have after-hour tickets," he says with a wink.

"Why do I get the feeling you're just going to portal through the front door?"

His lopsided, mischievous smile is all I need to confirm my assumption.

"Look at you, already a pro at portals." Ryne smiles wide as I step through the magical window he creates to sneak us in.

Once we're inside, he clasps his hands together eagerly. "So . . . Where do you want to go first?"

I glance around the empty marble hallway and shrug. "Surprise me."

His eyes light up. "Fun looks good on you, Brightheart. Follow me."

Ryne reaches for my hand again, and I allow him to take it. We race down the hall, trying our best to stifle the laughter. Ryne leads us up to the third floor, and when we cross the threshold, my jaw drops to the floor.

"Oh my suns," I gasp as I take in what lies before me.

Knights frozen in time are housed in glass casings, all wearing suits of armor from the mortal Renaissance era. Swords and shields adorn the walls. A larger knight riding an armored steed stands atop a platform.

Ryne meets my gaze from the other side of the glass compartment. "What do you think?" His grin softens, and his rosy cheeks brighten.

"This is fantastic," I say, wearing a smile so wide my cheeks start to hurt.

Ryne went out of his way to find something he thought I would enjoy. I know Marley told him how much time I spend in the library, so he knows I'm into books. A sting of guilt houses itself deep in my gut. This is fun for me, but is it fun for him?

We meet face to face; his eyes burn into my soul, and that strange flutter takes flight in my core again.

"Come here often?" I tease, earning myself a blush and a giddy chuckle from Ryne.

"Is that a pickup line?"

I lose all sense of sentence crafting when he looks at me.

"This is my quiet place when I need to get away," he says while looking straight ahead. "I thought you'd like it too."

We stroll into the next room, but neither of us drops the other's gaze.

"You didn't want to go out and celebrate with Machiis and the others?"

He shakes his head. "It wouldn't have been fun without you."

I scoff at his remark.

"What?" he laughs.

"I'm not *fun.*"

"I beg to differ."

We stop before the next room, neither of us sure what to say next. I'm not used to all this attention. Sure, Marley and I spend a lot of time together, but we never really hang out. I'm certainly not used to having a man's attention. It feels odd yet invigorating at the same time.

My head tilts on its own accord, thoughts running wild.

"What are you thinking about?" Ryne takes a step forward, and I take one step back.

My mouth doesn't open. All words escape me.

"You're not what I was expecting, Ayra," he says, sounding intrigued.

"What were you expecting? A stickler?"

He lets out a brief chuckle. "No, I never thought that. I guess I was expecting a grumpy gills."

My nose wrinkles. Marley calls me that all the time. The day I earned that nickname, she woke me up with her singing and clambering about. Sure, if she didn't wake me up, I would have been late to class. Being a night owl means I naturally loath morning people, and that day, Marley got to witness it.

Grumpy Gills. I can't seem to escape nicknames no matter where I go or who I'm with.

"Any particular reason?" I smile, curious about what he'll say.

"Well, for one, you shattered Machii's disk."

I hold up a finger and chuckle. "I fixed that, remember?"

"Only after I gave you my charming *Ryne gets whatever he wants* eyes."

"Huh, is that what you did?"

Ryne takes one more step forward.

My back hits the wall behind me.

"It's my specialty," he flirts.

"Anything else?" My voice is shaky from nerves.

He rests his chin on his hand and feigns deep thought. "The obvious, disappointed frown you threw at me when the mirror showed me your name. Oh, and when you set the table on fire."

I laugh when he starts to count on his fingers and place my hands over his. "Okay, whatever, I get it."

We stare at one another, and when he glances down at my lips, my heart stutters. Ryne takes another step forward, closing the brief distance between us. Our mouths are barely inches apart. If I stand on my tiptoes, I could kiss him.

A minute of silence passes before he speaks again. "You're much more than that, though, aren't you?" he says while brushing a strand of hair behind my ear, sending chills skittering over my skin.

Am I more than a stickler or grumpy gills? Is there more to me than perfection and rules? Before I met Ryne, I knew nothing of *fun* or smiling so wide my cheeks ached. Strange, how one minute you're *you*, and the next thing you know, you meet someone, and the person you once knew yourself to be is gone, like they never existed in the first place. It's not so bad, relying on someone else. It's actually quite nice.

I open my mouth to respond but shut it when flashes of light appear from around the corner.

"Oh, shit. We gotta go." He grabs my hand again just as shouting echoes behind us.

"Hey, stop!"

I can't help but grin and laugh as Ryne guides me through the halls, his own amusement brightening his face.

"Wait!" the stranger hollers.

As we round the bend Ryne shouts, "*Portalis Realasim!*"

A deep lavender portal materializes before us. Without wasting a second, we run through it.

Fraydora's natural eucalyptus scent envelopes me as we tumble across the academy's grounds. Ryne closes the portal as quickly as he opened it.

We lie on our backs, chests heaving up and down, trying to capture as much oxygen as possible. At the same time, we turn our heads to look at each other. Our laughter fills the air and bounces off the walls. I haven't laughed like this in ages.

"How's that for fun, Brightheart?" Ryne manages to get out through staggered chuckles.

I give him a thumbs-up, unable to form any words through my stomach-clenching laughter.

Ryne Gwydion is not what I was expecting. When I met him three days ago, I didn't think he would have an impact on my life. I thought he would get on my nerves and disappoint me. I thought I would have to carry my weight and his. Somehow, he's the exact opposite. I don't think the Glass of Prediction could have given me a better partner.

Ryne Gwydion, who would've thought?

Ryne

23

The first moment I met her, I knew Ayra was more than Cadie said she was. I could tell by the sparkle in her eyes. What I wasn't ready for was her willingness to step out of her comfort zone and try new things. When she saw the art museum, the world around us slowed, and the awe in her expression made my heart stop.

I can't stay away from her. Thank the gods we were partnered together. I'm positive she wouldn't have looked my way or wanted to be near me if we hadn't been.

I'm not sure if she feels the same way I do. After last night, though, before the guard almost caught us, I *felt* something between us. Her eyes glanced from mine to my lips, and I wanted to kiss her. I needed to feel her against me. My gut is telling me she might feel the same way. At least, I hope she does.

The next round of the games isn't for another couple of hours, but I find myself walking to her room. She might turn me away and ask me to return later. We were out late last night. If I weren't so excited to see her again, I would still be sleeping myself. My heart is calling for her, so I have to take the chance.

When her bedroom door comes into view, I run my hands through my hair. I can honestly say that nerves don't usually rile me up. Ayra seems to awaken strange feelings within me, just another reason why I want to be around her. I raise my fist to knock on the door, but before I make contact with the darkened wood, it swings open.

"Well, look who it is." Marley greets me with a cheery smile.

"Good morning, Marley." I offer her one in return while trying to peer into the room. "Is Ayra awake?" Curiosity and hope fill my tone.

"Not yet. Someone kept her out past her bedtime." She grins knowingly at me. "Any idea who's to blame?" she asks while crossing her arms over her chest.

My eyes widen. I'm not sure how protective Marley is, but I know she can kick my ass in more ways than one.

"It's fine, I forgive you."

I release a relieved chuckle. "Do you know when she'll wake up?"

I catch Kiki stretching at the foot of Ayra's bed. Butterflies whirl in my stomach, hoping Ayra will rise next, but Kiki slumps back down and goes back to sleep. Meaning Ayra isn't up yet.

"Knowing her, not for another hour," Marley says before looking back at Ayra. When she meets my gaze again, she smiles. "Why do you want to know, Mr. Gwydion?"

"I—"

"Did you plan on stealing her again?"

"Well, I—"

"Oh my gods, you were! Where were you going to take her!?"

"I was going to take her somewhere for breakfast."

Marley's eyes light up, and I know I just spewed the wrong words.

"Where? You know what, don't tell me. Let's go, we have to talk anyway."

She closes the door and links her arm through mine, pulling me farther down the hall.

"What about Ayra?" I ask while looking over my shoulder.

"She won't mind, trust me."

Her words go in one ear and out the other. I don't tear my eyes away from the door until we round the bend and approach the portal I made for Ayra and me.

"So, where did you plan on taking my best friend?" Marley asks with an arch in her brow.

"Well—"

Marley cuts me off and says, "Forget it. Don't tell me. Show me instead."

"I don't think you'll like it," I admit, and it earns me a cocky smile.

"I guess we'll see . . ."

Something tells me this is going to bite me in the ass.

When we lived in the mortal realm, my mom used to take me to this coffee shop on the outskirts of Killin, Scotland. I don't remember all the places my parents took me to when we lived here, but this place is special. The café is on the edge of a small town and is usually empty and quiet. The food is divine, and they make the best hot chocolate across all the realms.

Mom used to take me here every Sunday. We would order a drink and split a flaky, homemade croissant. And no matter the weather, we would sit outside under the wooden awning. In spring, tiny pink flowers grow around the wrought iron railing, and butterflies flutter around the wildflowers in the field farther down.

I didn't want to bring Ayra here because of the food and drinks. I wanted her to sit in the seat my mom used to sit in, admire the rolling fields, and sense the earth's magic that lingers in the air. I wanted to see her eyes sparkle when she saw the mountain range with snow-capped cliff tops that reach the clouds. I feel like Ayra and my mom would get along. The thought of them meeting makes my stomach jostle with excitement and anxiety.

I'm not with Ayra, though, and it's enough to make my chest ache.

"You're right," Marley starts as we step through the portal. "I don't like this."

"I tried to tell you—"

"Shh." She cuts me off again. "*I* don't like this, but Ayra would have loved it. Good job, Gwydion."

Marley's expression softens as she looks at me, and a surge of pride rushes through me.

"You've won the battle but not the war," she says before walking toward the café. "I'm a hard woman to impress. And you've got to impress me if you want to get on my good side," she calls over her shoulder, making me gulp.

With two cups of hot chocolate and a bag of croissants in hand, I lead Marley to the exact spot I had in mind. When we round the corner, she stops dead in her tracks, and her jaw drops.

"Wow," she mumbles in amazement.

"Did I impress you?" I tease as I place our mugs and pastries on the table.

"Not yet," she says as her eyes remain on the mountain range in the distance.

With an airy laugh, I pull out her chair and wait for her to sit.

"This is incredible. Ayra would have *loved* this. Please bring her as soon as you can." Her eyes lock with mine, pleading for me to make this vow.

"I will. I promise."

Marley drops her shoulders in relief before sitting down.

Once she's comfortable, I take my seat and sip my hot chocolate. Comfort immediately floods through my body. I'm brought back to the days of being a kid. Living in this realm was quiet and comfortable. My world was shaken when we moved to Hecatium Valora. Between the drastic change in environment, the teasing, and the strict and rather hectic lessons at the academy, I was lost, and I forgot who I was. Until Machiis stood up for me and reminded me of my true self.

With him by my side, we ruled the lower-level academy. I remembered who I was, and my light started to shine through again.

Machiis and I are drifting apart, but that doesn't mean he'll never be my friend again. Sometimes, friends drift away from you only to veer back into your life as a new and better version of themselves. I'm willing to let Machiis go and hope that means he'll return stronger and better than ever. I only hope a certain black-haired, lavender-scented witch doesn't trip him along his path.

"So, Ryne, tell me. What do you think of Ayra?" Marley asks while arching her brow.

"What do I think of her?" I repeat while trying to gather my thoughts because there are a lot of ways I can answer that question.

I can tell Marley how I felt a gravitational pull the second I saw her, like the universe was trying to bring us together. I could tell her that I adore Ayra's stubbornness, her brains, how strong-willed and powerful she is.

But the words aren't flowing, and Marley gives me a sly grin.

"You don't seem like someone who gets speechless. Has Ayra stolen your words? Or are you trying to formulate an answer that will make me happy? Because if I find out you're playing with my friend, trying to lead her astray, I will—"

"She's everything," I say without thinking, and she tilts her head. "The moment I saw her, I knew she was fierce, headstrong, brilliant beyond her years, but I saw behind the front she put on too. When I approached her, she faltered, just for a moment. But in that moment, I saw intrigue and curiosity. Yes, she's beautiful but that's not what keeps me coming back. As I've spent more time with her, I've seen her desire to be vulnerable. I'm drawn to the kindness she displays when Kiki runs up to her and when she's interacted with Maren. I witnessed her desire for knowledge and vast problem-solving skills. I'm being tugged closer to her every day, and that's not something I've ever felt before. She's someone who is going to change the world, and I'm not deserving to even stand beside her."

"You're not?" Marley retorts. "Why do you say that?"

Because the voices told me so, but if I say that, she'll think I'm nuts.

I look down and fidget with my cup. "How much do you know about me?"

"Very little, other than what Ayra says."

And that gets the wheels in my head turning. "What does she say about me?"

Marley chuckles, and her green eyes light up. "Well, remember the first day you two spent together? When she was getting ready, she looked like she was walking to her death bed."

My expression drops, and she snickers. "Wait, I wasn't done. When she returned to get ready for the interview, she was all smiles, and I could feel the shift in her energy. She then proceeded to tell me that you two went flying, and you showed her places on the grounds she'd never seen before. In a day, you showed her more than she's seen in years during her time here. If you ask me, you two are polar opposites, but the stars may have some secrets they're not willing to share yet."

I'm at a loss for words. I wasn't sure what to expect when she said Ayra talks about me, but it wasn't this.

Marley smirks like she knows exactly what she just did to me.

"Give yourself some credit, Gwydion. If I like you, that's a win. If Ayra likes you, that's a victory only I've known. And I can tell you, it feels pretty good."

A smile breaks out across my face, and my heart swells in my chest. The voices from the first match were harsh, and while I didn't give them the time of day, I felt their words stitching into my mind. Now? They've disappeared, and I'm confident in myself again.

"I'm sure you've noticed, but she's been through a lot. It's not my story to share, but I can tell you that she and Cadie used to butt heads more often than they do now. Things turned violent last year, but the headmistress threatened their chances to participate in the games if it kept up. Ayra used to go missing. When she returned, I healed her wounds and bruises. On the instances where I had to find her, well. . . I try not to think of those moments. Fraydora isn't all sunshine and rainbows, we have our own darkness."

I'm not surprised by Cadie's actions. What leaves me reeling is that Fraydora let something such as this go unpunished. With all the light that embraces this academy, there are bound to be shadows.

A pit forms in my stomach. The thought of Ayra in danger leaves me clenching my jaw. I wanted to protect her before, but now, the feeling is multiplied by ten. She can defend herself, I don't doubt that. It's the fact that she had to. . .

"I trust you won't hurt her. She's safe now. I doubt anything will occur during the games. Ready to go see our girl?" she asks while snatching her croissant and standing.

"Thanks, Marley."

She nudges my arm as she passes and winks at me. "Don't think I'll share her. That grumpy lady was mine first."

I chuckle as she summons a portal farther down the path.

"Don't worry. Something tells me she'll pick you over me every time."

Marley spins around and clicks her tongue. "See? You are smart. In your own way, of course."

When Marley steps through the portal, I turn around and focus on the mountain range. I thought my days here were over when we moved, but now I'm wondering if that's no longer the case. Something tells me I'll be back, and maybe I'll have the witch who lights up the evening sky with me.

Ugh, what time is it?

My head is throbbing. I don't know how late Ryne and I stayed out last night. What I do know is that by the time I walked into my room, Marley was sitting on the edge of her bed, waiting for me to tell her where I'd been. I tend to stay up past midnight, but last night, I was exhausted and ready for bed.

With a groan, my eyes blink open, slowly adjusting to the light around me. I peer over at the grandfather clock, releasing another grunt. The next game starts in an hour. I know if I go back to sleep, I'll only wake up at the last minute and rush around, just like yesterday morning.

Against my will, I sit up. I drag my hands across my scalp, willing this headache to go away. I'm starting to wonder if last night's fun was worth this morning's pain.

I stumble over to the herb cabinet and pull out a peppermint tea bag Marley made the other day. It won't be as good as her brewing, but I place the bag in a teacup. With a wave of my hand, boiling water fills the cup, releasing the aroma of mint in the air. With tiny sips, I let the natural remedy work its magic on me.

Walking past Marley's bed, I backtrack when I realize she's not there. *Where in the realms is she?* It's unlike her to leave without announcing where she's going. Well, on the bright side, this means I'll have a quiet morning.

I stroll over to the mirror while whispering the spells to change my clothes and fix my tangled locks.

Amethyst trousers and a matching tunic with embroidered stars and moons in various lunar cycles along the stitching comprise my outfit of choice. I'm unsure what kind of challenge awaits today, so I pair this set with matching heeled boots that can transform quickly into a set of running shoes. My hair is magically pulled back into an updo, held in place with an outfit-matching hair comb, and as always, I feather my bangs myself.

With time to spare, I sit in a chair in the corner of the room. Sipping on my tea, I close my eyes, breathing in the minty steam through my nose.

I wonder where Marley is. Knowing her, she's spreading her morning sunshine around campus like it's her job, making sure to smile at each and every witch or wizard who crosses her path. It must be nice being so happy all the time. Part of me wonders whether it can get tiresome, always having to smile even if you're down. Marley doesn't ever seem to have down days. I'm sure she does, even if they are once in a blue moon.

"Good morning, Ayra!"

The door flies open, hitting the wall with such force that I almost drop my porcelain teacup.

I take it all back. This woman never has bad days.

Marley walks in, wearing a broad, gleaming smile. To my surprise, Ryne comes into view next. He leans against the doorway, donning his casual grin. He's wearing similar attire to what he wore the first day I ran into him, except this set is black with silver threaded designs along the seams.

Anytime I catch him smiling or laughing, my heart flutters and swells in my chest. My bones melt, rendering me useless. And somehow, it's getting worse.

Must have been last night and the almost kiss. I never thought Ryne would go out of his way to bring me somewhere like that. I mean, who brings a woman to an art museum for fun? When did I let my guard down? He really worked some kind of strange magic on me.

"Ready to kick some butt today?"

My eyes flick back over to Marley. Zachii pops out of her hair and tilts his head.

"Where were you?" I ask while placing my now empty cup on the table next to me.

"Ryne stopped by, and you were sleeping, so we realm-hopped to a new world for breakfast. I wanted to get to know my best friend's new partner."

I peer over at Ryne, envy and disappointment settling in my stomach like acid.

"Oh," I respond plainly.

Ryne squints at me and mouths *"Are you okay?"* when he sees my expression, but I don't respond.

I was crazy to think I could be special in his eyes. We went on our adventure not even twelve hours ago, and he's already portal-hopped with another.

"Ready to go?" I ask, trying to push through my thoughts.

Marley jumps up and down with a broad smile.

Kiki leaps off the bookshelf's top ledge and trots along at

my side while Ryne steps back into the hallway, I feel him reach out for my hand, but I pull away.

Gathering outside the Grand Hall, we wait for the next two rounds to begin. Today's games are split into two, four teams in each match. After that, I'm unsure what will happen. This year is vastly different from years prior. I mean, look around the room, witches and wizards teaming up. Since when did this happen?

Speaking of wizards . . . Ryne won't stop looking at me. I feel his lingering gaze. It feels like his green-ember eyes are leaving tiny marks along my pale skin.

I won't give in to this pull that threatens my muscles. I let myself forget just how important these games are to me. I worked tirelessly for years, and I won't let a wizard ruin my future.

"Ayra," Ryne whispers as the doors to the Grand Hall creak open. "What's wrong?" he asks as Illana and Borrick step through the doors.

He reaches for my hand, but I snatch it away.

"Don't touch me," I mumble.

"Welcome, ladies and gentlemen!" Illana's voice carries down the hall.

"What's wrong, Ayra?" Ryne drops his normal grin and leans closer to me while drawing his eyebrows together.

"If you hear your name, please follow the hall to the left." Illana directs before Borrick starts listing names.

"Ayra, look at me."

I give into Ryne's request, ready to defend myself against his charm.

"I don't want to," I mutter.

"Brightheart and Gwydion."

My heels slam down against the stone tile, leaving Ryne

before he has the opportunity to snap back. I was a fool to think Ryne and I could be friends. Stupid to believe he would spend his free time with me without expecting something in return. I'm nothing like Marley. If he wants someone to swoon over his flawless smile, laugh at his ridiculous jokes, and worship the ground he walks on, he's bothering the wrong witch.

"Ayra, I don't understand." Ryne's voice floats in my ear. *Another spell . . .* "Please."

He can beg all he wants. I need to focus on the task at hand.

I don't spot Cadie at the end of the hall, which means we'll most likely face her and Machiis in the next round. That is, if we win this match.

The doors open as we approach the room, and Kiki's presence fades from my side. Just as I turn around to see where she's going, she leaps into Ryne's arms, comforting him like she normally does for me. *Traitor.*

Ryne falls in line behind me as we cross through the doorway. Just like yesterday, the room swells outward. Crowds cheer above us, seemingly more people than yesterday. A professor I don't recognize stands behind a podium, and wooden tables are set up on the stage, with chairs lined up across from one another.

"Do you know this guy?" I ask Ryne, hiding all emotion from my tone.

"Professor Xans, he teaches a few different classes at Traquore," Ryne says as we take our places at a table across from another team.

I glance to my left as Professor Xans pushes his glasses up the bridge of his nose. His neon-red hair coils around his forehead.

"Welcome to day two of The Academy Games!"

The crowd erupts in applause, the noise filling the empty spaces around us.

"Who's ready for some trivia?"

A sly grin spreads across my lips. I ignore the fact that Kiki is purring in Ryne's arms. I don't need him or her right now. Trivia is something I can handle myself.

"You'll face off with the team directly across from you," Professor Xans states loud and clear for everyone in the room.

My eyes lock with the witch sitting across from me. Sarris Drans. I only know her in passing, and she's someone I don't consider a threat. The wizard though? I know nothing about him. His silver snake-like eyes gloss over me, and his cocky sneer makes my lips purse. I would ask Ryne if he knows the wizard with the villainous gaze, but if I talk to him, his voice will work its natural magic on me, and I'll end up forgiving him. I'm not in a forgiving mood right now. I need all the rage boiling inside to fester. It will drive us to the next round and one step closer to victory.

"Once a team gets two answers correct, they move on. The remaining team is disqualified. Categories will range from mystical creatures to long and forgotten history. Shall we get started!?"

The crowd erupts once again, ready for another entertaining round.

Meanwhile, those on the stage, including myself, jostle our feet, unable to stay still. The anxiety will deter some, but not me. I'm used to feeling pressured. Perfection comes with a certain degree of internal drive, the need to be one hundred and ten percent, twenty-four seven. That feeling lives in my bones. Somedays, it's crushing, and it hinders my ability to stand upright. Other days? I use the pain to push myself to the next stage in my journey. I'm learning to grow around the lingering pain. In the end, it'll all be worth it.

"Ayra," Ryne whispers as Professor Xans asks the first question. "Did I do something to upset you?"

I never knew someone could be so in touch with their feelings. *Must be annoying.* Just like the feeling twirling in my stomach.

"Can we focus on the task at hand?" I look to my right, and Kiki blinks at me, her lime eyes judging me.

"Was it about this morning? What Marley said? Because —" He's cut off by Professor Xans.

"Nice to see you, Mr. Gwydion. Hope you'll pay attention today; we both know your mind tends to wander off," he says with a wink, igniting the room in snickers.

"Don't worry, Professor." Ryne taps his head. "You have my complete attention."

Professor Xans glances at me, squinting ever so slightly. "Somehow, I doubt that."

Ryne lets out a chuckle. One that I seem to feel in every cell of my body.

Focus, Ayra.

"Okay, the first team to release a spark gets to respond. If the team answers incorrectly, the second team will have a chance to answer. The first to answer two questions correctly moves on. Understood?"

I must have missed the rapid round of questioning for the first set of teams. We're already down to three teams, one team has been eliminated. Forget Ryne and his feelings. This moment is what I need to concern myself over, nothing else.

"In the mortal realm, there is a creature said to be the fiercest monster of Norse mythology, a gigantic wolf chained to a rock on an island. What is his name?"

Without wasting a second, I raise my hand and release a spark from my fingertips.

"Ms. Brightheart."

"Fenrir," I state in confidence.

"That is correct. If you get the next question right, you move on to the next round. Pay attention, Ms. Drans and Mr. Ivis. When is the best time to remove a poltergeist who is wreaking havoc?"

Before I can respond, the man with silver gleaming eyes shoots a spark in the air.

"Dusk." His voice is deep and smooth.

"That is correct. All right, last question. What would you fill a worry doll with if you were looking to soothe rising panic?"

I raise my hand just as Sarris raises hers, our sparks milliseconds apart. My chest heaves as I'm unsure who Professor Xans will determine was the first to light the air.

"Ms. Drans."

No. Overwhelming dread fills my chest. An iron fist wraps around my heart, increasing its pressure with each pulse.

"Saint John's wort."

I bite my lip, trying to suppress my relieved smile.

"Close, but not quite. Ms. Brightheart? What's your response?" the red-haired professor asks.

"Motherwort."

His right brow arches as I offer him my answer.

Saint John's wort is effective in lifting depression. Motherwort is what halts chaos and panic. Illana offered it to me years ago. I wasn't expecting it to work, but it did. I still have the doll under my bed, just in case.

"Correct! Ms. Brightheart and Mr. Gwydion move on to the next round."

I release the built-up tension in my lungs and shoulders, letting myself relax into the victory.

"Now that we have a moment," Ryne speaks up.

A groan sounds from my throat.

"I'm not doing this, Ryne," I grumble, irritated that he won't drop it.

"Doing what?" he asks, his brow wrinkling in confusion.

"Whatever this is." I gesture at him, unsure of what I actually mean.

He squints his eyes. "Is this about this morning? Because I came to your dorm for you, not for Marley. I wanted to take you somewhere special, but Marley wanted to interrogate me. She's very protective of you, you know. You have a great friend in her. I stopped by this morning because I wanted to see you, to be with you. Because you make me feel like I'm capable of anything. I feel it too, this . . . feeling. And it's terrifying."

His words hit me like a ton of anvils. "You wanted to take me?"

He nods. "Yes."

"Why? I'm no one special," I mumble.

"You are more than special. You're Ayra Brightheart. You deserve more than you realize, and you're worthy of everything and more."

Kiki meows at me as Ryne speaks those words, and it's like

he's pouring his magic into my soul, shooting sparks against the shield around my heart.

I hold on to his damning sea-green eyes as we jostle forward to sit closer to Professor Xans.

Two teams are left, and we're one of them.

"And just like that, we're left with our remaining teams! Only one pair will head into the final challenge. Who will it be!?"

Ryne and I now face the never-ending crowd. Portals remain open, letting mystical beings trickle in and out. Sorcery is thick in the air, and the sensation tickles my nose.

"Will it be Ms. Brightheart and Mr. Gwydion?"

I wiggle my nose in an attempt to scratch the lingering itch. The applause and hollering threaten to shatter my ear drums.

"Can we be friends again?" Ryne whispers as the professor introduces the remaining pair.

Kiki crawls onto my lap, nudging my hand to curl along her spine.

"I never said we were friends to begin with." I offer him a teasing smirk, and when he smiles back, I know it's enough.

I don't know if it's Ryne's magic coursing through my veins or some sort of love potion, but what I can say is, seeing his lips turn upward, and relief washing over his expression, I don't feel angry anymore.

"The first team to reach one hundred points wins! Are we ready?" Professor Xans is really taking the whole game host thing to another level. At least he's enjoying himself.

"Let's win this thing, Brightheart," Ryne murmurs before winking at me.

I don't groan at the explosion of winged fairies in my stomach. Instead, I let them run rampant and bask in the feeling. "First question, why must you avoid killing geckos?"

Ryne releases a spark in the air before I get the chance to register the question.

"They are believed to devour evil spirits," he states with such certainty that I wonder if he was lying when he told me he's failing all his classes back at Traquore.

"Correct, ten points on the board."

A tally board materializes out of thin air.

"Name one way to cleanse a crystal."

A tiny firework is blasted into the air by another witch.

"Place the crystal in a silk casing and let it rest in a stream overnight."

Ten points are granted to the team across the way.

I shift in my seat, readying myself for the next question, refusing to fall behind.

"The Salem witch trials were a devastating mark in history in the mortal realm. Who was the first witch the humans sentenced to hang?"

I don't waste a second. I ignite a flicker of light from my fingertips before Professor Xans finishes asking the question.

"Bridget Bishop."

Another ten points for us. The round goes by in a blur, and I lose track of how many points we have compared to the other team. If Ryne or I answer a question, the other pair responds to the following question, beating us by mere seconds.

Turning my head, I dare look at the score. We're tied, and the tension couldn't be thicker. My leg shakes restlessly; I'm unable to control the anxiety that rampages in my body.

Ryne places his hand on the spot just above my knee, squeezing it, and I freeze. His fingertips release a rush of warmth through the fabric of my pants.

I can't pretend Ryne's touch doesn't have an effect on me. My body's reaction and the relief that washes over me is undeniable. Does Traquore know some calming methods that we don't? Is Ryne more intelligent than I originally thought? Or is it something else entirely?

"This question could very well give us our first finalist. Listen closely and pay attention, witches and wizards."

The room falls silent, waiting in anticipation for what could be the final question.

"We've got this Ayra. Just breathe." Ryne offers me a warm grin, and when he removes his hand, I shiver, missing the warmth of his palm.

I force out a puff of air and nod my head. Don't focus on the what-ifs. Focus on the now.

"What is this flower?"

My brow creases. In Xans's palm, a white flower blooms, one I know doesn't grow in this realm. How do I know that? It was included in yesterday's potion-making challenge. It's the very same flower Ryne placed behind my ear.

Time slows, allowing me a second to catch my breath. No one flinches. Not a single hand flies in the air. Ryne is itching to move; he knows what the flower is. But I think he's waiting to see if I remember, and of course, I do. How could I forget?

When the flow of time resumes, I glance at Ryne and wink, letting my hand release a spark so bright the crowd squints from its intensity. I don't let go of Ryne's gaze.

With a smile, I say the answer I know will secure our spot in the next game. "Lpomoea alba, also known as a moonflower."

"That is . . ." Professor Xans draws out his response.

"You remembered."

My smile widens as Ryne beams at me.

Ryne doesn't care about winning. He only cares that I remembered something he taught me.

"Of course I did."

"Correct!"

An explosion of fireworks takes over the arena, booming along with the harsh clapping and shouts of approval from the crowd above.

"Ms. Brightheart and Mr. Gwydion move on to the semifinals tomorrow!"

I turn in my seat and wrap my arms around Ryne's neck. He doesn't waste any time in squeezing me back. His hair feels like silk against my cheek, and I inhale his natural orange and cedar aroma. I can't identify the reason for the upward turn of my previous scowl. Is it because we won or because Ryne's embrace is setting my entire body aflame?

"Looks like we have two sets of fireworks going off, if you know what I mean." Professor Xans's words send a flurry of chills up and down my spine. "Three teams survived the second set of games across the hall! Make sure to join us tomorrow to watch our final four teams compete for their spot in the finale!"

His words go in one ear and out the other.

I pull away from Ryne with burning red cheeks and brush a stray piece of hair behind my ear, wishing the shy smile on my face would fade, but it doesn't. I thought the feeling Ryne elicited in my stomach was irritation. Now, I'm starting to think it's worse than that.

This isn't irritation anymore. This is something deeper, and the unknown is throwing me off kilter.

The sound of my footsteps bounces off the walls around me. Ignoring the passing glares and muffled whispers has become a hobby of mine. If this was a normal day, I might have instructed the gathered crowd to return to class. Not today though.

Instead, unfamiliar feelings overwhelm me. My head is drowning in recollections. Ryne's eyes, his swoon-worthy lopsided smile, how he went out of his way to take me to an art museum, how close we were in the exhibit, all the giggling and wide grins. The memories alone are making me blush.

I near the end of the hall in a flurry. Normally, when you want to see the headmistress, you knock politely or make an appointment. I'm a rule follower, a "stickler," if you will. Not today. Today, all the rules are sucked into a tornado and blown right out the window.

"Illana?" I push the door open a little too swiftly.

It bangs against the bookshelf behind it, causing her

familiar to squawk and flap its wings at the disturbance. Illana appears from the other side of another bookshelf.

"Sorry," I say as I cringe.

I close the door gently behind me as Illana's lavender eyes search my face.

"Ayra, what in the underworld?"

Her black robes nearly swallow her whole, and her hair is neatly pulled back in a bun.

I release a sigh, trying to will my shoulders to relax.

"Are you okay?" She furrows her brow as she examines me before putting back the book she was holding and approaching me.

My chest heaves up and down as I try to get as much oxygen as I can into my lungs. But no matter what I do, I can't catch my breath.

The room begins to spin, Illana's numerous bookshelves whirling into one.

My hands fly to my head, trying to stabilize my balance.

Illana brings her hand to my back, urging me forward.

"Let's take a seat, come on. One step at a time."

Her words slow the world around me.

I sit in a plush chair in front of her desk. The cushion cradles my body, soothing the spinning that overpowers my head.

"Close your eyes."

I obey her request. Illana rests her fingertips on my temples as she whispers a chant, one I've grown quite familiar with. I join her in whispering to the witch goddess.

I call upon Hecate, asking for her guidance. The room is spinning, and I fear I may drown. I can't breathe. My heart is strained by an iron fist. Silence the world around me. Balance the earth, welcome air into my lungs, and let the moons' forces provide comfort and love. Hecate, goddess of all magic and witches, aid me in my time of need.

With each word, my body releases tension. My lungs inflate, catching up on the air I lost moments ago.

Through pursed lips, I release a shaky breath and blink my eyes open.

Once the room comes back into focus, the violent nerves that ravaged my body moments ago evaporate.

"Thank you," I sigh in relief.

I'm pretty good at keeping my composure. The only time I seem to lose my hold on it is when Illana asks me if I'm okay. It gets me every time.

"What's going on? It's very unlike you to storm in here without an appointment," she says while sitting in the chair across from me.

"There's something wrong with me."

Illana smiles and tilts her head, ignoring the panic lacing my words. "What do you think is wrong with you?"

I don't know what a motherly tone sounds like, but I think it would resemble something like this. Illana already has a natural, soothing nature, but when I get like this, she's even more gentle. Like she knows what she's about to say next will either ease my fears or send me into another breakdown.

"My stomach is a constant mess with what feels like a million winged insects fluttering in it." I wrap my arms around myself, the feeling returning as I voice it back to life.

"Does this have anything to do with Ryne Gwydion?" She arches her right brow.

"Please don't say his name," I groan before closing my eyes in defeat.

"Let me guess, along with your stomach troubles, you also can't focus, goose bumps cover your arms whenever he speaks, and you want to be around him nonstop?"

I squint my eyes open and nod.

"Well, it was bound to happen to someone. Although, I'm surprised it's you that it hit."

"What hit me? Is it a stomach bug? Did the wizards bring some sort of mysterious plague with them?"

Illana chuckles at my never-ending anxiety.

"I'm really glad my pain is entertaining you," I mumble, unamused.

"Oh, my dear," she says while wiping her eyes from laughing so hard. "It's not a stomach bug or the plague. . ."

I look at her with wide eyes. My nostrils flare as the thought crashes into me. No, not in a million centuries. Not now, not ever.

"Don't—" I point at her. "No. That is not what's happening."

"Tell me, what do you think I'm insinuating?"

"That I have a crush on Ryne Gwydion." At the sound of my own admission, I'm left spiraling. "No, there's no way." I shake my head in denial. There's no way I have a crush, especially not on Ryne. Absolutely not. "You're only saying that because Professor Xans made a stupid comment about fireworks."

My lips scrunch together. Illana is messing with me. There's no other explanation.

"I didn't need to hear his comment to see the fireworks you're referring to. I had the pleasure of witnessing it myself. That man is smitten with you. Knew it the moment he placed the moonflower behind your ear."

Her confession unleashes another series of questions in my head.

Is it possible Ryne has feelings for me? If he does, was it really obvious that soon? How can these feelings be so strong already? None of this is making any sense.

"I know what you're thinking, Ayra. Love doesn't have a timeline."

My eyes widen. "Love!?" I stand abruptly and pace around her office. I weave in between the rows of bookshelves aimlessly. "Love!?"

Illana's familiar, Zada, mimics me. She echoes the word, and I can't escape it.

"There's no way!" I shout.

"Ayra, that's not what I meant!" Illana chases me. "Love is merely a possibility." She catches up and places her hands on my shoulders, spinning me around to face her. "What I meant to say was that crushes are intense. The two of you have a spark, and it's growing rapidly because you're around one another every day. It's normal and completely okay."

Normal. Not once was I ever called *normal.* What a strange word.

"My feelings are normal?"

She nods. "You're always so perfect. Since you were a child, your feelings dominated you. Over the years, I watched you silence them. What you're feeling now is new and overwhelming. Don't silence it though. Go with the flow of it. Enjoy the moment. Forget about being perfect and have fun."

There's that word again, something I didn't experience until I met Ryne. But I can't drop being perfect. I have a point to prove. I need the academy to know that I'm not a waste of time. I will succeed in proving to the world that magic demands perfection, and that is something I won't forget.

"Okay, I'll try." I offer her a small smile, and she returns it.

"Now, you have a big day tomorrow. I knew this day would come, but now that it's here, I can't even begin to express how proud I am of you. Remember—" She taps the side of her head and winks at me. "Expect the unexpected."

"And let me guess, have fun?" I ask as I roll my eyes.

Her smile grows, exposing faint laugh lines along the corners of her mouth and eyes. "Now you're getting it."

Ryne

27

F*ireworks.*

The moment Professor Xans spoke that simple word, Ayra's smile warped into a worried frown, and her eyes widened. My suspicion that she may feel the same way I do was confirmed, but so was the lingering thought that her feelings for me are scaring her. That was solidified when she stormed down the hall after the game, hauling her ass to some unknown destination.

I don't want her to be afraid of any feelings that may be brewing between us. Hells, I want them to excite her. I've seen the look she gets when something intrigues her. I've seen her throw it at me more than once. She purses her lips together, and her eyes twinkle with curiosity as her forehead scrunches. She's stared at me more times than I can count, and I'd give anything to have it never end. I've been with two other witches before, both of whom I cared for. This level of connection I feel toward Ayra is different. It's *magical*, which is strange, given the fact that I see magic every day. It's a higher level of power resting deep in my chest, and she's the one awakening it.

I stroll through the halls, not watching where I'm going, my thoughts running wild. I don't notice where I wander until the blinding light from the suns shines brighter than before. Pulling my gaze from my feet to farther down the hall, I shield my eyes from the sudden change.

I haven't been to the North Wing before, solely because I tend to go where Ayra goes, and she hasn't come here.

I find it hard to believe Ayra and Cadie may have been friends at one point in time. They're so different, and frankly, Cadie is a cold-hearted bitch. Her expression when she torments Ayra is devilish. I fear what may happen if it continues. Cadie may be lost to the shadows of dark magic if she keeps it up.

Dark magic isn't something we see every day. Sure, a few witches and wizards perform the dark arts, but most don't believe the risk is worth the gain. The moment you cast a dark spell, it seeps into your veins, turning your skin black. You'll age and wrinkle faster than you normally would because dark magic comes with a cost, and that cost is your life force.

"Hey, lover boy," Cadie's voice sounds from behind me.

Turning around, I discover that I walked right past her and Machiis. He smiles at me while moving his arm from my waist.

"Ms. Blackwell," I greet her, trying my best to hide my distaste.

"What brings you to this part of the academy?" she asks while cocking her head to the side.

"I was lost in thought—"

"About Ayra?" Machiis asks.

"I heard what happened during your game. *Fireworks*, how adorable." Cadie clicks her tongue in painfully faux approval.

If I hadn't seen what transpired between Ayra and Cadie

the other day, I would believe her feigned cheerfulness. But I know how snake-like she can be, and I'm not buying it.

"I just lost my way, that's all." I take a step to walk away from them, but she blocks my path.

"Since you're here, can I show you something?" she offers, still pretending like we're friends.

"What is it?" I ask her while narrowing my eyes.

Her violet eyes glisten as the suns' rays trickle in through the glass ceiling. "Follow me." She heads down the hall.

Her familiar trots by her side, releasing strands of white fur into the air.

Machiis pats my back and ushers me forward. "You won't believe the stuff they have here, it's unbelievable."

I wish I could say my curiosity wasn't intense, but there's so much I don't know. The witching world is different from ours. I want to know everything, even if it means following the biggest snake within these castle walls.

The walls glisten here. Sparkles of light dance along the golden walls. Neatly trimmed rose bushes line the corridor, each velvet red rose is perfect, which seems strange and out of place.

Cadie leads us toward a courtyard. She leans against the banister before pulling something out of her bag.

My interest is piqued immediately.

"What is that?" I can't hide my wonder, and the question flows off my tongue effortlessly.

Cadie rolls the orb around in her palm. "It's supposed to bring good luck," she says.

My eyes never leave the orb. A swirling marigold hue swims within its depths.

"How does it work?" I ask while taking a step forward, nearing her before I can even comprehend how close I've gotten.

"It works off willpower. You think about the person or being you want to bestow luck on and let the magic work," Machiis tells me. "Cadie just showed this to me, it works wonders."

Hayes chirps as he flies away, and the movement makes my brow quiver, but it doesn't pull me away from staring at the orb.

"That's amazing," I mumble.

"Want to give it a try?" she asks, and I meet her gaze.

"Really?"

She places the orb in my hand and smiles. "Think about the one person you want to wish luck upon. A warm tingling sensation will fill your skin. That's how you know it's working. Give it a try." She gestures at my hand.

Cadie's familiar runs after Hayes, leaving them without their familiars. I should be focusing on that, but something is pulling me in, almost like the orb is calling my name.

I think of Ayra and the distress she was feeling when she fled after the game. I want nothing more than for her to be happy. While I don't think she needs luck for the games, I think she needs it for her feelings. Perhaps it would make her feel more confident. Maybe then she'd be ready to face the potential feelings she may have toward me.

I think of her eyes, how blue and silver they are. They remind me of the icy glaciers in the frozen lands of Zaffer, terrifying and beautiful. I think of her smile and how her cheeks turn red when she laughs. I think of my feelings for her and how I'd give anything to ensure her never-ending happiness.

Just as Cadie said, warmth spreads from my palm to my forearm and up to my shoulders. It slowly fills my body until it reaches my heart.

I meet her gaze and smile breathlessly.

"Is it working?" she asks, intrigued.

"It is," I say with a nod.

"Good." She grins.

I glance down at the orb, absorbed in its wonderfully beautiful magic, hoping Ayra will soon feel on top of the world. Because she deserves nothing less.

"Where did you go? I was looking for you." Marley almost jumps on me when I stroll through the opened bedroom door. Her arms rope around me, choking the air out of my chest. "I got worried when you weren't with Ryne. He said you got this weird face and walked toward the East Wing." Her words are laced with concern.

"I went to talk to Headmistress Illana. Nothing's wrong, I promise," I say while offering her a reassuring smile.

"Did it have anything to do with that firework comment?"

The floor under my feet feels like lit embers. Marley stares at me intently, waiting for an answer.

"Yeah." I shift in unease.

The temperature underneath my feet increases, slowly burning the soles of my boots. "Do you feel that?"

I bounce from foot to foot. No matter where I stand, the burning sensation gets stronger. It's nothing like the warmth that coats my hands when my flames take over. This pain is excruciating.

"Feel what?" Marley arches a brow.

I whirl around and scan the room. "The floor doesn't feel hot to you?" I ask as the temperature increases twofold.

"No . . ."

I huff. "Someone is fucking with me."

"Is that a raspie?" Marley's random question irks me.

"What are you talking about?"

She points at my feet, and I tilt my head as I glance at the floor.

"No, it's a lapwrin. More specifically, Ryne's familiar." I lower myself to my knees, offering Maren my finger.

He reaches out and holds my pointer finger, just like before. With a gentle tug, I get the signal he's trying to give.

"Where's Ryne?"

With a nose wiggle, he runs out of my room and down the hall. I don't know why Maren isn't with Ryne. What I do know is that he never leaves Ryne's side. The fact that he's here and Ryne isn't can only mean one thing.

I don't waste a second, and Marley doesn't question why I'm chasing Ryne's familiar down the corridors. Marley is good at figuring things out. She may not seem bright, but she's brilliant. She knows when to act and when to ask questions.

We follow Maren, barely able to keep up because his species is notorious for being fast. We must look crazy, two witches chasing a lapwrin down the halls. I can only imagine what others must think.

Maren leads the way like he's lived here his entire life. That, or he's following Ryne's scent. A thousand questions are running through my mind, but the heat under my feet is scrambling all rationale.

This confirms that Cadie is up to something. Only she can cast a spell from halls away and succeed. Whatever she's up to, she will pay for the havoc she is causing me.

Before long we cross the threshold into the North Wing. Immediately, light blinds me. I shield my eyes, letting myself adjust to the brightness. The walls and tile floors are gilded gold, and flecks of gold ore sparkle along the crevices. The scent of rose water reaches my nose. It's so strong my eyes start to water.

With another turn, I hear her, an irritated growl and screech. *Kiki...*

I don't know what I'm running into, but I don't care. The underworld is about to rupture through this hall like Hades himself is making an entrance.

Marley bumps into my back as I stumble to a halt. Kiki stretches along Ryne's leg, trying to bat the crimson crystal Orb of Molten Despair out of his hand. Cadie stands before him, smirking as her fingers dance along the smooth surface. Maren runs up Ryne's leg and settles on his shoulder before tugging on his earlobe.

"Fuck!" I scream as the tiles under my feet melt the soles of my boots.

"What in the underworld are you doing!?" Marley storms over and knocks the orb to the ground.

When it shatters, I collapse to my knees. Kiki scampers over to me, bumping her nose against mine.

"Ayra, what's wrong?" Ryne asks as he separates himself from Cadie's clutches.

"You don't know what that is?" Marley shouts, letting her usual, kind demeanor vaporize.

"Of course he doesn't!" I hiss.

I prop myself up using my hands, making eye contact with Cadie and side-eyeing Machiis, who looks concerned yet unbothered at the same time.

I don't blame Ryne; there are things we have here that he doesn't know about. This is all on Cadie.

"We were just having fun." Cadie chuckles, using her terrible attempt at an innocent tone.

"Ayra, are you hurt?" Ryne closes the small distance between us.

My chest is heaving, my breaths coming fast, as I ignore his worried gaze and focus all my energy on the one person who deserves my anger.

Flames overtake my hands. Instead of blistering heat, it's comforting.

"Ayra," Ryne whispers. "Don't do it."

I ignore his plea.

I lunge off the floor, bypassing Machiis, and wrap my hand around Cadie's throat, careful not to burn her. I want her scared. I want her to wither in fear and to beg for forgiveness.

"Let me go," she says with gritted teeth. "It was a joke."

"A joke!? I think we need to go back to year one, Cadie. Someone forgot what the term *joke* means," I hiss, fully aware that my skin is sticking to the soles of my shoes. "I'm sick of this. I'm tired of the constant torture from you and your lackeys."

Her eyes gloss over, and her gaze is full of pure hate. I don't know why our former friendship took a turn. I'll never know why she looks at me the way she does now.

But I do know why I feel this way. Her constant bullying and harsh words come to the forefront of my mind. I would have never noticed if Ryne hadn't pointed it out.

"What is going on here?"

I pull my hands from Cadie's throat and press them over my ears, protecting myself from Borrick's thunderous voice.

Cadie falls on her knees when my grasp around her releases. The flames on my hands flicker out, leaving the sleeves of my tunic fried.

"Cadie was using an Orb of Molten Despair on Ayra," Marley declares, unafraid to seek justice for me.

"It wasn't me," Cadie coughs, pretending like my grip on her throat injured her. "It was Ryne's idea."

"Explain yourself, Gwydion."

I meet Ryne's eyes as Borrick stares him down.

"He didn't know what it was." I butt in. "The orb is a tool witches use. He had no way of knowing the pain he was bestowing on me."

Borrick scans my facial features, and I gulp. This man's stare alone could halt armies. I would be foolish to lie to him.

"Ms. Brightheart, go seek medical attention. Ms. Blackwell, you're coming with me."

"What!?" Cadie screeches.

"Now!" Borrick's voice shatters a window down the hall. "Machiis Avium, go to your room. I don't want to see you again today. You've been nothing but trouble since we got here."

Cadie obeys, stomping down the hall as Borrick observes the three of us. "Talk to your headmistress before tomorrow."

I nod, knowing exactly why I have to follow up with Illana.

It doesn't matter that Cadie started it, or that I was defending myself. The integrity of the games is at stake. Cadie and I could be disqualified, and everything I worked toward could be over.

I groan as blisters form on the soles of my feet. Taking a step forward, I almost fall to the ground, and a scream builds in my chest from the pain.

"I've got you," Ryne says as he catches me.

I collapse into his embrace and let him support me.

"Thank you." I sniffle as tears start to trickle from my eyes.

Ryne offers me a sympathetic smile, his eyes glistening behind his ruffled hair. "I'm so sorry, Ayra. This is all my fault."

Before I can respond to him, Marley speaks up. "We need to get her to Professor Floris. Can you walk?"

I don't think walking is an option anymore, as I can hardly stand, so I shake my head in response.

"Ryne, can you carry her?"

"Just lead the way." Ryne scoops me in his arms.

I wrap my arms around his neck, fighting the desire to rest my head on his shoulder.

"Don't drop me," I whisper.

He tightens his arms around my body and clutches me against him. His lips brush my ear, and shivers run down my spine as he whispers, "I've got you, don't worry."

The healing waters are located in the West Wing. Professor Floris knows the only entrance that exists, and I know she'll escort us. She wouldn't let me suffer in pain just because she wants to keep the waters a secret.

Marley knocks on her office door politely. When Floris opens it, she locks her ivy-green eyes on mine, and all color drains from her face.

"What happened?" That grandmother-like tone fills her voice.

"Ayra needs the healing spring, please. We can explain along the way," Marley begs.

Floris jumps into action right away; she doesn't take time to question the direness of the situation.

After locking her office door, she opens a portal. "Follow me."

The four of us step through the portal, and Marley and Ryne pause as Floris walks ahead.

Plush green grass cushions their feet, and nature's song fills the air around us. Spring pollen dances in the air, landing on our cheeks and painting our skin daisy yellow.

"Come on, children," Professor Floris calls for us, beckoning us forward with her hand.

Marley and Ryne fall into step, and I snuggle into the crook of Ryne's neck. They dodge low-hanging tree branches, bending down to avoid vines of flowers that canopy the path. It doesn't take us long to reach a clearing.

The three of us gasp in awe.

I've only read about healing springs in books. There are only a few in all the realms, and pictures don't do it justice. The steady stream of water trickles over scattered crystalized pearl stones and boulders. Multicolored moss grows under the glass-clear water, reflecting azure, amethyst, and emerald around the spring's surface. Power floats in the atmosphere, and the air smells clean, like fresh water.

When I was younger, I had a hard time pinpointing what magic smelled like. It's different for everyone. Now, for me, magic smells like oranges and cedar . . .

Wait. . . with a tiny inhale, I smell Ryne's skin, and my stomach flips.

No . . . that can't be right. Why does Ryne smell like magic? More specifically, *my* magic? I look up at him, and my cheeks flush as he holds me close to his chest.

"Where are you hurt?" Floris approaches me, shaking me from my daze.

"My feet," I say before releasing a shaky breath.

"Ryne, place her by the spring's edge. Marley, help me with her shoes," Professor Floris instructs.

Ryne places me on the ground as gingerly as he can. Marley unties one boot as Professor Floris works on the other.

Once my boots are untied, I wince. Ryne reaches out for my hand, and I take it for support.

"This is going to hurt. Brace yourself."

I do just as Floris warns, but nothing could have prepared me for the amount of pain that shoots through my body.

"Third-degree burns on her soles." I hear her say, but my cries and the pain are all I can register.

Gripping Ryne, I shove my face into his chest as tears stream down my face.

"Are you ready, Ayra?" Professor Floris asks as she stands.

I nod against Ryne's chest.

He interlocks our fingers, and I scoot to the spring's edge.

"The water will be cold at first, but it'll adjust to your body temperature." Professor Floris tries to reassure me.

I sniffle before looking at Ryne for comfort. "Don't leave me," I beg him, sounding desperate.

Ryne makes me feel safe. He's the reason I'm hurt, but it's not his fault. My body wants him close, and I need to listen to it right now, especially if I want to heal properly.

"I'm not going anywhere," he says with a soft smile.

I stop before the water, unsure of what to expect. I don't think it'll hurt, but will it provide relief right away?

I squeeze Ryne's hand, and with a violent intake of air, I plunge my left foot into the spring. My jaw locks as I refuse to let any groans of pain slip through. I don't let another thought run through my mind.

The water wafts over my right foot as it sinks beneath the surface, and bubbles form around my ankles as the foreign heat trickles out, providing a cooling sensation. The moss under my feet sticks to the blisters, poking needle-sized pin holes through the skin to release the pressure and any toxins.

I meet Ryne's gaze and sigh. "Thank you."

With a nod, he releases my hand, not moving from my right side.

I rest my hands atop the moss under the water. After a few

muffled grunts from me, it doesn't take long for the water to reach my core temperature.

"This is going to take some time. Why don't you guys head back? I can watch her," Professor Floris offers.

I glance at Ryne from the corner of my eye, discovering he's shaking his head.

"I can stay and keep her company. I'm sure you're busy, Professor."

The suns' reflection bounces off his honey-shaded hair.

"Are you su—"

He doesn't even let her finish her question; he's nodding definitively. "I'm sure."

"Okay, I'll be back in an hour to check in. Coming Marley?"

I offer Marley a smile and nod as she looks over at me.

"I'll make sure Headmistress Illana punishes Cadie justly."

I mouth "*thank you*" to her, knowing the hell she's about to unleash back at the academy.

Ryne and I are left alone. The stream of water is soothing, and the flow is hypnotic. Kiki crawls onto my lap, purring and nuzzling against my palm. I release a sigh, thankful Kiki and no one else was hurt within that orb's radius.

"Ayra." Ryne twirls a piece of grass around his finger, never plucking it from the ground. "I'm sorry, I was stupid. I should have known Cadie was up to something. I should have known better than to listen to her." He doesn't meet my gaze, and he remains peering into his reflection in the water.

"You're not stupid," I say as I pull my hand from the water and rest it on his forearm.

His eyes finally meet mine, the dark embers dancing along his beautiful irises.

"You're many things, Ryne. But stupid isn't one of them. You're brilliant in your own wonderful, fun way," I say with a tired chuckle.

"Did you really just say that?" he asks with a hint of laughter.

Ryne is so much more than a carefree, fun-seeking wizard. I was wrong to assume he was.

"Shocking, right?"

We both smile and laugh in response to my change of perspective.

"More interesting than shocking, if you ask me."

I scrunch my nose at his words.

What an interesting witch.

"I mean that in the best way possible, of course," he says while wrapping his hand around mine. The way his eyes dance across my face sends butterflies fluttering through me. "You're something else, Brightheart." He curls his free hand into my hair.

I can't help but lean against his palm.

"More than a stickler or grumpy gills?" I stick my tongue out at him as I flick water in his face.

Next thing I know, he's scooping water in his hands and drizzling it over my head.

My mouth drops open, the cool water shocking my entire system before it adjusts to my body's temperature. "You're going to pay for that," I threaten with a teasing tone.

"Is that so?"

He smirks just as I whisper, "*Eathirum.*"

The ground beneath him launches him deep into the springs, and when he lands, a wave ripples to the bay where I'm sitting.

I'm giggling when he resurfaces, sputtering out water and shivering.

"Oh, you wanna play?" he shouts, and I can hear the mischief in his voice from here.

Ryne's mouth opens, but I don't hear any words. It's not

long before the water pulls me forward, slowly forming into a wave. Kiki leaps off my lap right before I'm hurled into the air. I let out a squeal, but it's muffled when my body splashes into the water. I swim to the surface, meeting Ryne and that chipper smile of his.

"You jerk." I spit a mouth full of water at him.

"You started it," he chuckles before splashing more water in my face.

We go back and forth, and with each spray of water, we dissolve into laughter. The current around us pushes us closer together, and as my feet brush against his, I freeze. A wave pushes me into Ryne's chest, and his arms wrap around me as the current relaxes.

"Did you do that?"

He shakes his head at my hushed question.

I peer into his eyes, letting his touch overwhelm my senses.

Being in his arms makes me feel secure, like he wouldn't let anyone or anything harm me. It's an unusual but welcome feeling, as I've always had to rely on myself for protection.

My breath catches as his lips part. I wonder if he can hear the pitter-patter of my heart. Does he know the effect he has on me? Is it possible I have the same effect on him?

"Ayra?" he whispers like it's a secret only the two of us know. I gulp past the lump in my throat. "What did you think of Xans's comment today?"

The one that sent me spiraling? The one that apparently wasn't even necessary because the fireworks are as clear as a sunny, cloudless day?

"I don't know what to think," I mutter.

Ryne brushes his nose against mine and glances down to my lips.

"What do you think?" I ask back.

His eyes lock on mine again, stirring up the feeling of those winged creatures in my stomach again.

"I think he's on to something." He weaves his hand into my hair, urging me closer.

I close my eyes as he closes his. Just as our lips feather against one another—

"How's it going?" Professor Floris's voice calls from the trees that protect the clearing.

I drop under the water, putting distance between Ryne and me. When I break through the spring's surface, Kiki is staring at me from the forest's edge.

"You didn't have to submerge yourself, Brightheart." Floris chuckles as she takes in the sight of a rather soaked set of students. "Mr. Gwydion, how did you end up in the spring?"

"Felt like taking a dip." He snickers before sloshing back onto the bank.

"What a funny pair you two are." Floris beams, shaking her head while she chuckles. "Anyway, feeling better?"

"Much, thank you." I nod and sigh in relief.

"Okay, you two, let's head back. You have a big day tomorrow," she says as she leads the way back through the trees.

Ryne and I follow her in silence, both too shy to admit to one another what just happened. Or, rather, what *might* have just happened.

When Professor Floris steps through the portal, Ryne places his hand on my lower back, ushering me to go through before him. Before I cross the portal, he squeezes my shoulder and I look back at him. A miniature show of fireworks leaves his fingertips, and his smile makes my heart weightless.

I thought fireworks were big explosions of light in the sky. Something that only happens during celebrations or parties. Is the feeling that's taken residence in my stomach what they're calling fireworks?

If so, I never want the feeling to end.

Ayra

29

R yne tried to insist on walking me back to my room, and as much as I wanted to let him, I didn't. I need time to think, to register the feelings circulating throughout my body.

I'm able to walk, thanks to the healing spring, but I'm mentally and physically drained. I keep stopping to catch my breath, using the walls for support. When I make it to my bedroom door, Kiki chirps by my side, and it opens. I stumble over to my bed and collapse face down, groaning into my pillow, happy to feel a sense of relief and comfort.

"You can thank me later." My back arches in response to Marley's voice.

As she skips into our room, I flip over and wrap my quilted blanket around myself, overwhelming exhaustion slowly staking a claim on my body.

"What are you talking about?" I say while trying to blink away my exhaustion.

Kiki curls in my lap, and her purring becomes a serene lullaby.

"I talked Headmistress Illana into letting you stay in the games."

"How did you manage that?"

She sways back and forth, and I watch the second her teeth meet the side of her cheek.

"We all have our skills, but . . ." She doesn't even have to finish her sentence; I know where she's going.

"But Cadie gets to stay too." The strength in my tone dissipates.

I succumb to the fatigue, falling against my pillows and letting the weight of my blanket cradle me.

"I'm sorry, Ayra," Marley whispers as she sits at the foot of my bed.

"Don't be. This will only give me the chance to put her in her place publicly," I mutter while stroking Kiki's velvet fur, letting her soothe me to sleep. "I won't be her toy anymore . . ."

Marley rests her hand on my leg and sighs. "Just don't let it turn you into her. Be you, Ayra. You are stronger than you think you are, and you will win. Just make sure it's for you and no one else."

My eyes flutter closed, but Marley's voice and the urgency of her tone still register.

I won't let Cadie Blackwell change me, but I also won't let her force me into a shell any longer. I'll become the best version of myself with the help of Ryne and Marley. I won't turn into a witch like her.

I'll become someone stronger.

"Today's challenge will determine who moves on to the finale."

I scan the empty field as a warm gust of wind wraps around me. Along with Ryne and myself, Cadie and Machiis and two additional teams I haven't seen before today are here. Cheering surrounds the empty grounds, but I can't see the audience. They're either cloaked with invisibility or watching from another part of the academy.

"First you need to obtain a golden key. Each team will start with a riddle. You are to figure out where the riddle is leading you and follow the clues."

Something brushes along my hand as Illana goes over the rules. I look down as Ryne's finger feathers around my thumb, but the second I notice it, he pulls away.

I gulp past a newly formed lump in my throat and release a shaky breath.

"The two teams who reach the goal first will advance to the final game."

"Are you ready?" Ryne asks.

I lock eyes with his. His accent still sends my brain into a frenzy; it's far too enjoyable to listen to his voice.

I give him a quick nod and grin before looking back at

Illana.

"Oh, and one more thing. Magic is prohibited during this game unless it is specified in your riddle. If you are caught using unsolicited spells, you will be disqualified."

My nose wrinkles in response, and I catch Ryne smiling out of the corner of my eye.

"With that being said, let the games begin!"

The applause reaches a crescendo, and the ground shakes, growing more unstable by the second. I lose my balance and stumble back, but Ryne catches me, wrapping his arms around me to ensure I don't fall. I don't think he realizes how close his lips are to my ear, their proximity sending a wake of goose bumps and chills down my body.

I lean into him, wanting to soak in this moment. I almost miss the second everything around us changes.

Neatly trimmed pillars of thick shrubbery shoot to the sky, interlocking and weaving together to create a wild maze.

"What the hells?" Ryne's whisper elicits a strange response from my body, and I'd give anything to hear that hint of curiosity in his tone again.

I shake my head, thankful the ground is no longer quaking.

Cadie scrambles into the entrance before her, prompting me to look around. Ahead of me is an entrance just like hers, and I don't waste a second.

"Let's go," I call back to Ryne, relieved that he's quick on his feet.

The maze is easy to follow. In fact, it seems to be leading us rather than tricking us into going in the wrong direction. With one final twist and turn, I halt in an empty clearing.

Scanning the area, I notice there's nothing. No hint or sign as to where to go next. Only when Ryne steps across the threshold does a portal open up.

"Oh, this is going to be so much fun." Ryne beams as he breathes deeply. "Ready?" He extends his hand to me.

Normally, I would resist, go my own way, and question his kindness. But I'm learning that this is who Ryne is. Not everyone is cruel and out to get me.

I place my hand in his and let the warmth spread from my hand to my heart.

"As I'll ever be," I say with a grin that matches his.

Ryne tugs on my hand and steps through the portal. When we emerge on the other side, it takes me more than a moment to process the vast change of scenery.

We're in a room brightly lit by the two burning suns streaming in through a window. Dust particles float through the air, along with the aroma of old books. When I step forward, the floorboards creak, but it doesn't stop my wonder. I run my finger along a book on top of a waist-high stack, and a thick layer of dust paints my fingertip.

"Have you ever seen this room before?" Ryne asks as he admires the space.

"No, never," I murmur.

The entire room is filled with stacks of books. I'm surprised a room like this even exists, and why are these books here and not in the library?

"What do you think we're looking for?" I glance around the room as Ryne looks for an answer to his question.

I rub my nose to relieve the tickle from the irritants. There must be something in here . . .

"Ayra, duck!" Ryne shouts.

I double over and cover my head, unsure of what I just avoided, but I know Ryne wouldn't just yell that at random.

"What is it?" I ask while righting my posture. When my eyes land on the ceiling, my eyes roll. "Really?" A chuckle leaves my chest while a sparrow flutters around the room.

"It was going for your head," Ryne responds, sounding out of breath. "What is it doing in here?"

We both watch the trapped creature, and I tilt my head and squint my eyes. "You see that, right?"

Around the bird's neck is a ribbon looped through a key.

"I see it." Ryne lowers his voice as the bird perches itself on a stack of books near the dirtied windows.

"How are we supposed to get it?" I ask.

We could cast a tranquilizing spell and subdue the creature until we get what we need from it, but we can't use magic.

"I don't know."

"Use your charm or something." As my voice raises, the bird's eyes land on us, and we freeze.

"Aw, does that mean you think I'm charming?"

I roll my eyes, trying my best to fight the smile that threatens my lips.

"Shut up, Ryne . . ." My breath hitches in my throat as his ear brushes along my cheek.

"It's the accent, isn't it?"

I side-eye him, wishing his closeness didn't make my cheeks blush hot.

"No, it's your carelessness." I try to add some bite to my words, but it doesn't work. My attempt ends up faltering and turning into a shy mumble.

"I knew you loved that about me."

I go to step away, desperate to regain my wits, but Ryne takes hold of my hand, securing me in my current predicament.

"You want to know what I like about you, Brightheart?" His eyes shimmer against the suns' rays, and the corner of his mouth forms a half smile. "You care, whether you want to admit it or not. You care immensely for your friends, and you would do anything to protect them."

He interlaces our fingers as he brushes his nose against mine. "You're brilliant, fierce, and willing to take risks. You're also the most beautiful woman I've ever seen." His free hand twitches, and I swear he's about to curl his fist in my hair and pull me into him, but he doesn't.

Instead, the sparrow flaps its wings and chirps, returning our attention to him. Ryne and I glance at the bird now perched on his finger.

I take a much-needed step back, secretly fighting to catch my breath.

"How did you do that?" I ask as he unties the ribbon and frees the key.

"We thought this was a sparrow at first, but it's not. This lovely is an adoring. I'm sure you can take a guess as to what it likes." He winks at me before moving to open the window across the room.

The bird flies away the moment the breeze enters the room.

When Ryne turns around, he offers me the key. "That doesn't mean everything I said wasn't true."

"Why do you think I care if you were telling the truth or not?" I ask with an arched brow.

"We've only known each other for a few days, but I know you, Brightheart. You care."

A door creaks open behind me.

Ryne smiles before reaching for my hand again. "And, like it or not, you could say the same about me."

"You know, maybe it *is* the accent . . ." I grin mischievously before taking his hand in mine.

I turn around, and we head down what looks like an endless hall with countless doors.

A lot can be said about Ryne Gwydion. One thing is for sure though: the accent isn't the only thing that makes him charming.

We enter another hall that isn't familiar. I'm beginning to wonder if these areas were made specifically for the games. That, or Fraydora Academy will always keep its secrets, and no matter how hard I try, I'll never be able to explore its grounds fully. As impressive as that fact is, it's also utterly frustrating.

After putting the key in multiple locks and turning the knobs with no luck each time, I'm wondering if this is some sick joke.

"Ayra, as much as I love strolling down this hall with you. I'm starting to worry you might jam that key into my chest if we don't get out of here soon."

I toss the key at him, and of course, he snatches it from the air with ease.

"There, now you have nothing to worry about." I groan in annoyance.

Ryne slides past me, trying the next door in this godforsaken corridor.

"We must be missing something," I mumble as Ryne tries to unlock another door. I turn around and stare at the door we entered, only to find it now closed. "Ryne?"

"Hmm?"

"Did you close the door behind you?" I ask while peering over my shoulder. The realization kicks in as he tilts his head.

"I most definitely did not." He starts back down the hall, tossing the key in the air.

"Ryne, I swear if that door opens—"

Ryne places the key in the door, and it swings open.

"You've got to be kidding me." I throw my hands in the hair as he spins around, wearing a bright, wide smile. "You're a piece of work." I point at him as I approach him.

"What did I do?" he asks with a hint of laughter.

I can't help but ruffle his hair as I pass him.

"Besides charming me senseless?" I wink at him, and his cheeks flush rosy pink.

My smile grows wider in return. Knowing I can affect him the way he affects me gives me nothing but satisfaction.

When I step across the threshold, the room we were in before is no longer there. The books that were coated in dust have disappeared, and in their place is an open field with an oak tree farther in the distance.

"I guess we don't need the key anymore," Ryne says.

As he shows me his hands, the key evaporates into thin air.

"What are we supposed to do?" I ask, feeling stumped.

"Go for a ride."

My nose wrinkles in deep thought. "What are you talking about?"

Ryne steps forward, pointing at a broom that floats in a field of knee-high bunny tail grass.

"Ready to have some fun?" He bounces up and down, wearing the brightest smile I've ever seen.

I'll never get sick of seeing his smile and how his eyes light up at the smallest things. I'll never get used to how he looks at me either, like I'm the most wonderful person in the world, someone he enjoys being around. I just hope he knows he's becoming that person for me too. He single-handedly changed my perspective, and because of him, I discovered my new favorite word.

"With you? I'm always ready." I jog toward him and settle on the broom behind him.

"Hold on, Brightheart," he whispers as the broom lifts from the ground.

I wrap my arms around his waist, nuzzling against his back and enjoying the way he feels against me. The scent of magic fills my senses, or rather, his scent does. I embrace him tighter and smile to myself.

Wind envelopes us as we rush forward, gaining speed within seconds. My stomach dips as we build momentum, soaring into the sky. The oak tree that once stood tall becomes nothing but a speck on the earth.

"I don't think we have to go this high." I raise my voice so Ryne can hear me.

"I know. I just wanted to do this."

Before I can ask what he means, he tilts the broom downward, and we rush back to the field.

"Ryne!" I squeal as my stomach lurches from the sudden descent.

I pull my arms tighter around him, and when we reach the ground, the grass tickles my ankles as we coast along the field. My hair unwinds from the ribbon I tied it in, flowing in the breeze.

Slowly, I let go of Ryne, trusting he won't let me fall, and I extend my arms out. Closing my eyes, laughter bubbles up from my chest and spills out of my mouth. It doesn't matter that we're in the middle of a competition. We could be falling behind, or we could have already lost, but I'm having fun. This feeling that warms my heart starts to alter my mindset.

As the broom slows and lowers back to the ground, Ryne

turns around, but he isn't wearing his signature smirk. His eyes settle on mine, and he inches closer as the shade from the oak tree covers us. "Are you okay?"

"Yes," I reply, breathless.

He hops off the broom, offering me his hands to assist me. When I stand before him, he weaves his hand into my hair, freezing my heart within this moment.

"Ayra—"

He brushes his nose against mine, igniting the same feelings that coursed through my veins the first time I saw him. His eyes linger down to my lips. A brief moment passes, and nothing happens. When his gaze meets mine again, I make the move I've been reluctant to admit I've wanted this whole time.

I close the agonizing distance between us and kiss him with the desire I've failed to ignore. My lips tingle against his, a sensation I've only felt along my fingertips when my flames take over, but this is stronger.

Ryne's kisses are full, soft, and addicting. I lean into him, needing more now that I have it.

When he pulls away and rests his forehead against mine, my body moves closer, like there's a tether pulling me to him. He presses his hands against my lower back, and his touch sends electric vibrations into my body. We fight for air, not moving our attention from one another. I glance down at his lips, wishing he would kiss me again.

"Fuck, Brightheart." He pulls me into him, and I let him hold me against his chest.

We both take in a long inhale of air as our lips meet again. Any remaining feeling of timidness fades away. I stand on my tiptoes, following his lead as he takes my mouth. I've never kissed anyone before, but I can already say for certain that Ryne knows what he's doing.

Our kiss turns feverish, hungry, and needy. New sensations

overtake my body, and it doesn't take a genius to connect the dots. This unfamiliar ache—it almost feels like a *need*—pulses low in my core, pushing me closer to Ryne. I never had the desire to touch myself, but Ryne is awakening this feeling within me. I thought the butterflies in my stomach were intense, but this is entirely different and not at all unpleasant.

Ryne rests his hand on the nape of my neck, urging me closer.

A moan escapes my mouth, and as it vibrates against him, he separates us but doesn't move away.

"What were they saying about fireworks?" I whisper through my heavy breathing.

Ryne chuckles in response, and just as he tries to continue the moment, a blast explodes around us.

"We've fallen behind," he mutters in concern.

Before I can tell him I don't care, he spins around and examines the tree. "Where do you think we're meant to go next?"

I shake my head to clear it and take a deep breath.

As I take a step forward, my foot meets the broom. For the first time, I examine it and squint as I notice something strange. I fall to my knees and trace my finger over the symbol carved into the wood. It's a sun with vines encircling it.

I glance back at the oak tree and approach it without thinking twice.

Only use the spells that are provided to you.

I don't know if this is the right move, but it's a chance we have to take. I raise my hands, letting the flames flicker along my fingertips.

"Ryne, I would back away if I were you."

Ryne looks back at me and nods.

Without a spell, I let the fire within my veins ignite the oak tree. It cracks and splinters under the heat's growing pressure.

"You're sure about this?" he asks with raised eyebrows.

I look over at him and shrug. "Honestly? No, but it's worth the risk."

Once the oak tree is engulfed in flames, I drop my hands.

We wait for a sign, something to tell us we've been disqualified. I don't think we will be, though, because if that symbol on the broom is what I think it is, this is what we were meant to do.

The fire dies, and black smoke trickles into the air, but it's not suffocating. The wind sweeps it away in one gust, leaving us staring at the burned oak tree.

"Do you think?" I hold my hand up as Ryne speaks.

I step closer to the tree as a flower bud sprouts on its splintered trunk. When it blossoms, more flowers grow in its wake, and it's not long before the tree's leaves turn from a crisp char to vibrant spring green.

"It wanted rebirth," I mumble in amazement.

"You're absolutely brilliant." Ryne matches my tone as a door materializes to my right.

"We still have a chance." Ryne jogs over to the door and opens it, but when I don't make my move, he arches his eyebrow.

"We don't have to, Ryne. I just want—"

"Are you giving up on me, Brightheart?" he teases.

"No, I just—"

"Are you afraid if you continue, you'll lose who you're becoming?" My silence is the only answer he needs. "This is your dream, and just because you continue down this path, it doesn't mean you'll lose yourself or me in the process."

I release a shaky exhale. "Are you sure?" I ask as I step forward.

"Positive. Besides, I won't let you go back." He reaches for my hand, and when I take it, he pulls me into his chest. "Especially after knowing how your lips feel against mine." My cheeks flush in response. "Let's go win this thing."

The portal that was disguised as a door isn't as stable as the ones prior. I am thrown back into the hedge maze, landing with an *oomph*. A series of groans leave my chest as my head spins. I dig my hands into the earth, trying to regain my composure and balance.

"Damn," I grunt into the grass as I glance around my surroundings, only to find that I'm alone. "Ryne?" I call out as I put pressure on my knees to sit up. "Ryne, where are you?"

Nothing, not even a chirp from a cricket.

Standing carefully, I make sure to give myself a moment before taking a step forward.

I scan the maze. At least I know where I am. *But where is Ryne?* As the thought enters my mind, an explosion sounds not too far off in the distance. *Does this mean we can use magic?*

"*Do you think she's catching on?*" The voice from the first day of the games returns.

"*I don't know . . . should we give her a hint?*" They tease me as I move toward the blast.

"It's a race to the end. There are only two spots left. You know what that means, interesting witch?"

I roll my eyes at the nickname the voices bestowed upon me.

"Give it your all."

"And remember . . ."

"Ah yes, remember—"

The voices cut out before they finish their rather irritating one-sided conversation.

"Oh, I'll give it my all," I whisper, knowing damn well they're still listening. "And I'll show you just how *interesting* I can be."

I weave through the maze, trying to follow the sound of the explosive fighting, but no matter how many times I think I make the right turn, I'm only dragged farther away from the battle.

I'm unsure how much time has passed or if I've seen this part of the maze before. Everything looks the same, and my mind is starting to play tricks on me. I make a sharp right turn but halt as the neatly trimmed hedges form a dead end.

"You've got to be kidding me." I groan in frustration.

Whirling around, I contemplate my next move.

The voices did say I can give it my all. Maybe that means I can use whatever magic I see fit? That, or they were trying to lead me astray. Something tells me they wouldn't do that; I think they get a kick out of watching me be *interesting*. There's only one way to find out.

I extend my arms, crossing my right hand over my left, and silently hope for the best.

"Revalis."

A pulse releases an orb of light from my palm, and it bounces off the greenery and makes a left.

I wait a brief moment for any sign of disqualification, but

when I'm met with silence, I jog after the pearlescent orb that will lead me out of here.

My eardrums pulsate as I near the continuous explosions. The orb leading me to the fighting slows down. As it makes a right turn, I peer around the corner just as it vanishes. The exit to the maze is right before me, along with Cadie and Machiis.

I step forward but stop when a hand grips my shoulder.

Ryne

30

"Fuck," I moan as I'm thrown back into what I presume is the hedge maze.

I dig my nails into the trimmed grass, trying to stabilize my balance. With a grunt, I roll on my back. My vision is blurry, and all I can make out are shapes.

"Ayra?" I call out for her, but she doesn't answer. "Bright-heart, are you there?"

I scramble to my knees, taking in my surroundings as my vision starts to defog. Ayra isn't here, but no one else is either. *Where the hells am I?*

A fiery explosion looms a few hundred feet in the distance. I wait for a sign of disqualification, but nothing happens, so that must mean we're allowed to use magic again. I need to find Ayra. Worry fills me when I realize she may be in the middle of that ongoing battle.

Shaking my head, I stand. I make sure to take my time until my vision fully clears, and once it does, I'm off. My legs carry me through the maze, weaving blindly. Any sense of direction I might have had is shot. My shoulders brush against the hedge as I lose my balance, bumping straight into the forest-green bushes.

"There's our ray of sunshine." The voice from the first day of the games returns.

"Look at him, he's worried about his witch." And there's the second.

"Welcome back." I smirk while steadying myself.

"I think he missed us." The first voice cackles.

"How darling."

I roll my eyes.

"Have you learned the lesson yet, ray of sunshine?"

"I don't think he has," the second voice counters.

"And what lesson would that be?" I ask, irritated.

"Should we tell him?"

"Hmm, maybe we should, maybe we shouldn't."

"How about a hint?"

"Ah, yes. A hint."

"The lesson, golden one, lies deep within you. Ayra knows who she is, but do you? Dig deep, and remember . . ."

"Ah, yes, remember—"

Another blast resonates in my ears, making the earth quake beneath my feet and shaking the voices away.

Their back-and-forth conversation leaves me reeling. I thought I knew who I was. Am I wrong? What am I missing, or am I missing anything?

Ayra comes to mind. She's so strong and willful. She knows who she is and what she wants. Do I know what I want? Do I know who I am and what I'm capable of?

An explosion rattles the hedges, pulling me from my musings.

If Cadie and Ayra are going at it, I don't know how this will end. They both have pent-up emotions toward one another.

I've seen Ayra's hands set themselves ablaze when she gets angry, so it wouldn't surprise me if those explosions were hers. I hope she doesn't let her fury carry her too far away. I don't want Cadie to take this opportunity away from her. This is Ayra's calling; it always has been. I won't let anything get in the way of her success.

Keep moving.

As I push myself deeper into the maze, my strength returns. I stop moving as the path I'm on splits into a fork. I could go left or right. The sounds of battle are intense, but I can't determine where they're coming from.

Following my gut instinct, I take the path to the left. The professors at Traquore often told me I shouldn't follow my gut. They say it's foolish and that a wizard worth his own salt follows the stars or facts. I never agreed with them; my gut has yet to fail me.

Maren leaps out of my pocket, and I halt as he raises his nose in the air, his whiskers swaying in the slight breeze.

"What is it?" I ask as he stops in the middle of the path. Leaning down, I brush my hand over the grass, but nothing seems out of place. "We need Ayra," I whisper, and he tilts his head at me.

Maren runs back up my sleeve and settles in my pocket. Once he's comfortable, I walk farther down the path. Not a second later, Ayra comes into view, and my muscles relax as the decision to trust my gut is confirmed.

I reach out for her, gently squeezing her shoulder. "There you are," I greet her, feeling more than relieved that she's not participating in the duel up ahead.

Ayra spins around and raises her fist, almost touching my nose.

"Fuck, Ryne. Where the hells have you been?" she whispers, hoping to keep our appearance discreet.

"Were you going to hit me?" My eyes widen as I fight an amused and impressed grin.

She drops her clenched fist. "You scared me. What was I supposed to do?" she hisses.

We stare at one another. A brief minute passes before our mouths turn upward, trying to hold back the laughter threatening to break free.

"So, what's our plan? Besides barging in with our fists raised?" I manage to ask before Cadie's voice fills the atmosphere.

"Had enough!?" she yells.

Ayra's head snaps around. The other team that managed to find the exit is motionless on the ground. Booming applause surrounds us, reminding me that we're being watched.

"That's what I thought," Cadie scoffs before turning to face Machiis.

"Where's the goal?" I whisper in Ayra's ear while scanning the field, looking for any sign or guaranteed progression onto the finale.

But there's nothing, no glimmer or sparkle to indicate where we're supposed to go next.

Cadie's eyes flick our way. "Brightheart! There you are."

"Oh, were you looking for me?" Ayra calls out as an obnoxious grin spreads across her lips. "Sorry to keep you waiting."

Cadie's pace quickens and her face contorts.

"If the goal was out there, why would she be trying to pick a fight with you in here?" I ask, hoping to pull Ayra out of her taunting trance.

She takes a step back and smirks at Cadie's red face. "Sorry, Blackwell, you'll have to find another entrance."

Ayra arches her fingers and raises them to the sky, letting the earth in front of us build until it creates a solid blockade.

"You think that will stop me!?" Cadie's voice cracks, and Machiis chuckles.

"Run!" I order before grabbing her hand, ensuring we don't lose each other again.

"Why—" When her attempt at a question comes out, a round of rapid explosions sounds behind us.

The ground shakes, but I don't let the quake knock us off our feet. I pull Ayra against my chest, shielding her ears.

"Machiis's specialty is explosive magic. Best not get in his way."

The blasts from earlier make sense now. Machiis was using his power against the other team, which seems like overkill if you ask me.

Once the ground stops shaking, I pull on Ayra's hand and lead us back to where Maren was sniffing around.

"Do you know where we're going?" she asks, raising her voice over the thundering booms behind us.

"Maren was sniffing something out up ahead. I didn't find anything, but it might require us both to be there. Here, this is the spot."

Ayra stumbles into my back as I stop in the middle of the path.

"This is the spot? Are you sure?" she asks, and I nod.

Maren peeks out of my pocket again, his nose wiggling up and down. He scampers down my sleeve while the earth beneath our feet shudders, and I glance over my shoulder to find fire creeping along the hedges.

"They're close. Whatever our next move is, we have to do it now."

As if Maren can understand her, he points to a groove in the grass, one so subtle you wouldn't notice it unless you were looking for it. I take a hesitant step forward, kneel down, and run my hand over the uneven strands of grass.

"Ayra—" My voice is cut off as another thunderous explosion echoes through the air.

I press my palm into the ground, and a muffled *click* averts my attention forward.

The leaves and vines that are twined around one another break apart, revealing a clearing with a pedestal in the center.

"The first two teams to reach the pedestal move on to the next round."

"Will the witch and her wizard make it?"

With a grunt, I push myself forward and call after Ryne. "Let's go!"

As I step into the clearing, the opposite side of the maze opens up, and another team appears a mere ten feet away.

"Shit." I spin around, and it feels like time slows.

Cadie's and my eyes lock, and Machiis's hands flicker as he casts another spell. My eyes widen when he aims for Ryne.

"No!" I call out as I launch my right hand forward. *"Eathirum!"*

As the spell leaves my lips, Ryne is launched into the air. I raise my left hand, creating a barricade of flames to prevent the other team from sneaking up on us on the other side.

Ryne hits the ground and lands at my feet. I pull him against my chest and meet his shocked gaze.

"Ready?" I ask him.

When he nods, I aim my palm toward our feet and shout, *"Earthirum."*

Ryne wraps his arms around me, maneuvering me against his chest so my back doesn't hit the pristine stone pedestal when we land.

"Stop them!" Cadie shouts, and a gust of wind follows suit.

It grazes my cheek a second too late. Ryne and I start our descent despite Cadie's attempt to deter us. Time resumes when Ryne's back hits the pedestal, and we're sucked through a vortex.

"Fuck," Ryne huffs as we're thrown across a sleek wooden floor.

I'm tossed to the side and land on my back. Sucking in as much air as I can, I try to brace against the pain of the growing bruises that begin to form throughout my pale body.

I don't notice the applause or the congratulations that thunder around the room. I only notice Ryne's look of concern, and when he realizes I'm okay, he offers me a breathless smile. I release a deep sigh and grin.

"And just like that, we have our finalists!" A voice from the ceiling circulates the room, barely audible above the applause. "Ayra Brightheart, Ryne Gwydion, Cadie Blackwell, and Machiis Avium!"

Ryne looks over at me, and his green eyes sparkle when he sees me looking at him. Every part of my body is sore, yet with one glance, Ryne steals my pain, and I feel cradled in the warmth of his gaze.

I should be over the moon about making it to the finale. Instead, I'm among the stars for another reason. And that reason is Ryne Gwydion.

Ryne and I walk side by side toward my room. Secretly, I'm hoping he wanted to escort me back because he didn't want to part ways with me just yet. The logical part of me knows it's most likely because I hit my head more than once when we were tossed in and out of portals.

My eyes keep trailing over him, and my stomach flutters when I catch his relaxed, carefree smile. Neither of us dare say anything about the moment under the oak tree, but I'd give anything to go back in time and relive it.

My whole life has been studying, memorizing spells and recipes, sleepless nights to prepare for practicals, and tolerating Cadie and her cronies. Now, it's different, and it's all thanks to Ryne.

I brushed it off when I first looked at him, calling it irritation. When the truth is, I knew what it was. I was just too afraid to admit it. I was terrified to think Ryne could become something more. Hells, he's a wizard and a mischievous one at that. He's so much more than that, though, and while our time together has been brief, I feel like I've known him for years.

My temper doesn't scare him. He doesn't listen to the stories about me. When I yelled at him during our first encounter, he didn't fight back or cower. He smiled, and it tilted my world on its side. Day by day, he's shown me what it truly means to live. He defined the term *fun* and made me laugh. He showed me that I'm not a stickler. I'm more than Cadie's harsh words. I'm more than my desire to be perfect.

"Ayra?"

I shake my head at his voice. Turning around, I notice I walked right past my room.

"Oh, sorry." I offer Ryne a shy smile.

"What were you thinking about?" he asks as I return to my bedroom door.

"Nothing," I admit with blushing cheeks.

Ryne places his hand on my waist and inches me closer toward him, and my breath hitches.

"About the celebration?" he asks as I get lost in his eyes.

"What celebration?"

He chuckles at my evident confusion.

That damn accent makes everything he says so dreamy.

"The celebration before the finale."

"Oh, right."

He traces tiny circles inside my wrist as his cheeks turn pink. "Will you go with me?" he whispers while feathering his nose over mine.

"Aren't we supposed to go together?" My gaze falls to his lips.

The desperate need to touch him again is overwhelming.

"Technically, yes, but will you go *with* me?" He kisses my top lip, and I shiver.

"Yes." The moment I answer his question, his lips overtake mine.

How could something as simple as a kiss feel this wonderful? How does he create these chills along my skin? How does he make my lungs forget how to breathe?

He traces his free hand up my back, his fingers gently

digging into my spine. The hand resting against my neck puts me at his mercy. I let him direct and control me in whatever way he wants. He leaves me practically boneless, and all I can focus on is the buzz humming through my body when he touches me.

It doesn't take me long to learn that he likes the little noises that leave my mouth or that he likes when I give in to his command.

I don't know if it's because of my inexperience, but I *like* not being in control of this.

When a moan of pleasure vibrates from my lips to his, he groans, and everything becomes a blur. His hands land on my hips, pressing me into his chest. Air becomes increasingly difficult to pull in as I feel his body pressed against mine.

I stand on my tiptoes, weaving my fingers through his blond hair. My breasts are pressed against him, and my nipples become sensitive underneath my bra. His length is hard, pressing into my upper thigh.

I want to reach down and please him. To feel him react under my touch. Allow him to take me right here against the wall.

"Fuck, Ayra," Ryne moans between kisses, a strange sensation whirling in my core.

"Fuck, Ayra, indeed."

I take a panicked step away from Ryne at the sound of Marley's voice.

"Hey Marley, when did you get here?" I ask while I catch my breath.

Her grin grows as my cheeks flush hotter.

"Wouldn't you like to know?" She throws a wink at me, and my eyes widen in response.

"See you tomorrow, Ryne!" I call over my shoulder as I link

my arm through Marley's and whisk her into our room, making sure to close the door behind us.

When I turn to face her, her smile grows. "You've got some explaining to do, missy."

Ayra

32

I had to give Marley every detail, and while doing so, I couldn't fight the smile that overtook my face. I had my first kiss . . . in front of millions. The reality of that should send me spiraling. I should want to hide in a corner, wrap myself tightly in a blanket, and never leave. I don't feel that way though. In fact, I feel the opposite.

I'm tired of fighting the universe. It seems to want Ryne and I to explore the spark it's lighting between the two of us. Sure, if I had a choice in the matter, I would have chosen different timing. I wouldn't have picked the week of the games to meet someone like him. But if the council didn't call for this change, I wouldn't have met him. I would have seen him, but I wouldn't have gotten to know him.

My goal would have been to destroy him, eliminate him from the games and erase him from my mind. I wouldn't have remembered him afterward, which makes my heart ache. In a twisted and complicated way, I'm happy the universe threw this curveball at me. Without him, I wouldn't be changing the way I am. With him, I'm becoming the person I'm meant to be in this world. I'm discovering who I am, and that's enough.

I'm someone worthy of fun and love; I don't have to prove myself to everyone. I'm a witch who wants to experience life and all its mysteries. See rare mythical creatures and adventure to unknown lands. I want to do it all, and I'm learning I can get what I want in life. Thanks to Ryne.

The second interview is today, and I don't feel the soul-crushing anxiety I felt from the first interview. I already know the questions that will be thrown at Ryne and me, with the kiss being the center of attention. He'll be with me, though, and with him, I know I can do anything. Plus, this interview won't be as grand as the first. Only the contestants who made it into the finale will be there. And while the questions will be more personal and direct, I know I'll be okay.

Marley isn't in our room while I finish getting ready. She said she had something exciting to do and that I could ask questions later.

She did, however, leave me a dress to wear tonight. She's taken it upon herself to become my personal fashion coordinator. The gown for this evening is simple. It's navy blue with long sleeves and a low neckline that drops to my upper waist, the swell of my breasts showing slightly. Intricate details of swirling flames and embers line the bodice. But the best part? It has pockets.

I place my hands in them and sway back and forth while looking at myself in the mirror. Marley told me to wear my hair up, so I cast a charm to style it to her wishes and fixed my bangs to my liking.

"What do you think, Kiki?" I ask the slumbering cat at the foot of my bed.

Without opening her eyes, she responds with a tired meow, giving me her approval.

"Ready, sleepy girl?"

She stretches her paws and arches her back with a big yawn. Kiki jumps off my bed and starts to make her way toward the door.

"That's my girl," I say with a smile before opening my door to step into the hall.

The interview will take place in the astrology room, so I walk toward the East Wing with some pep in my step. Not only am I excited to see Ryne again, I'm looking forward to his response to seeing me. I love when his eyes sparkle and his cheeks flush. He makes me feel like I'm the only one in the room, as if I'm the center of his world.

I'm realizing I feel that way about him as well, and he deserves to know that he's the first thing I look forward to when I wake up. He's my final thought before I fall asleep.

We may be on different wavelengths. I mean, he's radiant sunshine, and I'm a raging thunderstorm. He sees my flaws and scars, and they don't scare him. I'll never understand why someone like him wants someone like me. But who am I to question the universe and her grand scheme? If she feels I'm worthy of him, I should believe her.

The astronomy room appears in my line of sight, and so does Ryne. My heart speeds when I see him resting his back against the stone wall. His right foot is hitched up like he's getting ready to propel himself down the corridor, and his head is hanging low so he doesn't see me right away. I adore how his blond hair is messy on his casual days but slicked back for formal events. There's always one lone strand that rests on his forehead, and as small as it is, it makes butterflies spring to life in my chest.

I inhale a sharp breath to try and calm my body's reaction to him.

As I close the distance between us, I smile when he doesn't notice me. Bending over, I lean in close and try to meet his gaze.

"Whatcha looking at?" I snicker, and his lips quirk upward.

"There's something shimmering in the stone, right there." He points to a spot near his shoe.

I avert my gaze and observe the floor. I tilt my head when I don't see what he's talking about.

"I don't see—"

Ryne wraps his arms around my waist, lifts me in the air, and spins me around. My laugh dances down the hall as I hold onto him for dear life.

"Ryne!" I squeal while I wrap my arms around his neck.

With a chuckle, Ryne stops spinning and holds me against his chest, not letting my feet hit the ground.

"Hello, gorgeous," he greets me breathlessly.

"You tricked me." I poke his shoulder, feigning insult.

"I would never! I simply saw an opportunity to take you into my arms and hold you close."

"And the spinning?" I smile as the giddiness of being near him settles in my heart.

"That was for fun."

A tiny chuckle leaves my chest.

We stare at one another, savoring the silence and stillness of this moment.

Reaching forward, I brush the loose strand of hair off his forehead and let my fingertips trace his brow line.

"You're something else. Something I can't quite describe," I whisper.

"Is that a bad thing?" Ryne asks, matching my tone.

"Not at all." I offer him a loving smile before leaning in to kiss him.

The desperate desire to feel his touch leaves me in a state of wanting. My eyes close as our lips brush over one another. The mere contact awakens a blinding need in my core. It shoots down between my thighs and settles in my clit, throbbing. I've never felt this way, but I've heard enough from Marley to know Ryne's touches and kisses are stirring this need.

My breath hitches, and I'm panting as our lips toy with each other. I move to close the small gap, but my muscles freeze when I hear footsteps exiting the astrology room.

"There you are!"

My brow creases and my eyes widen when I hear Marley's voice. Ryne places me on the floor and ensures my balance before letting me go.

I stare at my friend, who is wearing a stunning one-sleeved, formfitting black gown with exquisite specks of stardust coated at the hem. Her hair is pulled into a neat, high ponytail, with Zachii acting as a barrette.

"What are you doing here?" I ask.

Ryne keeps his hand on the small of my back, tracing tiny circles along the base of my spine with his thumb. I have to suppress a shudder at the touch and force my attention on Marley.

"Remember how I said you could ask questions later?" she responds with a grin.

"Yeah."

"Well, now is the time for questions, my dear friend. Except I'll be the one asking them."

"Oh, fuck no—"

"Oh, fuck yes!" Marley beams as she clasps her hands together. "Let's go. I have a *million* questions for the two of you."

Marley takes my hand and pulls me forward. I glance back at Ryne, silently pleading for assistance. He throws his hands in the air and trails behind us. With a knowing smirk, he mouths, "*Sorry, Brightheart.*"

All I can do is groan.

Something tells me this evening is going to end up being too eventful for my liking . . .

T he astronomy room is empty of people except for the finalists, Marley, the headmistress, and the headmaster. They kept the telescopes, maps, and charts in the room. However, they've added royal-blue velvet-backed chairs for each of us to sit in.

This room is in my top ten favorite spots within the academy. The floors are constructed of pure crystal marble, and the walls are composed of floor to ceiling windows. There isn't a speck of free space. The drapes, which are normally cast aside to allow natural sun or moonlight to pour into the room, are pulled closed. There's a camera here, though, so I'm sure they don't want to cast a glare for the eager audience at home.

Cadie and Machiis are seated to the left. Ryne places himself next to Machiis so I don't have to sit beside them. With a silent thank you, I sit in the chair on the end and pat the wrinkles away on my dress. I rest my knee against Ryne's, and Marley offers me a warm smile as she takes her seat in front of the four of us.

"Do you remember what we talked about, Ms. Skylem?" Headmistress Illana asks with a hint of concern in her voice.

"To the commas and periods," Marley chimes.

"Okay, we go live in thirty seconds." Illana spins around. The worry lines near her mouth are apparent.

"How did you even get this responsibility?" I ask in a high-volume whisper.

Marley places her finger over her lips and fixes her posture. "Wouldn't you like to know?" she responds with a wink, leaving me more than confused.

"She's a woman full of mysteries," Ryne adds.

"You have no idea."

"Ten seconds!" Borrick calls out.

Ryne pulls my chair closer to him so our thighs are touching. I blush violently, ignoring the knowing snicker from Marley.

"Is this okay?" he mumbles in my ear, goose bumps erupting along my skin.

I nod and give him a shy smile. "Yes, it's perfect."

"Three! Two! One—"

Lights flare to life above us, increasing the temperature, and I have to resist the urge to shield my eyes against the sudden brightness.

Marley flashes us a flawless smile before starting. "Welcome to the pre-finale interview! My name is Marley Skylem, and I'll be your host for the evening. During the games, we've witnessed heartbreaking losses, moments of triumph, and, shall I say, fireworks?" She winks at Ryne and me before continuing. "Witches and wizards have been at odds for far too long. The Academy Games has proven that the two classes can work together. They can outsmart complicated puzzles, answer hard-hitting questions, and brew necessary potions with class. Our finale is approaching, and soon, we'll crown our victors! The final match will be a test of their true strength. Our victors will gain prestige and a scholarship to further their education. But before we get to that, why don't we get to know our final four?"

I close my eyes for a moment, focusing on the rise and fall of my chest.

I can do this, I repeat to myself until I believe it.

Ryne nudges my knee, and I look up at him. "You and me, right?" he mutters so only I can hear him.

"Right," I whisper back, and he gives me a reassuring smile. "That's my girl."

A whirlwind of emotions swarms in my mind and chest. Who knew such a simple word combination could make someone so warm and fuzzy?

Before I can give it another thought, Marley clears her throat and redirects her attention over to Ryne and me.

"Ms. Ayra Brightheart. You are at the top of your class here at Fraydora Academy. You excel in all your classes and possess knowledge and skill in everything you do. I've known you for seven years. You knew from day one that participating in the games was your goal. So, I have to ask, is it everything you thought it would be?" Her eyes flicker over to Ryne, and she smiles knowingly. "Or is it more than you expected?"

I offer a breathless smile before looking into her eyes. "It's more, there's no doubt about that. I worked tirelessly for years. I strived to be perfect—"

I can feel Cadie rolling her eyes, but it doesn't make my skin itch.

I keep my voice steady as I continue. "I was driving myself into a realm of mayhem. I thought in order to get into the games, I needed to be perfect in *everything* I did. But I was wrong, and someone showed me that."

"And his name is Ryne Gwydion," Marley says gently.

"Yes," I say, ducking my head and feeling my cheeks flush.

"Mr. Ryne Gwydion." Marley looks over at him, giving me a chance to compose myself. "You're just a ray of light. The first day I saw you, I knew you had tricks up your sleeve. The introductory interview didn't do you justice. Sure, you may not be the brightest or most powerful—"

"No offense taken," Ryne chuckles.

"You shouldn't take offense. If everyone was smart and full of magic, the world would be dull. You fill the world with light. You try to befriend everyone you meet. You see through their flaws. You see them as individuals who have emotions, needs, and desires. You see the good in people, and that in itself is a wonderful trait to have. But I have to know . . . what are *your* desires? What do you want after you graduate from Traquore Academy?"

Ryne drops his gaze to his hands, almost as if he's trying to formulate the right answer.

"Well, I want to be happy. I don't know what I want to do with my life after I receive my certification. But I do know I want to see it all. I want to adventure to uncharted territory, see mythical creatures, and eat food I've never tried before. I want to show the worlds kindness and light—if you want to stick with that term," Ryne answers as his expression lights up.

"Would that be with company or without?" Marley teases, and Ryne blushes.

"I'd prefer with . . . but that path hasn't been crossed yet."

My cheeks flush hot when he smiles to himself, and my heart thunders at the idea of traveling the world and going on adventures with Ryne. As much as I've always wanted to see the realms, I never toyed with the idea because my education always came first. But what if I follow my heart? What if I follow Ryne, and we have unforgettable journeys? The world won't end if I don't further my education right after Fraydora

Academy. There's nothing keeping me from doing what I want.

"The realms have fallen in love with the two of you. Personally, I saw the sparks from day one. The rest of the world followed suit during the first match. You two are a wonder, and I hope the fireworks continue to ignite in your hearts."

Without giving it a second thought, I take Ryne's hand and squeeze it firmly.

"Expect the unexpected, right?" I ask with a smirk of my own.

"Okay, enough with the love fest. I can't cry on camera." Marley wipes away her tears before readjusting herself to face Cadie and Machiis. "Mr. Machiis Avium, you're near the top of your class, confident, strong, and fierce. What has it been like to battle against your best friend? I'm sure it's not easy."

"It hasn't. I've known Ryne for over a decade. We've been lucky enough to avoid one another during the games, but with the last match approaching, I know it's bound to happen. The idea of beating him is a harsh possibility, but I won't let anything stand in my way." Machiis responds with poise.

Marley nods her head before looking at her next target. "Ms. Cadie Blackwell. You are the firstborn daughter of Vorne and Ramona Blackwell. You are smart, charismatic, stunning, powerful—"

"Oh, stop, you're making me blush," Cadie coos as I observe Marley closely.

"You're simply too good for us!" Marley smiles wide, shaking her head slightly. "So, tell me, how does it feel to have such power but lack talent?"

I press my lips together, holding back a laugh, as a stack of papers lands on the floor behind me. Peeking over my shoulder, I see Illana dragging her palms across her forehead, pulling at her hair.

This definitely wasn't part of the cue cards.

"Excuse me?" Cadie states with wide eyes. Her jaw drops open, but she quickly composes herself.

"I was just curious; do you bully those around you because you lack confidence, or is it something else entirely?"

I cover my mouth with my hand, trying my best to keep it together.

"I don't understand what's happening." Cadie's almost left speechless.

"I read in an old text about a soul mutation. They call it 'evil bitch syndrome.' Do you think you suffer from that?" Marley asks without a speck of amusement.

I can't take it anymore. Her seriousness has giggles bubbling out of my mouth, and Cadie's fury lands directly on me.

"You think this is funny? Did you put her up to this?"

I wrap my arms around my stomach to try and contain myself from further hysterics. "I did no such thing!"

"These are legitimate questions." Marley defends herself while maintaining a straight face.

"Headmistress!" Cadie calls, but it doesn't stop my best friend from continuing.

"Did you give Ryne the Orb of Molten Despair to hurt Ayra on purpose? Did you really think you'd get away with it? That her best friend wouldn't stick up for her?"

"Headmistress!" Cadie shrieks as her face reddens.

"Remember when you and your goons stalked Ayra? You followed her into the courtyard, froze her feet to the ground, and proceeded to leave her there until morning?"

The chair Cadie was sitting in screeches as she stands.

I'm on my feet, ready to defend my friend as Cadie storms over to Marley, who remains seated and coolheaded.

"Don't you dare—" I start to hiss, but Ryne grabs my wrist and stops me from intervening.

"Stay," he whispers in my ear, and my muscles stop me from moving another inch.

"Because *I* remember," Marley starts.

Cadie slowly stands toe to toe with Marley.

"I remember because I was the one who unthawed her. I was the one who cared for her when she got sick because of you. I'm sick of the professors giving you special treatment because of your last name. You are *no one* special, Cadie Blackwell. If anything, you are tainted and destined to be nothing more than a villain."

I try to pull away from Ryne, but his grasp is tight around my arm. My breaths come faster as I watch Cadie and Marley. From the corner of my eye, I see Machiis take a step forward, but Ryne raises his hand and prompts him to stop.

"You—" Cadie balls her fist at her side.

Marley looks down and smiles, then brings her gaze back up, locking eyes with Ayra.

"Do it. Show the worlds who you *really* are." Marley eggs her on, practically begging Cadie to hit her.

"Stop the transmission!" Borrick booms.

And like a bell signaling the start of a match, Cadie throws back her arm and aims it at my best friend.

I will the temperature in my veins to increase, and Ryne loosens his grip on me. Taking the opportunity, I burst forward and ignore Ryne as he pleads for me to stop. I dodge Machiis as he tries to hold me back.

Marley isn't used to Cadie's torment and violence like I am. I've had seven years to learn how to thicken my skin. Marley took it upon herself to try and get justice for me. This is the least I can do for her.

I arch my fingers, and a ball of swirling air forms in my

palm. I send the whirlwind flying toward Cadie. The blast blows her to the side, away from Marley, before her punch can land.

In a blur, Machiis runs toward Cadie while I stroll toward Marley. When I reach her, I take her face in my hands and examine her closely.

"Are you okay?" I ask.

She nods and covers my hands with hers.

"Are you crazy? Why would you do that?" I let out a slight laugh of disbelief.

"If the headmistress wasn't going to give her just punishment for what she's both done and did to you, then I was going to make all the realms aware of who she is and how the council holds her family in such high regard."

My shoulders drop, and tears sting my eyes. I rest my forehead against hers and let my tears roll down my cheeks and gather on my lips.

"She could have hurt you," I mumble.

"She would have tried, but you and I both know she wouldn't have gotten close to me. Not only can I stand up for myself, I have you as well."

I let out an airy chuckle, and the taste of my salty tears lands on my tongue. "You're right about that—"

"Cadie, no!"

Before I can register what Machiis is screaming about, a blinding white light explodes in the room.

My eyes slam shut, and my palms dig into my eye sockets to try and protect myself. As the room fills with pained screams, I groan as my body is shoved onto the marble floor. I roll onto my back, and someone digs their knee into my ribs and secures my wrists over my head. Heat burns the fabric of my dress and starts to singe my skin.

"Fuck!" I wince while blinking my eyes open.

"What's the matter, Ayra? Can't handle the heat?" Cadie hisses.

"You fucking bitch!" I holler before raising my knee to ram it into her hip.

Knocking her onto the floor, I roll on my opposite side and struggle to get up while the flash of light vanishes from the room. My hair dangles in front of my face while I turn my head to look at Cadie. She grunts and props herself up while setting her sights on me.

"Want to play dirty, huh? Well, let's play," she threatens.

She lunges forward but is stopped when Machiis catches her against his chest. Illana and Borrick enter the fray. Our headmistress walks over to Cadie, trying to soothe her anger as Machiis tries his best as well.

"That's enough. You're going to get yourself disqualified," he admonishes.

I scoff and roll my eyes. "Oh, please, the princess isn't going to get disqualified from anything. Let her show her true colors, and maybe they'll pay attention to her cruelty!" I scramble to my feet as she struggles to free herself from Machiis's grasp. "What's wrong, Cadie? Not used to people fighting back? Let's go!" I wave her toward me and huff when Machiis leans down to whisper in her ear. "Fucking pathe—"

"That is enough!" Borrick shouts.

Ryne spins me around and places his hands on my cheeks, forcing my attention on him. "You're stooping to her level. Stop this. Do not *become* someone like her."

I look into his sea-green eyes and focus on his cool palms, calming my frustration. My lungs stop gasping for air and, start to regulate, so I can breathe normally.

"You're better than that, you hear me?" he whispers again, and I nod.

"You're right, I'm sorry. I went too far," I mutter, feeling ashamed of myself.

"Don't be sorry. She's tormented you for years. You finally have the courage to stand up for yourself. It's normal. I just don't want to see you go down the wrong path. Be the change you want to see in the world, Ayra. Be the better witch."

Be the better witch.

During the first interview, I said that we need to be mindful of our own kind because we can be just as cruel as other classes of creatures. And here I am, doing the exact opposite of my supposed message.

I don't regret standing up for Marley, but I should have ended it with the first blast of air. I took things too far, which is exactly what Cadie has done to me time and time again.

"I'll be better," I say under my breath. "I promise."

"Cadie Blackwell, Ayra Brightheart, and Marley Skylem, I want to see you three in my office first thing tomorrow morning. Take the evening to calm yourselves. I am beyond disappointed in the three of you." Headmistress Illana looks at the three of us with a tired yet rageful expression.

"Yes, Headmistress," we respond simultaneously.

Ryne wraps his arms around me as Machiis escorts Cadie out of the room. I take in his scent and relax into his aura. I hold out my wrists and examine the burns. Thankfully, the marks on my first are superficial.

"Can you cast a healing spell for me?" I say into his chest, not ready to let him go.

He nods and begins to cast the charm that will heal the burns Cadie left on my skin.

Marley stands next to us, and when I look at her, I meet her smile with one of my own.

"How about I make the three of us some tea?" she offers.

"That would be lovely," I respond with a sigh of relief.

"Count me in. I'm going to need something to decompress. Something tells me the drama isn't over yet." Ryne kisses the top of my head before wrapping his arms over both Marley's and my shoulders.

"Oh, honey, you'll never rest with the two of us in your life. Better get used to it now," Marley teases as we stroll out of the room.

Ryne snickers before pulling me in again. I rest my head on his shoulder and close my eyes, letting him lead the way. While my eyes are closed, I make a vow to myself, one I intend never to break.

I won't turn into Cadie Blackwell. I'll be the best person I can be, no matter what.

I'm walking on air. That's what Ayra has done to me. I've kissed two other witches before, but kissing Ayra is different—in the most unbelievable way possible. She makes me feel like I can do anything, and I would give anything to keep her with me.

Machiis arrived without Hayes, and the sight was troubling. He and Hayes are always together, which can only mean his familiar senses darkness within him.

"Don't be a fool, Ryne," Machiis starts from the other side of my room.

I'm glad we're not sharing a room during this tournament. If we were, most of my nights would have ended with me sleeping in the hall.

"What are you talking about?" I ask as I clasp my black cape around my shoulders.

"You've got that look," he says before taking a bite out of a crisp fall apple.

"I don't know what you're talking about," I mutter with a groan as I run my hand through my hair, ruffling it.

"She's not anything special, you know," he says while chewing obnoxiously. "I say, fuck her out of your system and move on. There's no need to go any further than that."

"Did you really just say that?" I spit out.

He wasn't always like this. He used to be shy, kindhearted, and selfless. Now, he's a total twat. Confidence can go to your head if you don't keep it in check, and right now, it's doing just that. I've seen how the other witches grasp their chests when he walks by. He knows he's good-looking and that he could have any witch he wants. For some reason, the one he wants is a total bitch.

"She's nothing like the previous witches I've seen you with."

Maybe that's the point. The other women I've been with are nothing compared to Ayra. They weren't as bright, curious, or kind as her. Their smiles didn't light up a room. Their hearts didn't hold the passion that hers does. Ayra is a different kind of woman, and she's perfect. I would never fuck and dump her. The mere thought is an insult. Ayra deserves the stars. Nothing else will suffice.

"I'm going to ignore everything you just said. If I were you, I would stop talking about her around me. It won't end well." I drop my tone so he knows I'm serious.

I'm tired of hearing people talk shit about her. They only do it because they think it's funny, but I've seen the pain in her eyes when she catches them in the act. I won't let it happen, not anymore.

"I'm just saying—"

I point my finger at Machiis to cut him off. "Don't," is all I say before exiting my room.

"Whatever, man." Machiis shrugs before walking down the corridor.

I brush off his comments because I won't let him ruin tonight.

The thought of seeing Ayra is enough to ease my anger. I walk down the halls with my head held high, twirling the moonflower I wove into a bracelet.

When I make it to her bedroom door, I freeze. A smile spreads across my lips when I hear Ayra and Marley laughing on the other side. I wait a moment before knocking as I want them to finish the moment they're having.

I'm glad Ayra has such a devoted friend within Fraydora. We all need a friend like Marley. I had one, but he disappeared, and I'm not sure if I'll ever see him again.

Shaking my head, I tap on the door. Their voices soften as I wait outside anxiously. Light spills into the hall when the door opens.

My eyes meet hers, and my cheeks redden.

"I still can't believe you made it," Marley chimes as we finish preparing for the celebration. "Like, I *knew* you would. This is *you* we're talking about here, but it's so surreal!"

I smile at my reflection as she goes on and on about the match from two days ago. Apparently, my first kiss was heavily broadcasted. Marley said she almost lost her hearing from the excited hollering and applause. Ryne and I were at the center of attention, and I didn't care. I let my feelings and the desire overwhelm me, and I don't regret it.

"I can't believe you managed to host the interview and blast Cadie in front of millions," I quirk as I look at her through the reflection.

The three of us reported to Headmistress Illana this morning, and we all got an earful. I've never been summoned to her office for disciplinary action, and I can safely say I didn't like it. I'm not used to having people be disappointed in me. It made my skin crawl.

Marley did the right thing, and I stand by my actions. Illana allowed us both to stay in the games only because it's the eve of the finale, but if this had happened prior to the first game, we would have been disqualified and possibly expelled.

Even I knew that was a joke. She should have said that Marley and I would have been expelled while Cadie would still be walking the halls because of her parents' money . . .

Justice was served, though, even if we had to act as vigilantes.

Marley chose my gown again, and I happily obliged. When she first showed me the dress, I was intimidated. I didn't think I could pull it off, but now that I see myself, it's not half bad.

The gown is ebony velvet with shimmering silver stars sewn throughout it. Two pieces of sheer fabric cascade from my shoulders, creating a train down to my feet. The bodice hugs my curves, and small stars flicker around my waist and grow larger down the fabric. Marley cast "*Draso*," and my hair pinned itself back with a delicate gold crescent moon comb to secure it.

"So, how do I look?" I twirl around, hoping to get her mark of approval.

"Like a goddamn queen."

She should be saying that about herself. Marley curled her long hair, letting it flow down her bare back, and placed a simple gold circlet atop her head. She chose to wear a crimson-red formfitting gown with golden embellishments around her breast and waistline. If anyone is a queen, it's Marley. She's just too modest to see it.

I match her grin as a knock sounds from the other side of the door. Any semblance of confidence melts into pure anxiety.

"Wonder who that is." Marley shimmies her shoulders as she goes to the door.

"Wait." I raise my hand, pleading for her to stop.

"What's wrong?" The second she sees my expression, she walks over to me and takes my hands. "Breathe, Ayra."

I follow her direction and inhale deeply.

"Good, do one more."

I lock my eyes on hers and breathe, making sure to focus on my exhale.

"Are you nervous?"

I nod in response.

"It is very nerve-racking, it's understandable. So much has happened this week, and so much is changing. It's okay to want things to slow down."

I suck in a shaky breath and let it out.

"But you're doing fantastic, remember that, okay?"

I nod and let my shoulders relax.

"Okay." Zachii pops out of Marley's loose curls as Kiki rubs her body along the hem of my dress.

"Ready to have some fun?" With one last nod, Marley grins. "That's my girl. Now, let's go show these wizards who rules this world."

I bend over to pet Kiki, knowing she's here because she senses my growing anxiety. "Want to come with me?"

She winks at me as I pat down the invisible creases in my dress before looking at the door.

"I think you should get that," Marley says with a warm smile.

I walk forward and place my hand on the doorknob. It's now or never.

Swinging the door open, I freeze when I see Ryne. His hair is neatly slicked back, highlighting his sculpted jawline. He's wearing a black tunic with dark blue embroidery along the center seam, and his simple trousers somehow hug every curve and muscle. He complemented his tunic with an off-the-shoulder cape that has similar designs but with more along the hemline.

"Hey," I manage to say.

His green eyes widen, and his cheeks flush rosy red. I can tell he's fighting the desire to take in every inch of me.

"Wow." His whisper is barely audible. "You're gorgeous," he mutters, and I smile and duck my head to glance down at the floor.

With his hand under my chin, he tilts my head upward, and I gulp when his eyes meet mine.

"Never look down. You're too stunning to hide from the world."

I release a shaky breath when he shows me a moonflower twisted into a bracelet. "I see you, Ayra. I've seen you since the moment we first met." He slips the bracelet on my wrist with a shy grin. "Will you do me the honor?" He offers me his arm, and when I loop mine through his, my tension fades.

I feel seen and adored by him. I don't have to be nervous around him because I know he'll never purposely do anything to make me uncomfortable.

"I would love to."

When his fingertips touch my arm, goose bumps spread along my skin. His eyes trail down my body, almost like he's trying to find a way to memorize this moment forever.

"You're absolutely stunning." He wraps his hand around mine, holding me close by his side.

"Is the gawk fest over?" Marley asks as she peeks out into the hall. "Because I'm starving."

She steps through the door, accidentally bumping into me, and my breasts press against Ryne's arm. I swear he gulps, but maybe it's just my imagination.

Before the final game, the hosting academy is responsible for holding a grand ball to celebrate the competitors and the finalists. This is the event of the season, and everyone knows it. Every final-year witch and wizard will be here tonight, all dressed to impress, ready to eat and dance the night away, along with other things.

Ryne's hand tightens around mine as the thought crosses my mind. Kissing Ryne is enough to leave me speechless, but lying with him? The mere thought threatens to turn my bones to jelly.

"All right you two, don't have too much fun without me." Marley waves as we approach the Grand Hall door.

"We'll see you soon." Ryne offers her a kind smile as she walks farther down the hall. "Are you ready, Brightheart?"

I stare ahead at the massive door, my fingers fidgeting and picking at my dress.

The finalists are given a grand welcome. Our names will be called, and everyone will cheer and wish us luck in the final game tomorrow.

More attention. The one thing I can't seem to escape.

We stop in front of the double doors, and I can feel Ryne's eyes flicker over me, waiting for a response.

"As long as you're by my side, I'm ready for anything," I say with a soft smile.

He squeezes my hand before placing a gentle kiss on my forehead. "You keep on surprising me, Brightheart."

My attention is pulled toward the sound of heels clacking along the stone tile floor.

"Just remember, it's you and me. No one else matters."

I glance over my shoulder to find Cadie and Machiis approaching.

When she opens her mouth, a familiar, booming voice blares from the other side of the thick mahogany doors.

"It is my utmost pleasure to announce the first team to make it to the finale!" Borrick declares, riling the entire room.

"We witnessed their fiery start from the first game, the spark ignited in the second, and then fireworks in the third. They've captured our attention along with our hearts. Without further ado, Ayra Brightheart and Ryne Gwydion!"

The doors glide open, and a sudden burst of light forces me to squint. I have to blink a few times to adjust to it.

The Grand Hall is ever changing, and it never looks the same. The last time I was here, tables lined either side of the room, and the Glass of Prediction showed Ryne that I was to be his partner. Now, the room has been transformed into a ballroom straight out of a fantasy book.

Ryne leads me across the threshold and closer to the balcony overlooking the endless crowd. White quartz crystals shimmer across the pitch-black ceiling, and hints of amethyst and sapphire gems dance in the air.

Borrick gestures for us to take the staircase to our left. It curves down to the dance floor, where witches and wizards wait for us to join the festivities.

"Are you okay?" Ryne leans in closer to my ear.

"Just don't leave me." I don't mean for it to sound desperate, but of course, it does.

Ryne has this innate ability to silence my crippling nerves. I'm a powerful witch, but anxiety gets the best of us all every now and then.

"I'll never leave you."

I lean into his lips as he kisses my cheek. I don't even notice the thunderous applause until we step off the final stair.

"Now, let's add some spice to this slow-burning fire!" Borrick announces as Ryne and I settle in our spots in front of the crowd. "These two are the definition of fire and ice. They've dominated the competition and blasted their way through any obstacle that stood in their way. Here they are, Cadie Blackwell and Machiis Avium!"

As they step out onto the balcony, the room goes wild, and the clapping makes my eardrums pound.

Cadie's white dress is exquisite; no surprise there. The fabric is sheer, and it sparkles against the crystal's light along the ceiling.

When she steps off the last stair, I notice there's a slit that climbs up her thigh. The neckline is a deep V cut, showing her ample cleavage. Her long black hair is curled, and the locks bounce with each step she takes.

Machiis is wearing a navy-blue tunic and trousers with silver stitching along the seams. His dark hair is messy like someone was raking their hands through it.

"Let's hear it one last time for our finalists!" Illana's voice echoes from the balcony.

A sense of comfort washes over me at the sound of her voice.

"Before we begin tonight's celebrations, I have one final surprise!" Illana states as the applause dies down.

I catch Cadie side-eyeing me, a devilish smirk is painted on her face.

"We faced a huge change this year in the Academy Games. Witches and wizards partnering together was once an absurd thought, but look at us now. We've come a long way in such a short amount of time." Illana's gaze lands on me, a gentle sigh escaping her lips. "But that time is over. The next challenge will be witches versus wizards. Cadie will face off against Ryne and Ayra against Machiis. The two remaining winners will face off in one final duel. Only one winner will rise from the battle, so enjoy tonight because tomorrow will be a day we will *never* forget."

Marley found us not too long after Illana officially started the celebration. The three of us settle at a table in a corner, as far away from the crowd as possible. Food from various realms fills the table. Pastries from Paris, chocolate from the Land of Night, berry tarts from a town called Bexely in Altana, along with various meats, cheese, and vegetables. Marley is having the time of her life. She and Ryne are currently talking about taking me to that place they went to for breakfast before he leaves for Traquore Academy when this is all over.

I wish I could say I was enjoying myself as much as they are, but my mind is running through all the possibilities that could happen tomorrow. I don't want to part from Ryne. I wish we could finish the games and come out as victors together, which is a strange notion coming from me. Only a few days ago, the idea of being partners with him made my stomach churn. I thought he would weigh me down or ruin my chances of succeeding. I'm changed now, and that's all thanks to him.

I'm not concerned about dueling Machiis. I've seen the way he fights. He's a heavy hitter, but I could dodge his fire blasts in my sleep. My worry is Cadie battling Ryne. I don't think Ryne has a violent cell in his body, and I don't want to think about the damage she could inflict on him. Then there's the slim chance Ryne does win the duel, and that would only mean one thing. I would have to duel him.

"Are you okay, Ayra?" Marley asks.

I pull my gaze away from the glittery, tulle tablecloth and nod as Marley pops another sugar-coated strawberry in her mouth.

"I'm okay." I force a smile as Kiki leaps onto the table and grabs a piece of steak off my plate, making a genuine grin spread across my lips.

"Where do you think you're going?" Ryne asks Maren, who scampers down his sleeve to nibble on a piece of finely aged white cheddar.

"I think Kiki's antics are rubbing off on him," I say with a snicker while watching the two of them.

When I look up, I catch Ryne admiring me, and my stomach flutters.

"Would you like to dance, Brightheart?" Ryne offers me a lopsided smile along with his hand.

"I'm not the greatest dancer." My response doesn't stop him from standing.

"Don't worry, I'm not either," he says in reassurance.

I place my hand in his and let him lead the way to the dance floor made of thousands of stars. Galaxies swirl around the floor, undisturbed by the hundreds of feet that dance upon them.

I glance over my shoulder as a new song floats on the air, an orchestrated version of "Enchanted" by Taylor Swift. That woman has a chokehold on all the realms.

Ryne places his left hand on my waist, and I place my right hand on his shoulder. Our free hands intertwine as we sway with the music. I'm extra cautious not to step on his toes.

The music's tempo picks up, and Ryne leads me in a turn, making me smile ear to ear. He leads me back to him, and our chests press against one another. I don't stop myself from glancing at his full lips, wondering if or when I'll be able to kiss him again.

Could we find somewhere quiet? I've never craved someone's attention like this before, and while it's terrifying, it's also invigorating.

I'm pulled from my thoughts when he lifts me into the air, a tickling sensation spreading through my midsection. After each turn or lift, he pulls me back against his chest, making sure my balance is stable. We swirl around other couples, focusing on each other's eyes.

"Can I tell you a secret?" he whispers in my ear. "I only asked you to dance so I could hold you like this. Marley is fun and all, but I just want to be with you. You are magnificent."

We stop as the music does, and our chests heave as we catch our breath. His eyes sparkle, and I never want to look away. I could drown in his emerald eyes happily. A warm, tingling sensation spreads through my core, down to my thighs, then up to my heart.

Ryne has me firmly in his grasp.

"That was brilliant!" Marley shakes me out of my trance.

Her smile is wide and eager, and I can tell she wants to dance with someone. What she doesn't know is that every wizard in this room is looking at her, besides Ryne, of course. He seems to only have eyes for me, which leaves me dizzy and feeling marked by him.

"Did you want to dance, Marley?" Her eyes light up at my question.

"Pretty please!" she pleads, clasping her hands together, begging Ryne to dance with her.

I look at Ryne and smile when I catch him with his lopsided grin, but he doesn't respond. He looks like he's been hypnotized.

"Ryne?" I ask with a light snicker.

He shakes his head and his eyes flick between Marley and me. "I'm sorry. What did you say?"

Marley's smile widens in realization, and my cheeks flush with the knowledge that Ryne was stuck in his head while his eyes devoured me. I'd give anything to know what he was thinking about. The possibilities are endless.

"Will you dance with Marley?" I ask with a shy smile.

"Please, Ryne." She draws out his name and bats her eyelashes.

I catch Ryne scanning his eyes over me again.

I mouth, "*Please,*" and his expression softens.

"Marley, will you grant me the honor of this dance?" he asks as the next song fills the room.

Marley jumps up and down, nearly tackling him in the process.

They both smile and laugh, and I come to the realization that they make sense together. If a stranger looked at them, they would assume they were a couple. Hells, *I'm* almost convinced they're together. Two bubbly extroverts who fill whatever room they walk into with sunshine. I wonder what people think when they see Ryne and me. Do we make sense? Or are we so different that the thought doesn't even cross their minds? I want Ryne, but am I enough for someone like him? Am I deserving?

I turn around at that thought. With a gentle smile still on my lips, I walk back over to the table where Kiki and Maren are. We really shouldn't have left them alone. Kiki is nose deep in a plate of crispy bacon-crusted salmon, and Maren is swimming in the chocolate fountain.

"You two are too much," I say, trying my best to hold back my laughter.

Sipping on sparkling blueberry wine, I glance around the room. Witches and wizards alike are grinning, giggling, and gossiping amongst themselves. It doesn't take long for my eyes to land on Cadie and Machiis. She drags her fingers up and down his sleeve. His eyes are on her, while hers are on the wizard across from her. From here, I can see the glint of mischief in her violet eyes. Like always, she's up to no good. But right now, her attention isn't on me, and for that, I thank the stars.

As the song continues, I spot an open balcony door. Curiosity gets the best of me, so I stroll to the door, and a gust of fresh air welcomes me. I step out onto the balcony and place my hands on the marble rail, taking in the sight of the full moons.

One of the many things I love about Fraydora Academy is that you can see both the moon of Hecate and Looma. The moon of Hecate is light azure, while the moon of Looma is deep amethyst. They contrast one another, but they're beautiful nonetheless. The breeze is cool, and my eyes close when it envelopes me.

My breathing slows as chills climb up my arms. I don't allow my mind to wander or allow my nerves to settle in my core. Focusing on my breathing, my shoulders drop when I open my eyes again.

I didn't know the weight I was carrying until Ryne strolled into my life. Perfection is heavy, and it had settled deep in my bones. I thought the pain I walked around with was normal, but it wasn't. Ryne took it upon himself to show me the truth, and for that, I'll always be grateful. I don't know what will become of Ryne and me, but what I do know is that I'll always value him and our friendship. The idea of being more to him awakens new feelings in my body, though I don't want to get my hopes up.

Yes, the way he looks at me confirms that our feelings toward one another are growing, but I must prepare myself for the worst and hope for the best. I'm not worthy. I am destined to perfect my magic and studies. Perhaps love isn't in the cards for me.

I stare up at the sky and smile when I feel his presence behind me. I know it's him because if this were any other person, I would feel on edge and exposed. Ryne's gaze wraps my body in a sense of comfort, admiration, and love. He makes me feel safe and like I don't have to be on guard around him.

Most importantly, he makes me feel like I'm more. And that is worth more than I'll ever be able to put into words.

I like Marley. I really do, but I wish she had a date. Instead, we're dancing in the middle of the ballroom, and Ayra wanders back over to the table alone. Marley's a good-looking woman, and tonight is no exception. The color of the gown she chose complements her complexion. She could have asked anyone in this room to dance with her, yet she asked me, and I gave in because Ayra silently asked me to.

The song that fills the room is an orchestrated version of "Heaven" by Niall Horan. This is a nice moment, but I'd give anything to have Ayra back in my arms.

I lead Marley in a spin, and she laughs and beams with a wide, flawless grin. When I pull her back to me, her eyes lock on mine.

"Can I ask you something?" she asks as the final chords of the song ring out.

"Of course, you can," I say as the song ends, and she takes a tiny step back.

"Don't break her heart. Ayra's been through enough

heartache to last her multiple lifetimes. Please don't add to her pain."

There's that protective best friend I was waiting for. I offer her a soft smile. "I won't hurt her. You have my word."

She releases a sigh. "Good, but know that I've got my eye on you," she teases as she points two fingers from her eyes to mine. "Now, who can you hook me up with before you leave me to find your girl." She clicks her tongue as she scans the room, and I snicker before I join her.

"Let's see . . ." I mumble as my eyes land on Arlin Flore.

Redirecting Marley's direction to Arlin, I nudge her and subtly point in his direction. Her cheeks blush, and her smile grows when her eyes land on him. Arlin has slicked-back black hair. His eyes are piercing brown, and he's one of the kindest people I know. He won't sleep with Marley just for the hells of it, and he won't leave her high and dry.

Unlike another wizard I know.

"Arlin Flore. He's at the top of our class, he holds the record for the fastest time in flying, and he's looking right at you."

"Thanks for the dance, Ryne. Have a lovely night." Marley leaves me on that quick note.

I watch her approach him. Her confidence and giddiness can be felt from across the Grand Hall. Arlin's smile brightens when she extends her hand out to him, and with that, I'm off Marley watch duty.

When I walk back to our table, my hand flies to my forehead. "Maren, are you serious?" I mutter before looking at the scene that unfolds before me.

Kiki is on the table, belly up, snoring with crumbs surrounding her, and Maren is swimming laps in a chocolate fountain with his mouth open.

"You two are such a bad influence on one another." I sigh

as my hands land on my hips. "You know what, celebrate, eat everything. I'm going to find Ayra."

Leaving the table, I try my best to hide my growing smile.

I stroll over to an open door that leads outside, and I'm relieved to find Ayra alone. I'm glad Cadie or Machiis didn't find her. Ayra deserves this night. She worked her way to the top of her class and earned her spot in these games. She deserves at least one night of being carefree.

Her dress shimmers as the train that trails off her shoulders blows in the breeze. Her skin is flawless. My body is urging me to close the distance, to take her in my arms, and never let go.

Nothing comes out when I open my mouth to speak. I'm awestruck by her beauty. She's like the galaxy personified. The stars don't hold a candle to her.

I met Ayra almost a week ago, and she's done this to my heart. Love doesn't happen this fast, does it? It took months for me to feel a fleck of this emotion with my previous partner. This feeling can't be real, but my gut is telling me it is.

Growing up, I got to see what true love looked like. My mother and father have been together for nearly a century, and their eyes still light up when they see one another. Never in a thousand lifetimes did I expect to experience that level of affection. Yet here I am, and I can't help but wonder why the universe deemed me worthy. I take a step forward, and warmth flows into my chest.

Ayra was made for greatness. Surely that means I'm not enough for her. *Right?*

No, I need to remember I'm great in my own way. I won't hold her back. I'll support her to the end of time. As long as I'm with her and she's with me, we can change the realms.

"*Now you're getting it.*" The voice from before returns, and I grin at the compliment.

"There you are." Ryne's voice is smooth and luxurious.

A series of meteor showers shoot across the night sky when he approaches me.

"Are you okay?" he asks as he settles beside me, resting his arm against mine.

"I'm okay." Even I don't fall for it.

I tried to infuse my words with confidence, but in reality, I'm not okay. I'm worried about Ryne facing off against Cadie. I can't stomach the idea of him getting hurt or worse.

"You're a terrible liar." He reaches out to brush a stray piece of hair behind my ear. His fingers feather along my cheek as he goes back to admiring me. "Talk to me, Brightheart," he whispers.

"Can I show you something?"

He arches his eyebrows at my abrupt change in topic, but he doesn't push. "Lead the way."

I welcome the sudden silence when we enter the chilly

corridor outside the Grand Hall. Even though it's spring, the air is brisk. I run my hands over my bare arms, wishing this gown had some velvet sleeves.

"Are you cold?" Ryne asks as I shiver and my teeth begin to chatter. "Here." He unties his cape and drapes it over my shoulders. "There, it looks better on you anyway." He tugs on the clasp, forcing me to take a step closer.

We stand in the middle of the desolate hall, neither of us daring to break the silence. Ryne brushes his pointer finger along my jawline, leaving me flushed and out of breath. Feeling shy, I take a hesitant step back and drop my gaze to the floor.

"We're almost there." My tone softens while I force myself to start down the hall again.

Ryne catches up, and we walk to the East Wing in silence.

Not many people like the East Wing solely because it's dark, but that's why it's my favorite. The only light here comes from the moons and the floating candles that dance along the ceiling. The scents of ash and pine tickles my nose as we round the corner.

A pair of furry raspies wrestle in the middle of the corridor. Ryne chuckles at the sight of them, and I smile in turn. I could listen to him laugh all day; it's deep and comforting.

I lead Ryne to a door farther down the hall and look back at him before I open it.

"Remember when you took me to the art museum? You said it was somewhere you go to think."

Ryne grins at the memory. "Of course I remember."

"Well, this is my secret place." I open the door, already knowing the room will be empty.

I'm pretty sure no one but me knows this room exists. The room is dark, with a dimly lit chandelier hanging in the center of the ceiling. The walls are painted dark gray, and the windows are spaced about a foot away from each other. The floor is shiny, like it's been freshly polished, even though it hasn't.

I turn around to face Ryne as snowflakes begin to float down from the ceiling. "What do you think?" I ask, sounding out of breath.

He scans the room with a wide-eyed gaze.

"It's beautiful," he murmurs, stepping forward and meeting my gaze. "I was expecting more books though," he teases, and I smirk.

"Sometimes the best place to think is an empty room with only windows, nothing else."

Ryne closes the distance between us and brushes a snowflake off my cheek. "And the snow?" His eyes glimmer in wonder, but they don't stray from mine.

"It happens every now and then." I shrug. "That's the beauty of magic."

"Before I met you, I would have never described magic as beautiful."

I tilt my head and furrow my brow. I can't imagine describing magic any other way.

"Back at Traquore, the halls are dark. The curriculum is harsh and unforgiving. I started to resent the gift Hecate bestowed upon me. Then I met you." He presses his palm against my cheek, quickly warming my body from the chill. "I heard about you from the others. They said you were cold and a stickler for rules. But when I *saw* you, I knew none of it was true. The way you view magic isn't just about power, Ayra. You see it as a living, breathing entity. You show it the respect and love it deserves, and now I do too, because of you." He looks down at me, solidifying the feelings that have been growing within my soul.

Ryne is the light in the darkest depths. He is the sunshine

to my gloomy storm. The possibility of Cadie hurting him awakens an overpowering desire to protect him.

"Ryne—"

"You're worried about tomorrow, aren't you?"

I swallow hard and nod. The thought of Cadie throwing spells at him until he's too tired to fight back kills me. The thought of possibly having to duel him myself makes me sick.

"Just because I'm laid back doesn't mean I don't know how to fight. Cadie can handle her own, and I can handle mine."

I open my mouth to speak, but he cuts me off.

"And if we are to face each other one-on-one in the final battle, I'll give it my all. I know you won't accept my surrender or anything less."

I release a huff and wrap my arms around him, pressing my face in the crook of his neck and holding on to him for dear life.

"Will you dance with me?" His words float in the air like a melody.

"There's no music," I say into his shoulder.

"We'll make our own."

He places his left hand in mine and his other on my waist. Ryne leads the way, gently swaying us back and forth. The snow falls around us, landing gracefully at our feet.

I wrap my arms around his neck, and he pulls me closer.

"*Muse Evapora.*" Ryne casts a spell, and the room comes alive with the song "You Are The Reason" by Calum Scott. The harmony of violins and piano keys swirls around the room.

The snow billows around our feet, shimmering and sparkling in the candlelight. As we dance, Ryne keeps me tightly embraced against him.

I pull back and rest my forehead against his. His eyes seem to light up when I smile at him, and my heart yearns for him in a way I'm not accustomed to.

I don't know what love feels like. I only know the textbook

definition. Could this be it? Is love a feeling of excitement mixed with the sensation of a thousand butterflies? Is the look Ryne offers me a mixture of passion and true love?

We dance in silence, letting the song lead our bodies.

I move my head to his shoulder and shut my eyes, taking in a deep breath. Burnt citrus and cedar wash over me, and it comforts me, just as it always has. My muscles are constantly tense and ready to act, but with Ryne, I'm relaxed. I've only known him for a few days, but he's had an immense impact on my life. I feel myself falling, yet I don't worry about hitting the ground. Ryne will protect me, no matter what.

The song fades out, and we stop dancing, but I don't step away from him. I curl my hands into his golden hair as I open my eyes.

His green irises are like pools of summer green leaves, and I'd give anything to ensure he never loses his light.

"Thank you, Ryne. For everything," I whisper.

He smiles as I press my lips against his.

I lived without him for so long. Now, the thought of never seeing him again makes my heart ache. I can't imagine the day he has to return to Traquore, never seeing him in the halls or knocking on my door. Ryne melted the ice capsule I had shrouded my heart in, and now that it's thawed, things can't go back to the way they were.

Even if I could control it, I wouldn't change a thing.

I can't sleep. Ryne walked me back to my door not too long after I showed him my secret room. My finger feathers over my lips, remembering how his felt against mine.

I flip on my side and stare out the window. Kiki starts to purr as I cuddle close to her. Tomorrow is the day I either make or break my dream, yet, I don't feel the pressure I normally would before a test or high-pressure situation. Hells, I don't feel the weight to be perfect like I did before the first game. Instead, my mind wanders elsewhere.

Or rather, to *someone* else.

I'm dreadfully worried about Ryne. I know how Cadie can be. When her head is in the game, she won't let anything deter her. Ryne is her first obstacle to the final duel, and she will unleash all of her power against him. I've only seen her full potential one time when I accidentally shattered a sacred Blackwell heirloom that was kept in one of the North Wing classrooms.

We were learning a new spell, one that would bring an object to the caster's hands. I cast the spell correctly, but the thing with *Lunisim* is that you have to be able to *catch* the item. I'm not sure why we were using the heirloom. Probably to force us to be careful, but it was a bad idea. When the crystalized sunstone fell from my hands and shattered on the ground, all I could do was stare at it.

"What the fuck, Brightheart!" Those were Cadie's exact words.

At that time, our friendship was on the fritz. I was beating her in academics, and the defeat slowly punctured her thick skin.

"I'm sorry I—"

"You did that on purpose!" she fumed.

"Ladies, let's settle down. We can mend the object." The professor tried to cool Cadie's temper, but it didn't work.

"You will pay for this!" was the last thing I heard before a blinding white light slipped from her fingertips, filling the entire room.

The next thing I knew, her hand was wrapped around my throat, and she whispered a spell that slowly sucked the oxygen from my lungs.

"Cadie—" My vision faded in and out. "Stop—"

Fire burned my fingertips, begging to be released. I clawed at her hand in an attempt to free myself, and felt the flames melt her skin, but she didn't flinch. The pressure around my neck increased.

"That is enough!"

A gust of wind knocked Cadie onto her back. I fell to the floor, grasping my throat and coughing and gasping for air.

Everyone knows the Blackwell name is to be revered and that any witch in their bloodline is powerful. I don't think anyone actually believed it until that day.

I certainly didn't.

My stomach twists with worry, and as the stars rise, so do I. I slip out of bed and tiptoe to the front door. I don't know where Ryne's room is, but I can cast a locator spell to get me there.

Holding my breath, and hoping Marley doesn't wake up when I slip out. I pull the door's handle and glance over my shoulder. When she doesn't budge, I open the door.

"Where do you think you're going?" I jump and curse at the sound of Marley's voice in front of me.

"How did you get there?" I ask, grabbing at my chest from the fright. "Wait a minute . . . You weren't in bed? Where have you been?" I ask, feeling blindsided.

She's still in her gown, her hair is disheveled, and her lipstick is smudged.

"What have you been up to, missy?" I can't bite back the sass in my tone as Marley pushes past me with flushed cheeks.

"What we do in the dark is our secret." Her nose wrinkles as I continue to smirk at her.

"Fine, I'll be right back. I just need to clear my head," I say before stepping into the hallway.

"Ryne's room is in the West Wing," she tells me.

"That's not where—"

"Like I said, Ayra, what we do in the dark is our secret." With a wink, she creates a gust of wind to close the door.

I smile to myself, knowing I shouldn't do this, but for once, I'm listening to my heart.

Sleep is elusive, thanks to Ayra flooding my mind. I can't stop thinking about her. She was the embodiment of a queen tonight. My mind keeps replaying how her dress and skin glistened with every sway of her body, and I can't get the picture of her swollen lips from kissing me out of my head.

I wanted to make her mine in more ways than one, but I had to hold myself back in that room. The idea of laying her on the floor and positioning myself on top of her as the snow trickled down on us was fierce.

Kissing her is out of this world, and the way she makes me feel is unfathomable. Everything about her, everything she is —I *need* her. I don't know what will happen after tomorrow. We may continue as nothing more than friends. But my gut is telling me differently, and the feeling is comforting.

I'm not sure how I'm supposed to go back to my old life after this. The halls of Traquore were dim before. Now? They'll be covered in darkness. I'll miss the light that fills the halls at

Fraydora. I'll miss seeing the creatures and specks of magic. And most of all, I'll miss Ayra.

With a groan, I roll onto my back and stare at the ceiling. Maren made himself comfortable in a tiny hammock I crafted for him in the corner of the room. When I found him earlier, he was swimming on his back, nibbling on a piece of chocolate-dipped cheese.

Fuck, I need to clear my head. I swore to Ayra that I would give it my all tomorrow. Battle magic isn't my forte, but I did learn from one of the best, Machiis Avium; he dominates the dueling tournament back at Traquore. He's the reigning champion. I don't have his blast magic, but I have my own tricks.

I'm not worried about Cadie. That's the first rule Machiis taught me. If you go into a battle worried, you've already lost. There is one thing I'm concerned about though. If I win my duel tomorrow, I'll have to battle Ayra, and that possibility makes my stomach churn. That woman could blow me out of the water with her eyes closed—I have no doubt about that. She'll want a fight out of me, though, and I know I won't be able to give it to her. I could never hurt her, even if she made me swear not to hold back. My plan is to surrender immediately, even if it means she'll hate me for the rest of her life. I won't leave a mark on her, no matter what.

A shadow passes by my door, piquing my interest. I saw Machiis wander off after Cadie not long after Ayra and I left the Grand Hall, so I'm sure he's busy with Cadie or another witch. When the shadow passes by again, I swing my legs out from under my blanket. I catch the moment the figure stops moving as I drape my cape over my shoulders. If I didn't know someone was outside my room, I wouldn't have heard the knock. It's light, hesitant. As quickly as it happened, it fades, and the shadow disappears.

After pulling the door open, I step into the hall, and my heart falters.

"I just need to talk to him," I say to myself while I stroll down the main corridor in the West Wing, following the wispy trail of light to Ryne's room. "Warn him about Cadie's light magic, and then go back to bed."

I release a shaky breath as the wisp fades away, leaving me standing in front of Ryne's bedroom door.

What am I doing? He's probably sleeping. It's the middle of the night, after all. I release a muffled groan and fiddle with my thumbs.

Just knock.

I raise my hand and gently tap on the door. A few moments pass, and nothing happens. I could knock again . . . I shake my head, and any lingering courage flies right out the window.

I turn around and start back down the hall.

"Ayra?"

His voice stops me in my tracks.

My eyes widen as I face him. I have to fight my jaw from hitting the floor. Ryne's hair is ruffled like he was sleeping restlessly. He threw on a cape, but it only covers his shoulders, leaving his chest exposed.

Damn, I did not expect him to have muscles like that. How did he get his core to look so lean and rigid at the same time? His lounge pants hang low, and the waistband barely hanging onto his hips reveals a deep V toward his groin.

"Are you okay?" He takes a step closer, and I suck in a forceful gasp of air through my nose.

Fuck, I forgot how to breathe.

"Yeah, um—"

His eyes flicker down my body, and my eyes grow even wider.

I didn't grab a cape or blanket to cover myself with. I'm not as exposed as Ryne is, but this is the most skin he's seen from me. I replaced my velvet gown with a baggy T-shirt and paired it with a pair of loose, cotton shorts.

"Ayra, what's wrong?" he asks while taking another step forward.

I remind myself to breathe, focusing on my exhale rather than my inhale. I came here for a reason—to warn Ryne. So, why are my eyes scanning every inch of him? Why can't I focus on anything but how full his lips are? Or this strange feeling that seems to be buzzing in my veins?

"I—" I can't formulate a damn sentence.

He cocks his head to the side, and a lopsided smile forms on his face.

"Oh fuck it."

I take a few steps forward and close the agonizing distance between us. Pressing my chest against his, I tangle my hands in his hair and kiss him like I'll never get to again. I may have shocked him because he doesn't kiss me back at first, but when he understands what's happening, he gives me his all.

A groan vibrates from his chest as he presses his right hand against my lower back. We become a tangle of lips and limbs within seconds. Gripping, squeezing, exploring, but it's not enough. My hands trail from his hair to his chest and down his abdomen. His skin is so warm against my touch, and his muscles bunch and flex beneath my fingers. Getting to touch him only drives this unfamiliar need higher.

I'm not experienced by any means; I don't even pleasure myself, never had the need or desire to. Now? I *need* the weight of his body on top of me, and I *want* to feel him press himself inside me.

Fuck, just the thought of it pulls a moan from my core.

"Do you have a roommate?" I ask in between our hungry kisses.

"No," he mumbles.

"Good."

It's like Ryne's carefree nature is contagious. The old Ayra would scold me right now, telling me not to be reckless, not to lose my virginity to a wizard I technically just met. But I'm not the old Ayra anymore, and I trust this feeling. I want this, and I need to start taking life less seriously.

I need to start having fun.

Pressing my hands against his chest, I gently push him back as I step forward. Ryne doesn't question me. He walks blindly back into his room, never pulling his mouth from mine.

When we cross the threshold, he closes the door and presses me against it. He moves from my lips and places kisses down my neck. My vision hazes, and my head starts to spin. His touch, the way he feels, is addicting. Without thinking, I pull on the waistband of his pants, urging him closer. When he obliges, I suck in a sharp breath.

"Are you okay?" His voice is barely audible as he trails his nose along my jawline.

I meet his gaze and nod.

Ryne places a sweet kiss on my lips as he feathers his hands up and down my sides.

I swallow past the lump in my throat and shiver. My core is pulsing, traveling to the apex of my thighs. I want this. I want *him*. I want him to be the one to sate this need he keeps stirring within me.

Brushing my fingers along the waistband of his pants, I take a fortifying breath and search his eyes as I slip my hand beneath the elastic. When he makes no attempt to stop me, I reach farther down and take his cock in my hand.

He sucks in a sharp breath at the contact.

Watching him intently, I trace his length, unsure of what else to do.

My nerves must be evident because Ryne rests his forehead against mine. "Brightheart, how experienced are you?"

"Not at all." I drop my gaze from his and blow out a shaky exhale. Any semblance of confidence I had leaves my body. I stop moving my hand and ready myself to retreat. "I can go—"

"Don't," he states. "It's okay. If this is really what you want, I want it too. Could I . . . can I show you?" he offers, and my cheeks flush bright red.

I could run away; I have an out.

Yet, I don't want to. I want to stay and let him do whatever he wants to me. I need him to show me how to please him, so I nod my head.

He places his finger under my chin and grins. "Good girl."

Oh, fuck me.

Ryne captures my lips again. If he asked me to take over a country for him for a simple kiss in return, I would gladly do it.

We walk across the small living room, and the whole time, his hands are pulling on the drawstrings of my shorts. When his legs hit the edge of his bed, he steps back, leaving me in a daze.

My chest heaves up and down, and a potent mixture of nerves and excitement stirs in my body. Who knew the unknown was so . . . invigorating?

Ryne removes the cape around his shoulders, and I don't move when he steps forward or when he reaches for the waistline of my shorts.

"Can I take these off?" he asks.

My nod makes him smirk.

"Speak to me, Ayra."

"Yes," I breathe out.

He tugs them down, and my shorts fall to the ground. His breath hitches in his throat.

It's comforting to know he's just as nervous as I am. Although, he's better at masking it.

"And this?" He drags his hands up my stomach, taking my shirt along with it.

"Yes."

His eyes don't leave mine as he pulls my shirt over my head. A rush of cold air surrounds me, but Ryne quickly wraps me in his embrace.

"You're so beautiful," he rasps before kissing me again.

He moves his hands up to my bare breasts before he curses. "Fuck," he moans as he spins us around so the back of my legs are against the edge of his bed.

I bring my hands back down to his waistband and push his pants down his thighs until they pool at his feet, leaving him in only a pair of black boxer briefs.

My nerves have been replaced with adrenaline and my desire in this moment.

A surprised squeal leaves my lips when he scoops me into his arms, his hands firm under my thighs. I can feel his smile as he kisses me.

He places me near the top of his bed before settling over

me. I wrap my legs around him, arching into him, desperate for pressure against my clit. When he pulls back, I'm left needy and breathless. His eyes lock on mine, and I don't even notice his hand inching down my stomach to my underwear until it's too late.

"Have you ever touched yourself before?" He reaches into my underwear, hovering over where I'm aching but refusing to touch.

I turn my face away. "No."

With his free hand, he guides my eyes back to his. "Let me know what feels good, okay?"

I open my mouth to respond but release a gasp of shock. "Oh, fuck." I writhe as he brushes his thumb over my clit, warm, electrifying chills erupting in his wake.

"Is this okay?"

My spine arches as he makes tiny circles around the bundle of nerves, slowly satisfying the throbbing.

"Yes, don't stop," I beg him.

A proud gleam widens his smirk. "Careful, Brightheart. If you keep moaning like that, I'll take you faster than you can handle."

Goose bumps break out across my skin, and he adds another finger to the sensitive spot.

I whimper, "Ryne."

Desire fills his gaze as I cry his name. Just when I didn't think his touch could get any better, his finger drops lower.

"Fuck, Ayra."

My stomach tightens when he presses his finger a mere millimeter inside me, barely scratching the growing need building within me.

I glance down at his cock, and it's straining against the fabric of his boxers. Knowing he wants me as much as I want him is something I won't ever get over.

I reach down and place my palm against his length, still unsure how to please him.

"I want to touch you, Ryne. Tell me what to do."

"Is that what you want?"

I nod, and I swear his eyes darken.

"Please," I plead, and he bites his lower lip.

His lips clash against mine as he reaches down to free himself. When our lips part, we both struggle for air.

"Wrap your hand around it."

I meet his dark gaze and follow his directions. A groan leaves his chest when I do as he says. I have to hold back a gasp of shock when I touch him. His cock is . . . impressive, thick, and hard. When I glance down, my core starts to tickle and pulsate at the idea of him stretching me.

"Apply some pressure, not a lot, then stroke it from the base to the tip."

I tighten my grip around him, making sure to be gentle. His cock stiffens even more as I run my hand over him.

His eyes flutter closed. "Yes, just like that," he pants.

I thought his touch was a sensation I could never forget, but me touching him is another form of undiscovered magic. I love how his muscles flex as I find the right rhythm, how his breath catches, and how a moan follows shortly after.

And his eyes. When he opens them, the normal shade of green changes to a more commanding hue.

He moves his gaze to my breasts, admiring how they shift as I work him. He leans down and kisses the center of my chest, slowly traveling to my nipple.

"Don't stop, Ayra."

My breaths are becoming ragged as I observe him, unsure of what he plans to do.

"Let me know if you don't like this." He flicks his tongue over my nipple, sending a warm rush all over my body.

"Oh my—fuck, Ryne," I struggle out.

He takes my nipple in his mouth, gently sucking and licking it in time with my strokes.

A deep chuckle vibrates his chest. "I fucking love how your body reacts to me."

I increase my pressure around him, hoping to beat him at the game he's playing. But just as I think I'm starting to win, his fingers return to the spot he was rubbing moments before. I moan in pure bliss; never did I imagine a feeling such as this existed. My muscles tense as a flurry of chills spread down my thighs, my vision starts to fade in and out, and my breathing becomes erratic. Something is missing though—a carnal need.

"Ryne, I need you."

He kisses my nipple before slowing his touch.

"Say that again," he demands.

"Ryne, I *need* you," I whisper while wrapping my legs around him, urging him to close the gap.

"I need you to say it."

I lean up to kiss him, but he backs away. "Say it, Ayra." His lips hover over mine, teasing me.

"I need you to *fuck* me."

He shoves his face in the crook of my neck, sucking on my earlobe before biting it.

"It'll be uncomfortable at first," he says while pressing the tip of his cock against me.

"I don't care."

I need him to be my first. I can't imagine being with anyone else. I can't imagine being with anyone else ever again.

Hooking his thumbs on the edge of my underwear, he glides them off and tosses them on the floor.

I sit up and kiss his sculpted pecs, driven by the urgency to have him. He releases a groan as I tug his boxers over his thighs.

"Do you know the spell?" I ask, breathless, while looking up at him, and he nods.

I haven't done this before, but we were taught in class that there is a spell that must be cast before you lie with another. The spell lasts an entire day. It protects you against unwanted diseases and pregnancy.

"Give me your hand," he requests.

I don't look at him as he leads my hand over his lower stomach.

"You have to cast it, so repeat after me. *Lustiva Consetium.*"

"*Lustiva Consetium,*" I repeat.

Warm chills climb up my spine, spreading through my shoulders, down my arms, and right to my fingertips. When the heat dissipates, I lean back, settling on a pillow.

"Tell me if I should stop," Ryne says as he places his arms on either side of my body.

We lock eyes as he presses himself inside me. I feel myself stretch around him, and my jaw tightens as he settles in deeper. A mixture of nerves and pleasure swirls in my stomach. I remind myself that I have nothing to be nervous about, though, because this is Ryne, and Ryne has done everything up until now to make me feel safe and cared for.

Once he's fully inside me, he groans, and his chest heaves.

"I'm okay," I rasp.

He nods in response.

This time he's the one unable to form a legitimate sentence. Ryne pulls his hips back ever so slightly before pressing back into me with a grunt. After a few moments like this, the stretching no longer aches like it did, and I can tell he's holding back. He wants to go faster, harder, but he's putting me first.

Just when I think the cramping won't subside, it disappears, and in its place is something I can't describe.

The feeling from earlier returns. It creeps along my spine and travels down my hips. Ryne moans in pleasure, the muscles in his arms flex, and his cheeks burn.

"Ryne," I mumble, unsure of what's happening in my body.

He meets my gaze and slows down, the exact opposite of what I want him to do.

"What's wrong? I'll stop." He goes to pull out, but I stop him.

"No, don't stop," I urge.

He presses his forehead against mine. We watch each other before our lips meet again. I moan in between his kisses, the feeling between my legs growing stronger.

"Fuck," I cry out.

When Ryne notices, he increases his pace.

"Do you feel like you're about to explode?"

I can only nod.

"That's it, let it take over. Give me everything, Ayra."

I gently pull on his hair as the feeling spreads through my core.

"Oh my gods—"

"Yes, fuck yes." Ryne gives in to his desire.

His finger returns to my clit, rubbing against me. He dives into me harder; it hurts for a brief moment, but undeniable warmth and desire quickly replace it. My back arches off the bed, and as if Ryne knows the precise moment I need him to press into me, he does, and everything blurs.

My body erupts in both warm and cold chills, my muscles tense then relax simultaneously, and a series of incoherent whimpers escape my lips.

Just as these feelings blind me, Ryne presses into me and finishes.

"*Fuuuuck,*" he grunts as he collapses beside me.

We struggle to catch our breath, and I glance at him, admiring him. His cheeks are still flushed, his golden hair drapes across his forehead, and his eyes sparkle when he catches me.

"Come here," he says as he reaches out for me.

I roll onto my side and cuddle into his chest.

He wraps his arms around me and sighs. "Ayra?"

I glance up at him. The way he looks at me makes my heart skip a beat.

"I'm about to say something reckless."

"What is it?" I shift closer so we can meet eye to eye.

He runs his finger over my cheek, brushing a loose strand of hair off my face.

"You've had my heart since you shattered that Disk of Unyielding. I knew it from the start, and I think you did too. I've never been in love, but I'm falling in love with you. I think I may already be *in* love with you," he confesses.

I reach up and stroke his cheek, and he leans against my palm.

"I know what you're about to say. 'Ryne, you're so—'"

I kiss him, stopping him from finishing his sentence.

"I think I'm in love with you too, Ryne Gwydion. The second you smiled at me, I knew I was done for. I brushed it off as irritation, but you found a way into my heart. You left me impossibly helpless. I don't think you're a silly wizard. I think you're strong, charming, witty, and undeniably wonderful. Within a week's time, you've changed my life, and now, I can never go back to the days before I met you. Hells, I don't want to go back. I can't." I sniffle away the tears that threaten my eyes.

"You don't have to because you're stuck with me, Brightheart. That's just the way it is now. I also can't go back to the days before you. I can't live without seeing your smile, or how your eyes light up when you see a furry creature, or how your smile brightens a room. I refuse to even think about it."

I chuckle at his words, more than relieved to know I'm not alone in my feelings.

"It's settled then," I say with a grin.

"You and me." He places a kiss on my brow.

My eyes flutter closed as our breathing returns to normal. Ryne covers us with a blanket and plays with my hair, soothing me into a much-needed slumber.

"Goodnight, Brightheart," he whispers against my forehead.

"Goodnight," I mumble against his chest as sleep welcomes the both of us.

Ayra

42

The room is still dark when I open my eyes. Ryne is trailing two fingers up and down my bare back. I nuzzle closer to his chest, refusing to let this moment end. If it were up to me, I would never leave his bed. We would live out the rest of our lives here. But life isn't that simple. There is a game that must be played.

I wrap my arm around his waist, and he pulls me closer.

"Are you awake?" he asks.

I shake my head and bury myself against him.

"It's almost time." His voice is husky and quiet, making his accent even thicker.

"I don't want to," I whine, and his chest moves as he chuckles.

"Yes, you do. You want to show Machiis what you're made of."

Ryne rolls onto his back, earning himself more groans of displeasure.

"No, not yet," I moan as I shove my face into his shoulder.

He places his hands on my cheeks, forcing me to meet his gaze.

"Promise me something."

A soft smile plays on his expression. "Anything."

"Be careful. Cadie is more powerful than anyone can imagine. She's a Blackwell, after all. Don't let her beat you black and blue. Once you're out, you're out, deal?" I plead. "And if you defeat her, I expect you to give me your all."

"You have my word," Ryne says without a second thought.

I release a deep sigh, wishing this day was over.

"Don't worry, Brightheart. I can handle myself." He's trying to reassure me.

I give him a stiff nod in return.

"Come here." A devilish smirk plays on his face as he pulls me closer, momentarily melting my worry away.

"I thought you said it was almost time," I whisper as I feather my lips over his.

"Since when did you start listening to me?" He sucks on my lower lip before kissing me.

I melt into him, letting him ravage me like he did last night. My senses whirl until I'm left dizzy. He parts my lips with his tongue, slowly trailing over mine, awakening the same burning, needy sensation from hours ago.

I run my hands through his hair and moan. The second I do, his cock presses against my inner thigh.

"What time is it?" he asks, and I let out an incoherent groan, not caring about the time.

He shifts his head to the left, and I take advantage of his exposed neck, gently kissing and licking the spot beneath his jaw.

He releases a shaky groan, and I smile. Apparently, I found a sensitive spot.

"We have an hour before it starts." he manages to say before moaning in pleasure as I suck the underside of his jaw.

"That's plenty of time. Get on your back."

He rolls onto his back, so I take the opportunity to straddle him, seating myself over his hips before he has the chance to react.

"So demanding," he says with a chuckle.

My lips travel from his jaw to his mouth, and he kisses me in a frenzy. "Fuck me, Ayra. Now."

I need to be inside her. I'm losing the ounce of control I've been managing to keep in check. What's driving me even more insane? She's teasing me. For someone who isn't very experienced, she sure knows how to torture me.

We fell asleep naked, in each other's arms, and she's taking advantage of that. Placing herself over my cock, she moves her hips and slides her center along my length. Her gasp brings a knowing smile to my face.

"Does that feel good?" I ask, knowing damn well it does, solely by her expression.

"Yes," she hums. "Really good."

I grip her hips and guide her, ensuring she's applying the right amount of pressure against her clit.

"Ryne, fuck, that's so good."

My teeth meet my lower lip. I love it when she says my name. Knowing I create a growing need inside her, knowing I've been the only one she's been with, makes me want her more.

"Lift your hips for me." My tone is deep and commanding.

Her swollen lips and fluttering eyes add to her lustful expression.

To my surprise, she obeys.

"Like this?" She's out of breath and red.

And, gods, is she a sight. The ends of her hair curl, partly because I couldn't stop running my fingers through it last night. Ayra's blue and silver eyes glint, waiting for me to tell her what to do next.

I don't utter a word. Instead, I press the tip of my cock inside her and slowly guide her down my shaft.

"Fuck me," I groan loudly, trying to stop myself from thrusting into her until we're both screaming each other's names.

Her muscles contract around me, hugging every inch. Her warmth alone is enough to make me come.

"Tell me what to do," she pleads as I trail my hands up her waist and over her curves.

"Ride me," I rasp.

"I don't know h—"

"Trust yourself." I cut her off, curious to see what her body wants to do to mine.

And to my pleasant surprise, she lifts her hips ever so slightly and crashes back into me. Her pleasing smile mirrors mine.

"Just like that, don't stop," I order as my eyes travel to her breasts. Her nipples are peaked, and my mouth begins to water.

She grips the sides of my waist, gently digging her nails into my skin as she bounces on my dick. When her eyes flutter closed, I sit up and take her lips against mine. Her moan fills my mouth, stirring my growing need to ravage her. Before I can explore her mouth with my tongue, she pushes me back and smirks.

"So bossy," I whisper with a grin, and she whimpers.

Fuck, she's going to be the death of me. I raise my hips and press into her. Her back arches forward as her hands grip on the mahogany headboard.

"You like that?" I ask as I thrust into her again. Her cry of pleasure is like music to my ears. "Answer me." Her eyes find mine, but she's struggling to find her words.

"Yes, for fuck's sake, yes."

I grunt and flip her onto her back, and she squeals in delight. I settle over her and guide my cock back inside her. She cries out, and her pussy squeezes my length.

"Sorry, baby. It's my turn." Pulling out and pressing in, I fill her.

With one last passionate kiss, I part our touch as the desperate need to taste her nipple overpowers me. I trail my kisses down her chest, looking up into her eyes, and wrap my lips around her raised peak, sucking and savoring how sweet she tastes.

Ayra curls her hands into my hair, pulling on my locks as I time my tongue with her grinding, and my abdomen tenses in pleasure. I'm trying to hold back. I'm not done with her yet. Hovering over her breast, I lick my thumb and start to feather it over her left nipple. Her body reacts just as I hoped it would.

"Oh my gods—" I interrupt her by kissing her in desperation.

"Look at me, Brightheart."

When her eyes open, they're glossed over in a drunken haze.

"I'm the one fucking you. No god could *ever* make you feel this way." As I dive in and out of her, I run my finger over her clit. "Do you feel that?"

Her eyes close again, but I stop her.

"Look at me, Ayra," I demand, and her eyes shoot back open. "Are you going to come for me?" I growl.

The overwhelming urge to fill her makes my body temperature increase.

She nods, but I need more.

"Say it," I command, and her eyes sparkle.

"Yes." Her moan fills the room, and I curse.

"Give it to me. That feeling brewing in your stomach is *mine*. Come for me, Brightheart."

"Say it again," she calls out as her eyes close.

"You like when I boss you around, don't you?" I chuckle before biting her lower lip.

With a whimper, she nods.

"Come for me, Brightheart. Right now."

As if her body was awaiting permission, her hips lift off the bed. I ram my cock inside her, pressing and holding myself still as she writhes around me.

"Hells," I moan before getting ready to pull out, but she wraps her legs around my waist, holding me hostage, and her eyes flutter open. "Ayra," I warn her.

"It's okay. The spell lasts a full day. I want to feel you, Ryne."

"For fuck's sake." I thrust into her, and when I do, I fill her.

I groan in her ear, muttering her name and incoherent curses until my cock stops pulsing and her pussy stops sucking me off. When I pull out, I rest my hand against her throat, kissing her with fierce desire.

"You really are something else," I manage to say before collapsing on my back.

We're both silent as we catch our breath. I get a glimpse of her from the corner of my eye, and I'm smiling like a lovesick fool within seconds.

"What are you looking at?" she asks while turning her head to look at me.

"The most beautiful witch to walk across all the realms," I confess.

"You're such a charmer," she squeals as I pull her against my chest.

"Is that what I am?" I trace my fingertips over her waistline, spurring her into a giddy defense.

"Ryne, stop!" Her laugh fills the room as the suns rise.

She captures my hands in hers and attempts to hold me off. "I don't want to kick you out of reflex," she says midlaugh.

I pin her arms over her head and kiss her. "I take back what I said last night," I whisper against her lips.

"Which part?" she mumbles.

"I don't think I'm falling in love with you, Ayra. I've *already* fallen."

Her smile brightens the room, and I run my thumb over her cheekbone. I don't want this moment to end. I need to relish in her existence forever.

"Ryne, I—"

"**R**yne, get your ass up!"

I jolt from the sudden banging against Ryne's bedroom door, our brief hour of solitude coming to an abrupt end.

"You've got to be shitting me." Ryne runs his hand over his eyes and groans.

"I'll never understand why you two are friends," I blurt out.

Machiis is the last person I thought Ryne would ever align himself with. The first day I met him, when he threw the Disk of Unyielding at my face, I made up my mind about him. He's an ass.

"He wasn't always like this; he used to be nice and fun. He stood up for me when I was getting bullied when we were younger."

A forlorn look settles on his face, like memories of their friendship are running amuck through his head.

"He's changed, though, and not for the good."

Before I can respond, the rampant tapping returns.

"Dude, come on, we've got some witch ass kicking to do!"

My brow raises, and I scoff.

"Don't, Ayra."

I crawl off Ryne and hop out of his bed.

"Ayra." A knowing smile takes over his lips.

I whisper, "*Changesis.*"

A not-so-subtle frown replaces the smile on his face as a set of casual clothes settles on my figure.

"Ayra," he repeats as I back away from him.

"What? I'm just going back to my room," I tease, knowing damn well what I'm really about to do.

"I can create a portal for you," Ryne says as he gets out of bed, slowly stalking toward me.

"I don't want a portal."

The banging returns, widening my mischievous smirk.

"Ryne, what are you doing? We've got to go!" Machiis shouts.

I reach for the door handle, ready to see his face when he sees me and more than ready to call him out on his bullshit and give him the word lashing he deserves.

"Ayra, get your ass over here." Ryne is trying to sound intimating, but I can hear the hint of laughter in his whisper.

I chuckle when a pair of joggers materializes over his legs, but I continue to back away from him.

"*Make me,*" I mouth before spinning around to crack open the door.

The moment it opens, Ryne closes it, and I stifle a laugh when he spins me around and presses his chest against mine.

"You're looking for trouble," he growls before kissing me.

Ryne's body shifts above me, and the sound of the deadbolt locking the door punctuates the otherwise quiet of the room.

"Ryne, do you have someone in there?" Machiis calls behind the door. "It's that *witch,* isn't it?"

Normally, a comment like that would get under my skin, but Ryne's bare upper body is pressed against me, and I'm focusing on how his lips move against mine, how his touch makes me feel like an all-powerful being. The comment barely registers.

"Be right out, Machiis!"

I whimper when Ryne pulls away to answer his friend.

Noticing my pout, he picks me up and squeezes my ass before devouring me again. "You're going to pay for all of this . . . later," he grunts as the hum of a portal lingers in my ears.

Ryne carries me through it, but I refuse to stop kissing him.

"Not later, *now*," I retort.

He smiles against my lips before pulling away. I groan when I notice we're back in my room.

"Later, after you win. We can celebrate *all* night."

"I'd like that." I lean to kiss him again, but he places me on the floor instead.

"Marley, Ayra's back," he calls out, and something clatters on the floor.

"Where the hells have you been!?"

I point at Ryne as he steps through the portal. "You're gonna pay for this," I say before Marley makes her entrance, and he fucking winks at me before he closes the portal.

Marley trips over her feet when she sees me, excitement and curiosity etched into her expression.

"Spill it," she says out of breath.

"Whatever happened to 'what we do in the dark is our secret'?"

"Fuck that!"

I snicker as her voice raises.

"I'll tell you later. I've got a finale to win." I stand before the floor-length mirror, casting *Changesis* to prepare myself for today.

First things first, I head into the bathroom to relieve myself I and to take a quick shower. With time crunching, I wash myself as quickly as possible before returning to my side of the room.

A royal-blue coat that flares around my hips replaces my plain T-shirt, a matching set of trousers glide over my legs, a brown leather belt ties around my waist, and a pair of matching fingerless gloves cover my hands and wrists. I step into a pair of dark chestnut boots as my hair ties itself back. After messing with my bangs, I give myself a firm nod.

I can do this.

"Ready to kick Machiis's ass?"

I smile at Marley through the mirror's reflection.

"Always."

I hold my head high as I approach the Grand Hall. The air feels different now. I don't feel the weight of the world on my shoulders, nor the crippling pressure to succeed. Granted, I wouldn't be upset if I win, but I don't think I'll be devastated if I lose because in the end, I've won either way.

I won the chance to understand what it really means to live. Not everyone gets a second chance like this. If I hadn't met Ryne, I would still believe I'm nothing more than the drive to be perfect. I would have run myself into my grave, thinking I failed simply because I could never reach my own expectations. The thing with perfection is that once you try to grasp it, the standard rises, and it never stops. Ryne helped me see that, and he'll have my gratitude and heart long after my dying breath.

When I lift my gaze, I see him. An aura of light surrounds him, like the suns know he's worth the energy and warmth. He's already in his position before the entrance. As if he can sense my presence, he glances over his shoulder, offering me a lopsided smile.

I know exactly where I'd be if I hadn't met Ryne. I'd be walking to the final game, but my expression would be focused and stern. For certain, I would be putting myself under immense pressure to win because if I failed, the crushing weight of disappointment would follow. Now, I know if I lose, no one will care. The academy certainly won't. I may feel sad for a moment, mainly because I've worked so hard to get where I am today, but at the end of the day, I get to be with the one person who has opened realms of possibility for me.

Machiis turns around to say something to Ryne, but when he notices Ryne's attention is elsewhere, he rolls his eyes and scoffs. Cadie must have heard him because she spins around and offers me a stomach-churning grin.

"Brightheart," she chimes as I stand in my spot behind her. "How are you feeling? The day after losing your virginity can sometimes be rather . . . *uncomfortable*."

I poke my cheek with my tongue and flick my eyes over to Machiis. He knew I was in Ryne's room last night; it doesn't take a genius to put two and two together.

"I guess you would be a pro at that, considering you've *lost* your virginity more than five times."

I'm not a fool. I've heard the gossip. The one thing about staying in the shadows is that you hear everything. Cadie has had a good number of boyfriends, if you want to call them that. Her friends were whispering one day in the library, saying she got a kick out of pretending to be a virgin. And while I'm not one to judge, this "kink" of hers sounds more like deceit.

Cadie's face flushes, and rage furrows lines in her forehead.

Ryne whistles and turns around; he knows he doesn't need to stick up for me. I can do it all on my own.

"Wait, you're *not* a virgin? You said I was your first."

I would feel bad for Machiis if he wasn't such a prick.

"I don't know what she's talking about." Cadie's voice rises. "You've heard the stories. She's completely mental."

Ryne's shoulders stiffen.

"For all we know, she sneaks out in the middle of the night just to fuck anything that crosses her path."

I roll my eyes at her attempt to deflect, but Ryne balls his hand into a fist.

"Good point. I've never heard a virgin moan the way she did last night."

Ryne whirls around, grabs Machiis by his collar, and slams him against the wall.

"Dude, what the fuck!?"

"Want to say that again?" Ryne seethes with rage, a tone I've never heard from him before.

"It was just a joke."

Ryne forces him against the wall again, unhappy with his response.

"I'm starting to wonder why I still put up with you. Something about you changed this year, and a certain *someone* has only made it worse." Ryne cocks his head toward Cadie.

"Put me down, Gwydion," Machiis orders, his brown eyes narrowing in fury.

"Apologize to Ayra."

I really don't want his apology, but Ryne does, and something about that is endearing.

"Fuck you," he spits out.

"That's enough!"

My hands fly to my ears as Borrick thunders down the corridor.

Ryne drops Machiis to his feet before standing firm.

"You have been nothing but trouble since we got here,"

Borrick declares as Machiis scrambles to his feet, placing his hands behind his back as Ryne does.

"Ryne was only defending me; it wasn't his fault." I can't help but flinch when Borrick directs his attention to me.

"You two have caused some headaches as well. I'm going to be so relieved when this is over. I don't care what or who started it. You're about to duel anyway. Unleash your anger in the arena," Borrick says before opening two portals in front of the towering Grand Hall doors. "Ladies to the left, gentlemen to the right. Your battles will happen simultaneously. Whoever wins can head to the next arena even if the fight isn't over. Cadie will duel against Ryne, Ayra will duel against Machiis. The last person standing wins. Any questions?"

"No, sir," Ryne and Machiis call out as Cadie and I shake our heads.

"Then let the games begin."

The portals pulsate, and cheering erupts around us. Cadie steps through the portal without another thought. Ryne and I lock eyes before heading into our separate arenas. With a grunt, Machiis pushes past Ryne and strolls through his designated vortex.

"*Give him hell,*" he mouths.

I smile softly and nod my head at Ryne.

"See you soon." With my final words, we both take a step forward, ready to face whatever comes next.

Let the games begin.

T he world opens around me, and stray pebbles crunch under my feet. We're surrounded by boulders that are centuries older than myself. The suns hang in the center of the sky, blaring white and hot. Machiis steps out of his whirling violet portal ahead of me, his hands balling into fists like he's stretching his fingers for battle.

I take in a deep breath of brisk air and let it out.

Show them how interesting you can be.

The voices I'm expecting to return don't. Instead, my internal monologue welcomes me as I ready myself for the duel. One step closer, one more obstacle, *I can do this.*

"Contestants, are you ready!?" Borrick calls out.

Applause erupts, and I glance around the arena. The shimmer of a protective barrier separates the growing crowd from Machiis and me.

I plant my feet in the red rock below me, my knees slightly bent. Machiis rolls his neck and faces me with a devilish smirk.

"This is not a battle to the death. Whoever is incapacitated first is out. The other contestant can rush to the other battle and jump in if it's still in process. The last one standing wins."

My eyes pierce Machiis's empty gaze. My muscles twitch, and adrenaline rushes through my veins.

"Let the battle begin!"

Fireworks skyrocket into the air.

Machiis pulls his arm back, launching a fireball at my head, but I manage to dodge it in time. His feet clamber along the rock as I roll across the ground. He moves his hands to create another blast.

Slamming my hand into the terrain, I splinter the ground. It cracks and crumbles all the way to the strip of land between Machiis's feet. He loses his balance, and the fire in his hands extinguishes as he leaps out of the way to find stable ground.

I take the opportunity to gain some distance. After pushing myself to my feet, I run across the arena. I'm willing to bet Machiis wants distance between us, but so do I. He's not the only one good at hurling fireballs.

"Where ya going, Ayra?" he calls after me with a sardonic chuckle.

I skid to a stop and face him, only to find another explosion coming my way. I bend backward to narrowly avoid his shot, the fire singeing pieces of my hair in the process.

He's fast, I'll give him that.

"You know, I knew you were trouble that first day I saw you in the courtyard. I warned Ryne you were a piece of work," he taunts as we dance around one another.

I guide my fingers behind my back, creating a mix of fire and earth.

"And why is that?" I shout back, a bit of cockiness in my tone.

"Ryne likes pretty things, even if that *pretty thing* is a rule-obeying bitch."

I grin at him as the magic whirls around my right hand. "Aw, so you think I'm pretty?"

He opens his mouth to respond, but my movement distracts him. I raise my left hand, pretending to pull the rock above him down. He launches a blast above him only to find an empty sky. With his attention diverted, I launch the fiery earth from my right hand.

Machiis is fast, but I'm faster. His eyes widen in realization when he notices the magic whirling toward his chest. He doesn't get the chance to react. The fire hits him dead center, and the force of the throw pushes him against the rocky terrain.

He releases an "*oomph*" when his spine makes contact with the jagged wall.

His knees hit the ground first, and his eyes scan over me as I near him. I can't help but chuckle as he struggles to stand.

"Don't get cocky, Ayra," he seethes. Blood cakes his mouth as he smiles at me. "I'm not out yet."

Lightning cracks down at my feet. I leap out of the way but scream out in pain as a spark catches my shoulder.

"Fuck!" I shout as I collapse to the ground.

The lightning jolts along my skin, growing more intense by the second. My back arches off the ground, and my teeth meet the side of my cheek as the sparks spread. I try to roll onto my side, but the pain grows. My eyes flick around the sky, only to focus in on Machiis as he looms above me.

"Looking hot, Ayra."

I groan as my fingernails dig into the earth. Spit bubbles past my lips as the lightning spreads to my toes.

"Still not my type though. I'm not into smoked witch." He laughs before planting his foot on my chest.

"*Are you really going to go down like this?*" The voices return.

"*Hmm, strange. I thought she was more interesting than this.*"

"Such a disappointment."

I suck in a deep breath and my eyes scan the area to my right, focusing on a precarious boulder.

"Ah, now she gets it."

"Careful, Machiis," I hiss as flames encase my pointer finger.

His smirk diminishes as he follows my gaze.

"I'm not out yet," I mutter as the flames launch from my fingertip.

It creates an avalanche of rocks and boulders tumbling down. Machiis tries to scramble out of the way, but I take hold of his wrist.

"Where do you think you're going?"

The earthfall crashes to the ground, dust and debris surrounding us within seconds.

"Protectium!" I cast a shield right before the earth collides with us.

I want to scare him, not decapitate him.

As the rumble dissipates, I let a moment of silence pass. I haven't lost Machiis because my hand is still wrapped around his wrist. With a twirl of my finger, the cloud of rocky smoke disappears. I glance down at my body, thankful the lightning curse has run its course.

His chest is heaving, and his eyes are stuck on the suns above us.

"Frostarius." I cast a bracelet of ice around his wrist, one so heavy he couldn't stand no matter how hard he tried.

When I sit up, my head spins, and the world around me becomes unsteady. I take a brief moment to collect myself before standing, doubling over to rest my palms against my knees while catching my breath.

"Fucking bitch," Machiis curses as he fights against his restraint.

"Funny, I thought you said you were going to kick *my* ass," I say while meeting his eye. "Not too bad . . . for a *stickler*." I step away from him, ready to be done with him.

"Ayra Brightheart has defeated Machiis Avium!"

The applause reaches a crescendo, and I walk forward as a portal appears in front of me.

"Cadie Blackwell and Ryne Gwydion's arena is straight ahead. I have a feeling things are about to get heated!"

I run right into the vortex, unsure what I'm about to walk into. All I know is if Cadie hurt Ryne, if she went too far, she will have more than hell to pay.

Ryne

46

Light magic isn't the only thing Cadie Blackwell exceeds in. With every cast I throw at her, she deflects it or throws it back at me. I grunt as my back hits a nearby tree, my body rolling across the field as she cackles to herself. She's toying with me, and she's enjoying every second of it.

"Is this the best Traquore has to offer? What a pity."

I spit out a mouthful of blood as she yawns.

I whisper, *"Earthiarm Polis."* And a sword made of solid rock flies into my hands. Ignoring the shaking in my knees, I stand upright.

Before she can cast another spell, I arch my fingers, pulling a series of hardened rocks from the ground. I push them forward to create a diversion. As Cadie shields herself with a barrier of light, I charge forward. Driving the tip of the sword into her shield, I watch it crack like glass, slowly splintering until it breaks. When it shatters, a gust of wind pushes me back, forcing my body onto the ground in an instant.

"Now, that's more like it," Cadie calls out in excitement.

I roll onto my side, my eyes blurring and my head throbbing. I'm not sure how much more of this I can take.

"Aw, are you done already?" she coos.

Taking a trick out of Ayra's book, I coat my hands in flames.

"*Blaze Vapado,*" I grunt while extending my right arm and aiming my shot at her.

She's encircled in flames in a matter of milliseconds.

I take the brief opening to stand, but my balance threatens to betray me. Standing as tall as I can, I meet her eyes through the fire.

She raises her hands, whispering a spell I can't make out.

The sky darkens, and thunder rolls in, crashing in the sky. Rain pours down onto the field, extinguishing the flames I created in the blink of an eye.

"I'm used to fire. You can thank your girlfriend for that," Cadie hisses as she steps over the burnt spring grass. "Do you think you really stand a chance against me?"

I stifle a groan. One of my ribs must be broken because it's poking against my skin.

"Probably not." I smile, knowing damn well I don't stand a chance.

My goal was never to win this duel. It was to exhaust her. Let her throw me around until Ayra shows up. The sweat across her brow signifies that my plan is working.

"You're so cute. Shame you fell for the wrong witch."

Ignoring her words is easy, and the familiar *whoosh* of a portal opening relaxes my shoulders just a smidge.

Right on time, Brightheart.

"I didn't fall for the wrong witch. I fell for the perfect one."

She's behind me, I can sense her, but I'm not done with Cadie yet. Ayra will have to wait one more moment.

"*Electriciar!*" I pull a strand of lightning from the sky and aim it at her chest.

When it crashes into her, my knees buckle. Ayra peeks into the clearing, but she doesn't make a move. Her face is caked in dust and soot. I hope she gave Machiis the beating he deserved; this is the least I can do for her. I'll fight until my body gives out. I'll do whatever it takes to get her across the finish line.

I blink numerous times when I step through the portal. The sounds of water splashing, rocks hitting the ground, and the hum of electricity echo in my ears. I stride across the grassy field but come to an abrupt stop when I find Cadie and Ryne. They're both banged up, their cheeks smeared with dirt and blood.

Cadie's normally perfect hair is tangled, and her brow is wrinkled as she gasps for air. Ryne is holding his own. He lasted a lot longer than I expected him to. Not that I ever thought he wasn't strong, it's just that I didn't trust Cadie to play fair. He looks tired though. Blood drips from his lips, and his body looks crooked.

I observe them as they circle one another, unsure of what I should do. I could leap in there and take her out myself, but then I'd have to duel Ryne, and the thought shatters my heart into a million unrepairable pieces. I could help Cadie defeat Ryne, but why on earth would I do that?

Ryne notices my appearance in his peripheral vision. The corners of his eyes wrinkle he smiles softly.

"*Electriciar!*" Ryne summons a strand of lightning it surges toward her chest.

When it makes contact, she screams in agony, and Ryne drops to his knees.

"Ryne!" I shout without thinking.

I run onto the battlefield, ignoring Cadie, and fall in front of Ryne.

"Are you insane?" I choke out at the sight of him.

His chest rises and falls in an irregular pattern, and his breathing sounds more like a whistle while his face turns black and blue.

"Is that you, Ayra?" Cadie spits out.

"You must be tired, Cadie. No one's there," Ryne grunts while he fights to stay awake.

"You made it just in time. I'm about to kick this wizard into a realm where he can never return," she cackles.

"You won't get the chance! I won't let you near him!" I scream as my tears drop on his face. I trace his jawline, and I struggle to breathe. "It's going to be okay; just hang on."

Ryne's emerald eyes glaze over, and in that brief moment, everything flashes.

I cover my eyes with my arm as a blinding white light shoots from Cadie's body, the same kind of magic she used on me all those years ago.

I slam my hand into the grass, hoping to ruin her balance.

When the light dims, I look forward, and my body reacts before my brain commands it to. "No!" My voice is strained.

Cadie's hand is wrapped around Ryne's neck, blocking air from entering his lungs. I lunge forward only to be knocked back by a gust of wind that Cadie throws at me with her free hand. I'm thrown across the field, tumbling and groaning until I come to a stop.

When I look up, I scream again. Ryne's lips have turned blue, his eyes bloodshot, his hands desperately clawing at Cadie's fist.

"You're killing him! Let him go. He's out! Fight *me*!" But she doesn't acknowledge me. "Headmistress!" I shout, hoping she'll stop Cadie before she kills the one wizard I care about.

When I look past the protection barrier, I find her slamming against the shield. Her mouth is forming words, but I can't make them out.

What in the underworld is happening? Why can't she get in?

"Cadie! What did you do!?" I holler, but she doesn't budge.

No one beyond the barrier can stop Cadie from murdering a wizard in front of millions.

But I can.

With a strained scream, I dig my feet into the ground and charge toward them again, desperation filling my veins. I just need to get close enough to cast this spell. *Hang on, Ryne.*

His eyes start to close, forcing mine to widen in despair. I'm not remotely where I need to be to know this spell will work, but it's now or never.

"*Eathirum Goliums!*" I slam my foot on the ground, nodding my head from the left to the right, begging to the goddess Hecate that this spell works.

As my gaze slides over Cadie, a rocky creation I crafted in my mind strikes her, knocking her off her feet and slamming her across the field.

Ryne's body slumps to the ground, and he lands face-first in the grass, motionless.

"Ryne!" I cry as I close the distance between us.

I drop to my knees and lift his head onto my lap. "Ryne, can you hear me?" Hot tears spill from my eyes as I look down at him.

My breathing turns violent and shaky at the sight of him. Cadie left her handprint on his throat, indicating she had a deathly grip on him. His eyes are closed, his cheeks have lost their natural blush, and his mouth is set in a frown.

"Ryne, please wake up."

His chest is barely moving, but it is moving. Air whirls around my fingers, and I make sure the magic is full of pure oxygen.

"Hecate, please let this work," I plead with the goddess before setting the air in a gentle stream through his nose. My tears spill from my eyes and land on his mouth, smearing the dirt in the process. "Please." I choke on a sob as the magic leaves my fingers.

I rest my hand on his cheek and press my forehead against his. "Please wake up, Ryne. I can't do this without you. I can't *live* without you. I need you. You're the light in my never-ending rainstorm. You are the sunshine to my cloudy day. I can't imagine you not holding my hand when I need you the most. Never seeing your smile or hearing your voice again. Ryne, you're *it* for me. Please."

A wisp of air leaves his chest, and his chest goes still.

"I love you, dammit," I sob as I rest my hand over his heart, willing it to flutter awake.

The slightest inhale fills his lungs. When his chest moves, I open my eyes to find him watching me.

"I love you too, Brightheart," he forces out.

I press my lips against his, not caring about the snot and tears that cover my mouth.

"Damn you, Gwydion," I choke out.

He tries to chuckle but ends up wincing instead. "You weren't kidding about her."

Shuffling comes from behind me.

"She was toying with me until you got here. And . . . I think she cast a barrier around the arena."

That would explain why the headmistress can't come in.

Cadie moans as rocks crumble around her.

I press my lips against Ryne's again and offer him a reassuring smile. "Stay here and don't move. I'm going to finish this."

Ryne squeezes my hand and offers me a weak smile. "That's my girl."

I shift Ryne's head off my lap as carefully as I can. Out of the corner of my eye, I spot Cadie limping toward me. As fast as I can, I raise my hands, creating a rock-solid earth tent around Ryne. I don't trust Cadie not to try and kill him again. I need to make sure he's safe.

"Always love to ruin a good time, don't you, Brightheart?" she sneers.

"You almost killed him!" I spit as I turn to face her. "In front of millions!" I gesture to the crowd around us, hoping to bring her to her senses.

"One less wizard in the world wouldn't be such a bad thing. I thought you would agree."

"Since when did you hate wizards? I thought you and Machiis were friends."

Her snort of disgust is all I need for an answer. "He was nothing more than a tool to get me here today. Although I didn't really need him, he was fun to play with."

She goes to move toward Ryne, but I block her path, earning myself another sickly grin.

"I thought *you* hated wizards; this is certainly a turn of events. Ayra Brightheart, the rule-abiding witch, fell in love with a happy-go-lucky wizard. How sweet." She presses her lips together and clasps her hands. "Let me finish him," she growls.

"Never." I stand my ground, ready to place my life in the line of fire to protect Ryne. "Darkness has consumed you," I spit out. "Have you not noticed? Venus isn't around you anymore. Your once vibrant eyes are dull. You're stepping into dark magic, and it *will* consume you!"

With a menacing smirk, Cadie takes a step forward. "I'll do whatever it takes to win. Even if it means succumbing to the dark arts." She attempts to approach Ryne again, but I block her.

"Not a chance in hell."

"Fine, want to play hardball? Let's play. *Blizarra!*"

An icy wind slams into my body, launching me across the field. My back hits the ground right as jolts of lightning fill the sky. I roll to my left, dodging the spark just in time, but before I can react, another strike spills from the sky, aimed right at my heart.

"*Protectium!*" I shout, raising my hands in time to block the curse from hitting my core.

The shield above me splinters, cracking like broken glass. It shatters around me, cutting my cheek and leaving other superficial cuts in my skin.

"Nice catch, Ayra," Cadie chimes.

I sit up with a groan.

"But I'm not done."

My eyes widen as she hurls a stream of light magic at my chest.

"*Protect—*" My cast is cut short as the spell hits me dead on. My body rolls farther down the field, and my tunic catches aflame, leaving my hips raw and bloody.

"Isn't this what we always wanted? Isn't this what we worked so hard for? It was always meant to be you and me in the finale, and you're throwing it away!" Cadie shouts, her tone emotionless. "I think love *softened* you."

Images flash before me: the Ayra from the start of the year, her head held high, determination written in her blank expression. Nothing could stand in her way of success. No one could stop her.

Visions of me crying in the library's depths appear next, attempting to hide from the never-ending taunts and whispers. I held my emotions in and let them become my armor until it was too late. I hid from the world when everything became too much. No one could see me cry because if they did, I wouldn't be a threat, and that was all I had. Ayra the wise, Ayra the stickler, Ayra the powerful, Ayra the *broken* . . .

A memory of Ryne appears next. How he looked at me in the courtyard, how his eyes sparkled when I gave into his charm and fixed his unruly disk. When he first spoke, I felt the spark. His accent didn't hurt. His smirk and confidence burrowed under my armor, slowly chipping it away. No matter how hard I tried to push him away, he came back harder and pushed me further into the unknown.

Did his love soften me?

I tilt my head toward the earth barrier I cast to protect him. A rush of magic seeps into my body, and the strength I lost moments ago slowly returns.

Ryne helped me through my first portal. He brought me to an art museum because he knew I would love it. He charmed his way to my heart because he knew I was more than my desire for perfection. He knew I was worth saving, that I was worth loving.

"No." I clench my jaw as I stand.

Cadie scoffs at me as I stumble. "No, what?" She plays with an orb of blinding light in her hand.

"Love didn't soften me, Blackwell," I state, solidifying my

tone and my body. "It saved me." I stand firm, ready to end this once and for all.

"How touching." She clicks her tongue.

Flames crawl up my arm, but she'll know my next move. I need to be unpredictable. I need to—

"*Remember . . .*"

"*Ah, yes, remember.*"

I shake my head as the voices converge into one.

"*Have fun.*"

I smirk as my eyes land on a body of water to my left. Cadie knows my go-to spell is fire. She can guess my next move with ease. I let the flames continue up my arm, and her smile grows when I pull my arm back. We open our mouths at the same time.

"*Aquaias Elementium!*"

"*Tornadium Ev—*" Her sentence is cut off as water from the lake splashes into her.

I pull the remnants toward me; it pools under my feet and lifts me off the ground. I rush for her, knowing I must take this opportunity while she's down. One cast of her light magic, and I'm done for. No one would be able to rescue me.

Cadie plants her palms in the muddy earth and hoists herself up, but I'm faster. My fingers weave and dance in the air, forming a molten orb of fire and ice from the water beneath my feet. I hit the ground and charge for her, putting pressure on my right leg. I leap into the air, and as I hit the ground, I slam my left foot down, ruining her stability just as quickly as it returned to her. With a curse, she slips on the wet earth. My feet splash in the puddles around her, and Cadie rolls onto her back and grunts.

"Is that all you've got?" she chuckles.

I shake my head. "Not even close." I ram the fire-coated icicles into her palms.

The light that covered her hands disappears as her pained screams fill the arena.

"I hate you!" she cries, tears spilling from her eyes.

I kneel beside her, and the mud soaks through my leggings.

"I don't know what happened between us. Something tells me it was more than me breaking the Blackwell crest in class all those years ago."

She flails, her legs kicking in an attempt to free herself.

"Maybe we let the academy get the best of us. Maybe if we weren't so hyperfocused on success, we'd still be friends." My tone softens. "And as much as I want to say we still could be, I know it's a lie."

Her eyes meet mine. Her hatred is real and practically tangible.

"Maybe in another life, Blackwell, perhaps we could try again."

Her scream nearly shatters my eardrums as I stand.

I don't notice the growing applause as I walk toward Ryne. I don't care about the announcement I've been waiting to hear for years. None of it matters.

"Ladies and gentlemen, we have our victor! Ayra Brightheart!" Illana declares, pride evident in her voice.

I bring down the rocky shield around Ryne, and he manages to rise to his feet as I near him. His smile welcomes me. I rush into his arms, not bothering to hold my tears back.

"You did it," he whispers as he cups my cheeks, pulling me from his chest to meet his gaze. "Your dream came true."

I shake my head, and he raises his brow curiously. "This *was* my dream. It's not anymore," I admit, even though I know the entire arena can hear me.

"Then what is your dream?" Ryne asks.

"You."

Carefully, I press my lips against his. The cheering grows,

and Illana's voice comes next, but I don't register what she says. None of it matters anymore. All my life, I've fought for a feeling I didn't know existed. I sought approval from the academy, the headmistress, and the professors. I wanted them to know I wasn't a waste of space and resources.

Now I know I never was. I wish I had known it sooner, but maybe if I had, I wouldn't be where I am today. I wouldn't have met Ryne or participated in the games. I wouldn't have fallen in love or know what it feels like to be loved in return.

I wouldn't be as interesting as the voices claim I am.

Ryne pulls back and rests his forehead against mine. His mouth curves in a grin. "So, Brightheart. What's next?"

I smirk. "Now that, Mr. Gwydion, is a surprise."

"Ayra! Ayra!" Reporters from other worlds call for her as she walks beside the gunnery I'm lying in.

"Ayra! How does it feel to be crowned the victor after such a grueling duel?"

"Tell us how it felt seeing the man you love nearly die right in front of you!"

Damn, that's harsh.

"How did it feel when you saved him!?"

"How does it feel to be the most beloved witch in all the realms!?"

The last comment makes Ayra roll her eyes, and I chuckle. Upon hearing me, Ayra looks down and smiles in relief as I stare up at her.

The second the barrier was down, a team of healers swept in and lifted me with air magic to rush me to the infirmary. They tried to hold Ayra back, but she didn't listen. They insisted she needed her own medical evaluation, but she fought with an iron fist. They don't know her as well as I do. If they did, they would know that Ayra wasn't going to leave my side. Not until she knew I'd be okay.

Taking her hand, I squeeze it in reassurance. I'm going to be okay *because* of her. She saved me. It's because of her that I can breathe and stare into her gorgeous eyes. I never doubted her, not for one second.

"I'll be fine," I try to say but end up wincing in pain from my broken ribs.

With a brief nod, tears start to flow from her eyes. "I know. But if you die, I will find a way to resurrect you just so I can kill you myself."

I laugh but wince again as the pain in my upper abdomen shoots across my body. "No need for that, my love. You'll have me for many years to come."

Her expression softens, and she smiles at me with a loving smile. "I'm going to hold you to that."

We pass under an archway, and before I know it, Ayra is gone and screaming, "Let me through! I have to be with him!"

I'm laid on top of a bed in the medical ward, where healers and physicians surround me to perform diagnostics.

"Please!" she sobs.

I want to sit up and show her I'm going to be okay. But before I can offer Ayra any comfort, a wave of nausea surges through me and the pain in my chest becomes unbearable.

"*Fuck!*" I scream as the physician places her hands over my ribcage to perform a healing enchantment.

While the charm is supposed to offer pain relief, every inch of my skin begins to itch and crawl.

"Shh, I know. Just hang on for a few more moments," the healer whispers, but all I can register is Ayra's reaction to my cry.

"Ryne!? Ryne, can you hear me!? It's going to be okay. I'll be right there." Anguish fills her tone, and it makes my heart ache.

My jaw clenches, and my teeth meet the side of my cheek. The taste of blood fills my mouth as my vision starts to fade.

"It's going to be okay," the healer and Ayra's voices merge into one.

The world around me sways, and just as the pain starts to fade, my eyes close, and I'm met with nothingness.

"Is he going to be okay?"

My eyes start to peel open. I wasn't expecting to hear his voice. Curiosity is giving me the strength to see if what I'm hearing is real or not.

"He's going to be fine."

There she is. I would recognize that natural bite in her tone from miles away. Stiff silence fills the air. I want to turn and face my girl, but I've wondered how this scene will play out.

"He doesn't look well," Machiis says with concern.

"He was beaten to near death by your girlfriend. Of course he doesn't *look well*."

"She's not my girlfriend," he retorts, but Ayra scoffs.

"Could've fooled me. From the moment you stepped onto the academy's grounds, you've trailed behind her like a lost soul. I don't know why Ryne gives you any time of day. You are foul, pretentious, and a bully, just like Cadie Blackwell, minus the psychotic mental break."

"I'm nothing like her—"

"That's the lie of the century. Prove it to me. Why aren't you like her?"

"I don't have to prove anything to you."

"No, you don't. I couldn't care less what you think of me or what I think of you. But I'll tell you this. This man, your supposed friend, is someone I care deeply about. He's the only one I give two shits about, and if he cares about you, that *must* mean something. When he wakes up, I want you to think really hard about whether or not you're worthy of his friendship. If you deem yourself worthy, you should reevaluate. If you determine you are indeed not worthy to be in his light, then become the type of person who is."

Ayra's statement almost makes me break my cover. I wasn't ready for her to say that. I was preparing to hurl myself at her to save Machiis from her wrath. He's a dickhead, but there's a reason I can't let him go. Something is telling me he's worth saving.

The universe is pleading with me to help change him, and I think Ayra sees it too. The last time they talked was the day of the one-on-ones. All those days ago, Machiis was wrapped around Cadie's finger. Now, he's freeing himself. I'm curious to see what he realizes and what he does with this newfound information.

Silence welcomes me again, but I know the two people who care about me are here, debating whether or not the other is here for the right reasons.

"You know, Ayra Brightheart, you are everything they say about you. You're hardheaded, a rule follower, strict, and cold."

I can feel Ayra roll her eyes, but before she can say anything, Machiis continues.

"But you are also fierce, loyal, and protective, and I can tell you care about Ryne. You *love* him. We didn't get off on the right foot, but I hope you grant me the chance to make it up to you. Because you're right, I'm not worthy of his friendship, but I want to be, and I feel like that's a good start."

Giving in, I open my eyes and look at Machiis. The first thing I notice are the bags under his eyes. I don't know how their duel went, other than Ayra winning. He doesn't look too banged up, nothing a simple spell couldn't fix.

Tears slide from his brown eyes, trickling down his cheeks. He's quick to wipe them away, but not fast enough before Ayra and I notice.

"I agree with you," Ayra responds with a hint of smugness. "You aren't worth his friendship."

His expression falls, and more tears follow suit.

"But I also agree that you can fix it. And I know you'll get there. Because honestly? I don't deem myself worthy to be with someone like him either. But somehow, he sees potential in us, and I get the feeling we'll live up to his expectations. And maybe, just maybe, we can become friends too. Isn't that right, Ryne?"

I turn my head, and she smiles at me like she knew I was awake the entire time.

"Now, that would be a wonder. It might even make it into history texts." My voice is hoarse when I speak.

"I would punch your arm if you weren't currently lying in the medical ward," she chuckles before her eyes sparkle back to life.

"I know, trust me." My lips curl into a loving smile, and my heart flutters as she offers me one in response.

"Ryne?"

"Machiis?" I chime back, meeting his pained gaze.

"I fucked up . . . again," he manages to say before choking on tears that he doesn't bother wiping away.

Before I can try to reassure him that everything will be okay, a certain furry familiar trots into the room and jumps onto Machiis's lap.

"You've got to be kidding me," Ayra says in disbelief.

I suppress a chuckle when Kiki nudges her nose against his, urging him to pet her.

"It seems like Kiki has a thing for wizards. Who would have known," I tell Ayra, who is currently resting her hand against her forehead.

When Kiki looks at her, Ayra looks back and mouths, *"Traitor."*

"I like her, she's nice." Machiis sniffles through his tears as he runs his fingers through Kiki's fur. "She reminds me of my mom's familiar."

A flap of wings echoes down the corridor, and Hayes flies through the entryway, chirping as he settles on a vaulted perch. Machiis smiles at the sight of him, and I'm thankful he's not completely lost to the dark.

"You can keep her," Ayra sighs while trying not to smile at the sight. "Oh! Before I forget—" Ayra stands up, reaches into her jacket pocket, and pulls out a sleeping Maren.

"Thank the stars," I mutter while reaching for the small lapwrin.

When he lands in my palms, he perks up and chirps. Scurrying up my sleeve, he nuzzles and rams his nose against my cheek while trying to crawl up my face.

"Okay, okay," I snicker before holding him again. I lift him up to my nose and rest mine against his. "I'm okay, buddy. I wouldn't leave you."

Maren's whiskers wiggle as he lets out a tiny breath and closes his black eyes. The pit in my heart slowly begins to close, and the pain that lingers in my muscles fades. Maren and I have been through everything together. He's the second half of my soul. And now that I have Ayra, I feel complete. I don't think I could be any happier.

Looking back at Machiis, I smile at him, and he releases a shaky breath.

"One step at a time, right?"

He nods and wipes his nose on his sleeve. "And don't let them see your nerves because if they do—"

"You've already lost," Ayra chimes in, surprising us both. "What?" she asks with a wide smile. "I pay attention." She taps the side of her head.

I look over at Machiis, not letting my grin drop. "I told you she was something else."

"Yes, yes, you did," he says with a light laugh.

"Well, you better get used to it, gentlemen, because I'm not going anywhere." Ayra crosses her arms over her chest and pretends to be serious.

Not a second passes before her lips curl upward, and she's laughing.

"I wouldn't want it any other way, Brightheart."

Because whether she knows it or not, I plan on sticking by her side for centuries to come. I will find her when my magic fades, and my soul departs this realm. I will reunite with her when the stars vanish, and the planets collide. She is my true love, my gravity, my stability. I may have only known her for a matter of days, but I know she's the one because my gut tells me she is. The one thing I learned while at Traquore is to trust my gut. No matter what.

"And that, Mr. Gwydion, is how you'll change the world." The voices echo before fading away with their final message.

"So, Ms. Brightheart," Mera Zelds begins the final interview.

I can't wait for all this to be over.

"I have an endless list of questions for you, but I know what it's like to be in your shoes. You want nothing more than to leave this room, graduate from the academy, and breathe fresh air. Everything leading up to the games is thrilling and new, but now that it's over, you want it to be over."

"I couldn't have said it better myself," I answer with a breathless chuckle.

Pulling at the sleeves of my gown anxiously, I let out a puff of air through my lips.

Marley chose my gown for the final time. It's gorgeous with long, sheer, black lacy sleeves and a corset bodice that pushes up my breasts and forms around my curves. There's a slit near my right upper thigh, but the tule doesn't let a lot of my lower body show. There are specks of silver gems embedded into the dress, and they sparkle with the slightest movement. My hair is half up, held in place with a matching silver crescent moon hairclip.

My leg jostles, and I miss the presence of a certain someone who has been with me during these interviews up until this point. If he were here, his knee would be resting against mine. He would whisper reassuring words in my ear and make me smile without effort. Just the thought of him brings a soft grin to my face, as embarrassing as it is to confess.

"Based on your smile, I have a feeling you have someone to see rather than somewhere to be," Zela chimes, and my blush grows hotter.

"Right again," I respond nervously.

"Well, let's get started. When the realms first met you, you made a rather sly comment about watching our own kind. It's safe to assume, based on the trials and previous interviews, that you were talking about Cadie Blackwell. How do you feel about the turn of events? Did you worry her mind was slipping? Or that she may truly hurt someone else?"

I open my mouth but then close it.

Be the better witch.

Thinking back, I could never have imagined Cadie hurting anyone. But that changed when we stopped being friends. We became academic rivals, and her personality switched. In the blink of an eye, she became my villain, but I wonder if I was the villain in her story as well.

"Cadie Blackwell is a phenomenal witch. I truly believe she lost herself, but with time and the right care, she can turn around. There's always a speck of light in the dark. And that's all I'll say on the matter."

"Very admirable of you to believe in someone like that. I commend your good nature, given everything that happened during the final game. Speaking of which, let's talk about Ryne Gwydion. He quickly became a crowd favorite. He won over the hearts of everyone during the first interview and sealed the deal when he placed the moonflower in your hair during the potion trial. Tell me, how is he doing now? After the duel with Cadie Blackwell?"

I don't want to think back, but the images of Ryne beaten flash in my mind. I have to remind myself that he's safe and on the mend. He's waiting for me in the infirmary ward, and I'll see him as soon as I'm done here.

"He's healing remarkably well. He'll be able to return to Traquore within the next few days. He's stronger than anyone gives him credit for."

"His performance in the games shocked many. I personally wondered how someone like him got into The Academy Games in the first place, but his skills rivaled a lot of the competitors. He has a unique mindset—"

"He does, but that doesn't mean he's not up to par with the rest of us. In fact, he's more intelligent and powerful than anyone I know. Knowledge doesn't just come from texts or genetics. It comes from experiences and, most importantly, how you decide to view the world. Ryne sees the best in people, refusing to believe anyone can be inherently bad. He listens to his gut, and it has yet to fail him. Ryne is more than his grades and statistics. It's people like him who are going to change the realms." Passion runs through me as I talk about the man who changed my life.

More people need to be like Ryne Gwydion. That includes me as well.

"You really love him, don't you?" Mera asks with a soft smile.

I meet her gaze, and my heart is pounding in my ears. Everyone saw the first kiss Ryne and I shared. Everyone heard me profess my love for him when he was near death. This kind of thing has never happened before, so of course it would be a hot topic.

"He's everything," I respond honestly. "I wasn't prepared to meet someone like him, especially not during the games. I had a one-track mind, but he swooped in and set me off course. Little did I know that road would teach me the most important lessons in life. It's important to remember to let go. I'll never stop being a perfectionist. It's a part of my soul and engraved in my mindset, but I can remind myself that I'll never be perfect. It's not possible. I can be myself, smile, laugh, and have fun. I don't have to strive to know everything. I can simply exist, and that's enough."

"You've learned and changed a lot; be sure to credit yourself as well. Your change isn't all because you met a wizard. It's because you were willing to adapt for the better. To save yourself. More people need someone like Ryne Gwydion in their lives. Luck was on your side when you two met, Ms. Brightheart."

"I don't think luck had anything to do with it," I answer under my breath, but she still hears me.

"No? If it wasn't luck, what was it?" She arches her brow as she examines me.

"Sometimes, the universe creates two souls that are meant to be together. They may not make sense to other people. They can be complete opposites. A grumpy gills and a ray of sunshine, if you will. But the two of them know the truth, and they see past the other's flaws. The universe knows exactly what you can handle before you do. And she knew Ryne and I were ready for one another. Call it luck or destiny, but either way, Ryne changed my life. I would be just as lost as Cadie if he didn't come into my life when he did."

"So, not only did you win the Academy Games, but you also

met your person. I guess my last question is, what can we expect from Ayra Brightheart?"

I purse my lips as I try to conjure an answer to her question. The old Ayra would want to start her next level of education immediately. I would have thrown myself into books and, soon after, into a mental break. But I'm different now, and that's not what I want anymore.

"How do you feel about surprises?" I ask her with a slight smile.

"I love them," she beams.

"I used to hate them, but I'm learning to appreciate the unknown." I fix my posture and smirk at Mera, just as Ryne would smirk at me. "I guess you'll have to wait and see . . ."

The celebrations lasted for weeks after the finale of The Academy Games. Fraydora Academy for Witches was granted the prestige it deserves. Applicants began rolling in the moment I was crowned the victor, and the halls became crowded with potential students who wanted to see the witch who saved the wizard she loved from death.

Rumblings around the realms picked up after I defeated Cadie, or rather, after she tried to kill Ryne. The professors flooded in after the battle, providing medical treatment to Ryne and binding Cadie's hands behind her back as she screamed and fought back.

I wish I could say for certain what happened to her. It seemed her mental state had withered away. Perhaps it all became too much, the constant pressure to do better than me, to succeed at everything. I would know because I was the same way. Cadie and I have a lot in common, I just wish she'd noticed her downfall sooner. Maybe she would have been crowned the victor instead of me.

Also, if I knew the amount of attention winning entailed, I would have reconsidered. I didn't care about winning in the end. I just wanted to save Ryne. Winning was a bonus, I guess . . .

I'm happy to have won for the academy. For years I wanted to prove myself to this school, show the halls I was worth their time and protection. Now that I have done it, I feel like my job is done, and I can move on to the next step in my life with no regrets or setbacks.

"Are you ready?" Marley asks as she peeks around the dressing divider in our room.

I take one final look in the mirror. My dark brunette hair flows down my back, curling at the ends. Star-jeweled barrettes are secured at the back of my head, offering a hint of shine. I pat down the wrinkles along my midnight-blue gown. The sleeves are sheer, swimming around my wrists. I stare at my eyes in the reflection. The only thing I recognize is the color —blue with flecks of silver. Everything else is foreign to me. The gleam of wonder and curiosity is something I'm not used to.

I have Ryne to thank for that.

"Ayra?" Marley calls again.

With a sigh, I relax my shoulders and turn to Kiki, who is sprawled along the foot of my bed.

"Ready, girl?"

With a gentle shake of her head, she stands, stretching with a yawn. She leaps onto the floor and nudges my ankle, and I lean over to pick her up.

"Ready, Marley."

With Kiki in my arms, I turn around and find Marley in a similar gown to my own. Her silver hair is pinned delicately around golden suns encrusted in diamonds. Zachii rests on her shoulder, and he winks his beady eye when he sees me.

"Damn, we look good," she says.

I offer her a small smile as my stomach starts to flip-flop.

"Are you ready?" she inquires.

I purse my lips and shake my head. "No, but I'm ready to get this over with."

She beams at my response. "That's my girl."

Ryne

51

Cadie really did a number on me. I stayed in the infirmary for a couple of days for observation. Parties and celebrations took place every single night, but Ayra skipped every one of them. Honestly, she may have been using my state as an excuse, but I was happy to have her with me. I'm convinced that her company healed me faster than our modern-day medicine and healing enchantments.

Our bliss was cut short though. I didn't return with the others the day after the finale, but once I got a clean bill of health, it was time to leave. The look on her face destroyed me, just as mine did to her. I wanted to stay at Fraydora forever, hide away from the world with Ayra. We could have lived in the library for years without anyone finding us. But I was being selfish. The world needs to know of Ayra's brilliance and compassion. I couldn't take that away from the future of this realm.

Goodbyes are never easy, but this wasn't a goodbye. It was

a see you later. The conversation replays in my head twenty-four seven.

Ayra and I are wrapped in one another's arms in my bed at Fraydora. I'm packed and ready to go for the morning, but I'm not ready to leave Ayra.

"I don't want you to go," she mumbles into my chest.

"I don't want to go," I whisper against the top of her head before placing a small kiss there. "But we have to finish our education. It's only another month before we get our certifications."

I feel her release a deep breath before snuggling closer. "A month is too long."

With a knowing smile, I rest my forehead against hers and meet her gaze. "And to think, you once couldn't wait to be rid of me."

"Shush, you," she laughs lightly before wrapping her arms around me and nuzzling into the crook of my neck.

"Nothing will change between us. You know that, right?"

She nods as her tears dampen my skin.

"We'll send one another letters, and before we know it, we'll be together again. You'll miss the days when we were apart."

"That's impossible," she says while pulling back to meet my gaze again.

We just look at one another for a moment.

I reach forward and trace her jawline with my knuckles. "I'm so proud of you. You've come so far."

"Because of you."

I shake my head. "No, that was all you, my love. I was just a simple guide; you did all the work."

"I'm afraid," she mutters. "What if while you're gone, I fall back and become who I used to be?"

"You won't," I say with a confident smile.

"How do you know that?"

"Because my girl is far too hardheaded to allow herself to revert."

She chuckles, and I continue to smile at her.

"This will work. I have confidence in us."

Ayra nods and places a soft kiss on my lips. "I do too. I love you, Ryne."

"I love you, Ayra. I always will."

I left the following morning, and I haven't been back since. Ayra and I've exchanged a few letters, and they're the only things that have kept me going until today.

"Are you ready, Gwydion?" Arlin calls from the other side of my door.

He and Marley have gotten close over this past month. I had a feeling they would make a good match. He blushes whenever he receives a letter from her, and I can only imagine the amount of squealing Ayra has to listen to on a daily basis.

"Almost!" I answer as I secure my cloak's clasp under my left arm.

Looking in the mirror, I make sure I'm decent for the day. The corset that hugs my figure is forest green with hints of gold. My cape is black with gold chains and embellishments.

Running my fingers through my hair, I turn to face Maren. "Ready, boy?"

He squeaks in response, running up my sleeve to settle himself in the inside pocket of my cape.

"Dude, we're going to be late." Arlin charges in, his brow furrowing at the sight of me.

I'm still not used to not seeing Machiis as often as I used to. After our moment in the medical ward, he started a journey of self-discovery. He knows what Cadie said about him during the game, and he's recovering from her deceit, along with the repercussions of his actions. I'm giving him the space he needs. When he's ready, I know he'll return, and we can try our hand at friendship again.

"That's a bit formal, even for the end-of-year ceremony, don't you think?" Arlin asks as his brows arch.

"I'm not going to the ceremony." I smile at him while I open a portal in the middle of my empty room.

"What about your degree?"

"Borrick gave it to me early. I have an urgent matter to attend to." I match Arlin's knowing look before placing one foot through the portal. "I'm sure I'll see you around. I don't think Marley plans on giving you up anytime soon."

I leave him with those words. Ready to see the one person I've been dying to reunite with for weeks.

y foot jostles up and down, and I have to remind myself to breathe. I take in as much air as possible while scanning the crowd from my seat on the stage in the center of the courtyard. Including myself, there are a total of sixty witches graduating this year. Cadie isn't amongst the crowd. She was expelled after her violence in the arena, but I have a feeling her father will make sure she gets her degree one way or another.

I run my hands through Kiki's velvety fur, trying to focus on Illana's voice.

"Seven years ago, you first walked through the doors of Fraydora. Now you're about to walk out of them as a new witch, someone you don't fully know yet. I can honestly say that each and every one of you has been a joy to teach. Seeing you grow up in front of my eyes is the biggest joy of my life."

My eyes flick around the crowd, looking for a certain blond wizard. I know he won't be here though—

"I know you're itching to get out of here, so without further ado, our victor and head witch, Ayra Brightheart."

Applause fills the courtyard, and Kiki jumps to the ground as I stand. Illana and I lock eyes, and she pulls me into a hug and sniffles.

"I'm going to miss you most of all," she whispers before pulling back.

I match her solemn expression with one of my own. "You think you can get rid of me that easily?"

She smiles wide in response.

I step toward the podium, trying my best not to get overwhelmed. Kiki leaps onto the tribune and lays down, earning a few chuckles from the crowd.

"Sorry about her," I start, my voice slowly rising in volume. "Most of you may know that I don't have parents. The people responsible for my existence left me on the doorstep of this academy. The professors and corridors raised me until it was time to start my education. I didn't walk through those doors again until I was fourteen." My eyes glance over the witches seated before me.

"Some people think I was only accepted into this academy because I was abandoned here, and I can honestly tell you that this fact used to bother me, but it doesn't anymore. I could go on and on telling you how I earned my place here, but I won't bore you with my life story."

A few snickers fill the air.

"What I can tell you is that people change."

Two raspies catch my attention, wrestling along the border of the courtyard.

"Some change we find on our own, but change can also be influenced by someone else."

A different kind of scurrying makes my head tilt to the right. A lapwrin bolts past the tumbling puffs of fur, and I smile wide when the familiar's wizard chases him down the corridor.

Ryne scoops him in his hands and places him in his pocket. He runs his hand through his hair and smiles when he notices my eyes are on him.

"*Hi*," he mouths and offers me a tiny wave.

"I used to be a stickler, or so I'm told."

The witches around me chuckle, and Ryne's expression lights up.

"I used to think I had to be perfect at everything I did. If I fell short, I was a failure, a waste of space, someone who wasn't worthy of her position or power. I used to think magic required nothing but absolute perfection." I meet the eyes in the crowd before continuing. "That is until I met a certain wizard. He showed me that it's okay to simply *live*. I didn't have to know everything or be perfect. He went out of his way to show me how to have fun. Hells, I didn't know what that was until I met him. Sorry, Marley."

"It's okay!" she shouts out from the crowd.

"He helped me realize that magic can't be perfect because magic is pure chaos. Ryne was the influence for my change. All I had to do was light the spark and watch it catch. When you leave today, I want you to remember that it's okay if you don't succeed the first time around. It's okay to fall flat on your face and let fear take over. As long as you get back up, face those fears, and try again, you're not a failure. You're a witch."

Fireworks fill the sky above me, followed by thunderous applause. Kiki leaps into my arms at the sudden blasts, and Illana steps forward.

"Remember, my fellow witches, change the world and always keep them guessing!"

I take the two stairs off the stage, and Kiki jumps out of my arms, throwing her body against Ryne's leg. His cheeks flush as I approach him.

"What are you doing here? I thought you had your own graduation to attend."

He looks around the courtyard and shrugs. "I had a feeling this one would be more entertaining."

A dragon made of crimson lanternflies weaves around the pillars in the room, and jubilant music fills the air.

"And?" I ask with a grin.

"I was right, per usual."

I gently punch his arm. He winces with a chuckle before tilting his head to the side. His hair is slicked back, but that tiny stray piece of hair rests on his brow.

"Congratulations, Ms. Brightheart."

"Congratulations, Mr. Gwydion."

He pulls me into his chest, wrapping his arms around my body. I breathe in his natural scent—burnt orange, cedar, and magic.

Everything in my world settles.

He tilts my chin upward, kissing me. A swirl of warmth and devotion floods through me.

When he pulls away, he smiles against my lips, and his eyes shimmer. "So, I was thinking . . ." He steps back and walks down the corridor.

I trail after him, grinning ear to ear.

He spins around and walks backward, winking at me as he opens a portal at the end of the hall. "We should go on an adventure."

Maren pops out of his suit pocket and wiggles his nose.

"What kind of an adventure?" I ask as Kiki trots alongside Ryne.

"Now that, my love, is a surprise." He comes to a stop and reaches for my hand. "How does that sound?"

I glance over his shoulder before locking my eyes on his. Overwhelming excitement and love fill my core. Ryne might not know this, but I'd go anywhere with him. I'd do anything for him. He's the light to my shadow, the fire to my ice. He's the love I never expected to find.

My lips curve into a smile, and he winks at me. I don't even have to think twice about my answer.

"Sounds like fun."

Two Months Later

I t turns out that when you fall in love in front of an audience, people tend to spot you from miles away. Ryne and I should have known we'd be the center of attention once we stepped through that portal.

Over these last few months, we've received requests for interviews, statements, and live commentary of the broadcasted games, and I'm sure we'll give in at some point, but now isn't the time. We're too busy exploring the depths of unknown castles built in stone, hiking through haunted forests in the Land of the Night, and combing through the Grand Library of Aethrial.

Ryne's parents gifted him a cottage after he graduated. When we're not on grand adventures, we spend most of our time there. His new home is cozy. It's settled along a forest's edge near the realm's border. We planted a garden in the front yard, mostly necessary supplies for potions and tonics. Ryne did insist on a bed of moonflowers, and who am I to deny him of that? The spacious cottage has a living room, a simple kitchen, a small library, and two bedrooms on the second floor. We could have had our own rooms, but where's the fun in that?

Rain droplets splatter against the window pane, creating a soothing ambiance. Kiki scurries down the hall, Maren trailing right behind her. They love playing cat and mouse, or rather, mouse and cat.

I smile to myself as I flip to the next page of my book, *The History of Altana*. It's about one of my favorite queens. I can read her story repeatedly and never grow tired of it. Her and King Alden's love story and how they saved a crumbling kingdom went down in history. Thunder shudders in the sky, and I jolt from the sudden boom.

"Didn't think you were scared of thunder," Ryne teases as he strolls into the room.

"I'm not," I say as I turn the page of my book. "I just don't like surprises," I sass while giving him the side-eye, instantly regretting it.

Ryne's hair is drenched from his shower, and his T-shirt sticks to his subtle abs and the curve of his waist. His joggers hang long on his hips, revealing the V of his lower stomach.

"Did you plan on reading all day?" he asks.

Months have passed since we first met, and I still can't get over the lovely cadence of his voice. It puts me in a trance every time.

"Ayra?"

"Hmm, did you say something?"

With a smirk, he walks over to me and taps on my book.

"Did you plan on reading all day?"

I did . . . now I can't even think straight.

"My love?" he chuckles.

"Yes?"

One inch at a time, I raise my eyes to meet his. He swipes his tongue over his lips, sending a tidal wave of butterflies fluttering in my stomach.

"I know that look." He plucks my book from my hands, placing it on a nearby table.

"What look?" I play innocent, but deep down, I know I have a *look*.

"You want me to say it?" His tone turns darker and hungry.

"Say what?" My voice softens as I shift off the bed and stand before him.

He feathers his nose across mine. Our lips touch, but we don't make full contact.

"On your knees, Brightheart," he orders.

I take his mouth against mine, kissing him desperately. Another adventure Ryne and I have taken full advantage of is exploring one another's bodies. Discovering what we like, finding out how to make one another moan and plead for more. Apparently, I like when he takes control, and fuck, he does it well.

He wraps his hand around my throat, urging me closer, and he groans when my tongue parts his lips.

"Is that what you want? Me on my knees?" I ask while running my hands up his body, taking his shirt with me.

"Yes," he moans before tossing his shirt across the room.

My hands slide under his joggers, pulling on them until they drop around his ankles. A gentle chuckle rolls off my tongue when I notice he's not wearing any boxers, like he had this planned from the start.

I take his cock in my hand and start to stroke him. "How's this?" I ask.

He pulls me against him again, gently squeezing my neck and kissing me with pure desire. We become a bubble of incoherent moans and whispers in moments. When I pull away, he moves forward to continue, but I trail my lips down his chest instead.

"Fuck, Ayra," he mutters.

I settle on my knees, still running my hand over his cock. Looking up at him, I kiss his length, starting from the base and stopping at the tip.

He weaves his fingers into my hair, holding it back in his fists.

Taking my time, I wrap my lips around him, taking him inch by inch. Once he's fully in my mouth, my eyes start to water.

"That's my girl." He thumbs the tears from my eyes as I flick my tongue around him.

His eyes flutter closed, and a groan vibrates from his core.

I glide my mouth from his shaft just before the tip, sucking and moaning.

I love how he reacts to me, how his body craves me, and never seems to stop. I would never have thought I'd have this kind of effect on a man, but I'm so glad it's Ryne.

Warmth spreads through me, trickling down to my clit, and he knows it. My movements become less teasing and more sensual. My eyes start to close, but he catches me in time.

"Look at me when I fuck your mouth." He thrusts his cock into my mouth, making me gag. Pulling back, he growls as I continue to suck.

"Such pretty eyes." He hums while drying the tears that remain near my eyelids. "You should see how good you look. How perfect your lips fit around me. You're a fucking goddess."

He thrusts one more time before withdrawing completely. "Get on the bed," he orders, and his eyes fade to a darker shade of green.

Backing away, I untie my lounge shorts and step out of

them. Ryne's eyes devour me, practically leaving burn marks along my bare skin.

I toss my baggy shirt aside, exposing my bare chest to the chill in the air. Ryne scoops me into his arms, and a needy moan escapes when he kisses me. I'll never get used to the tingle he leaves on my body from his touch.

I wrap my legs around his waist, but when my back hits the plush comforter, he pulls away. His chest heaves up and down, matching my own. He hooks his thumbs around the waistband of my panties, and I lift my hips so he can glide them over my legs. He throws them across the room.

"Oh shit, one second."

I tilt my head and notice we left the door open, which usually wouldn't be a problem, but we have a pair of nosey familiars on our hands.

"*Aerosera.*" With a gust of air, he pushes the door closed, and just as quickly as his gaze left, it returns, warming me with a single look.

Keeping eye contact, he kisses my stomach while feathering his fingers along the underside of my thighs. He lays on his chest, pulling my legs over his shoulders in the process.

"You're so gorgeous," he mumbles as he kisses my inner thigh.

His breath is hot and rapid. I gasp when his thumb hovers over my swollen clit. His mouth curls, knowing he's taking an agonizingly painful amount of time. The second I open my mouth, his lips envelop my pussy, and my back arches.

"*Yes*, Ryne." My moan heightens when he sucks my clit, slowly pulling back just to return with his tongue.

His eyes close, his groan vibrating into me. A gentle grin spreads across my face, and my core tightens with each caress of his tongue.

"Don't stop," I plead.

He adds his thumb to the fray, moving it in time with his tongue. I grind against his face, needing more, needing him to get me across the finish line before the feeling that boils inside bubbles over.

He smiles against me and shakes his head, pinning my hips down with nothing but his arms. "Not yet, Brightheart."

He leaves a longing, butterfly-inducing kiss against my folds before settling on his knees.

I sit up and glance at his lips. He places his hand under my chin, tilting my head upward. "I fucking love you," he whispers against me before devouring my mouth with his.

Ryne guides me back against the bed, positioning himself between my legs. His fingertips rest on my abdomen, and I return the favor.

We both whisper, "*Lustiva Consetium.*"

The tips of my fingers heat up as his fingers warm against my skin.

There is no doubt in this world or any other that I *love* Ryne Gwydion. If I had never met him, I would still be striving for the absolute best, running myself dry. I wouldn't be *here* with him, and I wouldn't be *this* happy. I would have driven myself off the cliff I was teetering on, falling and crumbling until I was past the point of saving. When I look into his eyes, I know he loves me. I hope he knows just how much I love him.

"I love you," I whisper.

He brushes his knuckles along my cheek, grinning that damn grin of his.

"I know, Brightheart, I know." He retakes my lips, slowly pressing his cock inside me.

My walls contract around him, and the contact is enough to make me finish before we get started. He kisses the underside of my jaw as he backs up, only to press into me again. We become a tangle of skin and desperation. I wrap my left leg around his waist, allowing him to go deeper, and he groans, stirring more need inside me.

"Harder," I mutter.

Smirking down at me, he increases his pace, diving and pressing into me at the right moments. My muscles tighten, and my vision becomes hazy as I'm brought closer to the edge.

"Ryne," I cry.

He presses his forehead against mine and places his hand over my throat.

"Come for me, Ayra," he urges.

My head tilts back as he fucks me harder. He pulls me against him, lifting my hips off the bed.

"Ryne—oh fuck!"

Blinding supernovas fill my eyes as he hits my G-spot. My muscles spasm before they relax, and a wave of hot chills rolls through my body.

Ryne kisses me before cursing against my lips.

"Give me everything." I pull on his lower lip with mine. "Mark me as yours."

He growls before kissing me furiously.

"You're already mine, Brightheart. You were mine since day one," he grunts, slamming into me and whirling my senses. His cheeks flush red, his jaw clenches, and his eyes darken. "Fuck," he curses loudly as his back tenses under my hands.

His cock flexes as he fills me, and a deep warmth covers every inch of me.

We're both completely out of breath when he collapses next to me. I jolt as rolling thunder booms in the sky. With a chuckle, Ryne pulls me against his chest. I roll on my side and face him. His gaze is content and loving.

"Do you think we'll always end up together? No matter the dimension, realm, or time? Are we written in the stars?" I ask out of the blue.

"If we're not, we'll write our names ourselves." He grins and runs his hands through my hair. "We are meant to be no matter what the universe may say."

I release a deep sigh, my eyelids growing heavy. "Never let me go," I whisper as I nuzzle into his chest.

He wraps his arms around me, securing me in this moment forever.

"Never."

Ryne
54

I never want to leave this bed. I would watch Ayra sleep forever if I could, but I have a more important task at hand. Slipping away, careful not to wake her, I grab my shirt that I threw across the room. I dress as swiftly and as quietly as I can, but thunder booms and lightning strikes right outside the window, causing Ayra to stir in her sleep. Tiptoeing over to her, I place the quilt over her shoulder.

"I'll be right back, my love," I whisper, hoping she's still asleep.

When she doesn't respond, I leave the room, careful to close the door with a muffled click. I take the stairs down to the first floor and smile at the sight of Marley drenched in the middle of the foyer.

"What took you so long?" she asks in a hushed, irritated tone.

"You don't want to know." My confession makes her face contort.

"Absolutely disgusting. I get the feeling you two will never grow tired of one another," she says as I grab my cloak.

"Gods, I hope not," I tease her as I open the front door, letting the rain soak the floor.

"You're lucky I like you, Ryne," she threatens as she steps back outside.

"Oh, trust me. I know."

The rain really put a damper on my plan. I recruited Marley to help me with a secret mission, and she accepted without a second thought. The time I've spent with Ayra has been the best of my life. I can't imagine living without her, and knowing she feels the same settled the decision. I'm not sure how she'll react. She might punch me or call me stupid. Or she'll kiss me until our lips swell, and she'll stay in my arms until the chill sets in our bones. Either way, this is something I have to do.

"Did you bring the supplies?" I ask Marley as we step into the clearing.

"All set up and ready to go." Marley gives me a thumbs-up.

"How are you and Arlin?" The mention of his name makes her cheeks turn rosy.

"We're good, and that's all I'll say. I don't kiss and tell, unlike you two." She points her finger at me playfully.

"Does Ayra tell you what we do? I'm surprised. I thought our trip to the library was our little sec—"

Marley shushes me before I can continue. "Don't say another word!" She covers her ears and hums.

"Okay, missy. Let's get started." I clasp my hands together as we reach the part of the clearing that will serve as the beginning of the next chapter with Ayra.

Fairy lights weave around soaked tree branches, emitting soft light. The moons rise as the rain starts to slow down. Traces of storm clouds hang low in the sky, so I'll have to do this quickly. Knowing Ayra, she's bound to wake up any moment now.

"Okay, I think we're ready." I turn to Marley as she beams. "It's showtime."

"Kiki, stop." I shift away from the furry paw that won't stop hitting my face.

I roll over to the side, patting the bed for Ryne, and my eyes open when I realize he's not there. "Where did he go?" I ask my familiar, who is most likely only bothering me because she's hungry.

Sitting up, I scan the dark room. The rain stopped, but the clouds are hanging low, hinting that another storm is on the way.

"Where in the hells did you go?" I whisper to myself.

It's not late in the evening. He could have gone downstairs for a snack. I get out of bed and toss one of his stray long-sleeved sweaters on and a pair of my loose-fitting shorts. Chills run up my spine as I walk across the cold floor. It's empty in the hallway, so I head down the stairs.

"Ryne?" I call out but I'm met with silence.

When I step off the staircase, I walk toward the kitchen. A blinding, fiery blast fills my vision, followed by an ear-shattering explosion. An invisible force pushes me backward, and my back slams against the floor.

"What the fuck?" I curse, my muscles aching and my back scratched raw from the aged hardwood flooring.

Ryne.

Where the *fuck* is Ryne!?

I scramble to my feet, adrenaline rushing through my veins, urging me to run harder, faster. I barrel out the back door, straight toward the remnants of the explosion. The forest tree line crackles in flames, slowly growing and spreading. I raise my hands and push an unearthly chill at the fire, extinguishing it immediately. My legs carry me past the burned trees and ground. Everything becomes a blur as I scan my surroundings.

"Ryne!?" My throat turns raw from screaming. "Ryne!?" I stumble to a stop when I enter a clearing. "What the fuck is going on?" I shoot my confusion at Marley, who smiles innocently and sways back and forth.

"Long time no see," she chimes as Zachii pops out of her messy bun.

The foliage around her is also burned. The trees are singed to a crisp.

"Damn, you're fast."

I spin around and face Ryne. Our chests are both heaving as we attempt to catch our breath.

"What is happening?" I ask with both rage and panic.

Ryne looks over my shoulder at Marley. "Help me out here?"

Marley appears behind me in an instant, covering my eyes with her hands.

"Marley—" I fight against her, but she keeps up with my flailing, making sure to keep my eyes closed.

"Just stay still," she giggles.

"I swear, if someone doesn't tell me what's going on, I'm going to—"

Marley spins me around and removes her hands from my face.

"Kill you . . ." I mutter under my breath, my anger disappearing the second Ryne drops to his knee. "What are you doing?" I whisper in disbelief.

"The explosion wasn't part of the plan. I guess there's a reason they say to be careful with fireworks." He chuckles.

Maren crawls out of Ryne's shirt pocket with a ring in his mouth. He drops it in Ryne's hand and wiggles his pink nose at me. "These last few months with you have been a dream, Ayra. One I don't want to wake up from. I know our lives are going to look different in a few months, with you starting at Velar University and me exploring the realms. What I do know is that we won't change. The universe made us for one another, and I'll be forever grateful. You tell me time and time again that I changed your life, but I don't think you know that you also changed mine. Everyone back at Traquore thought I wouldn't amount to anything, and that mentality seeped in, and I accepted it. Because of you, I know that isn't true. I can make a difference across the realms, just as I know you will."

The thunder from the impending storm booms in the sky, and drizzle starts to trickle from the swollen clouds.

"I need you, Ayra. I want you for as long as you'll have me." Ryne's cheeks flush red as he offers me a silver ring with intricate leaf designs. Small midnight-blue gems lay delicately along the band. "You said to make you mine."

I chuckle, tears running down my cheeks.

"I know I'm nothing more than a carefree wizard, but I will love you far longer than time may allow us. I will love you in every life we live, and I will always find you. Ayra Brightheart, will you bind your soul to mine?"

I drop to my knees in front of him, sobbing. "You scared the shit out of me, you know that?"

We both laugh, and I rest my forehead against him as we brush our noses over one another.

"You're willing to put up with me forever?"

His eyes shimmer, and the ember flecks swirling around his irises lighten.

"And some," he whispers.

I curl my hands in his hair and smile against his lips. "Yes, Ryne. I will marry you in this life and the next—"

He kisses me abruptly, cleaving my sentence.

"And the next." I chuckle between our kisses. "And the next."

The rain returns, soaking us in a matter of moments. Ryne and I stay locked in each other's gazes, knees in the mud, not caring about the rain or the threat of lightning.

"You guys are cute and all, but I'm headed back to the cottage," Marley states as she jogs out of the clearing.

"I guess this means we'll have to go to those interviews now," I say with another laugh, knowing the crowd will see the ring on my finger the moment I walk through Fraydora's doors for the next annual games.

"Something tells me we'll crush it." Ryne's smile melts all doubt and anxiety away, just like it always does. "We'll give them a show."

"Fireworks?" I ask with a knowing smirk.

"Fireworks."

Ten Months Later

"Kiki, stay close. The last thing I need is for you to venture off today," I whisper against her head before giving her a final scratch.

Kiki gives me a meow of excitement in response, and the carriage door opens by itself, prompting me to step out. The only reason I'm doing this is because I'll get to see Ryne for the first time since last month. I started to further my education at Velar Academy, focusing on elemental magic. Ryne has been touring the mountains in Scotland, more specifically, the range outside his, his mother's, and now my favorite café. When he first brought me there, I was transfixed. Magic hummed in the air and settled in my veins. That mountain range has been explored, but both Ryne and I agreed that something must have been missed. So, he's been hiking the trail with Maren and camping there at night.

I still live in the cottage, and I travel back and forth

between home and the academy. Once Ryne is done with his research, we'll see one another more. I'm beyond ready to see him today. I want to hold him in my arms, kiss every inch of his face and body, and breathe in his familiar scent. I couldn't figure out why Ryne smelled like my magic until I started at Velar. According to scholars, rare instances of magic smelling like your soulmate occur. It doesn't happen to everyone, but it's aimed to help those two souls reconnect. The moment I discovered that information, I sent Ryne a letter, and we both couldn't believe it. To think we were always meant to find one another is unbelievable.

Ryne is my person, my other half, and knowing I am his makes my heart swell. But first, I have an unknown castle that requires my attention.

This year's games are being held at Traquore. I've never been here. Ryne has told me a little bit about this academy, but it's more menacing in person. The entire infrastructure is volcanic stone, Gothic tower points, and iron fences with pointed tips. There are no wildflowers, only precisely trimmed hedges. A few ravens squawk and perch themselves on the roof, adding to the ominous atmosphere.

I understand why Ryne was so enchanted by Fraydora's grounds. I can't imagine waking up in a place like this every day, walking through dark corridors only lit by torches, and seeing little to no sunlight or lively creatures. I don't blame Ryne for wanting to leave Traquore as fast as he could. I want to hightail it out of here, and I just got here.

Kiki stays by my side, although I feel her attention gravitating toward the crows as they chatter above us. The looming doors open, and my eyes take a moment to adjust to the darkness as I step inside. There's a raging fire within a hearth in the back center of the room, and above the fireplace is the head of an elder elk. His antlers are grand, weaving and arching to points. His eyes are pitch black, and the flames reflect in them. I wonder if the students here name this creature. And if they do, how many names does he have? If I were to name him, his name would be Hank. No questions asked.

Dark gray cobblestone is under my feet, straight from the medieval era, and a few lingering wizards catch sight of me and start to whisper. The participating witches arrived a couple of days ago. The same rules from last year will be applied to this year, and I can't wait to see what follows.

I glance around the room, Ryne said he would be here by the time I got here . . . where in the underworld is he?

My robes swirl around me as I begin to pace. Kiki follows me, keeping in step and being on her best behavior, which I am beyond thankful for. My fingers arch and weave in the air, stretching like I'm preparing for battle.

I come to a halt as a rush of warmth I've missed dearly pebbles up and down my spine. When I turn around, we lock eyes, and a wide smile plasters on my face.

Not caring about the crowd, I run toward Ryne and crash into his arms. He releases an *oof* and squeezes me as I embrace him.

"Fuck, I missed you," he murmurs in my ear.

I weave my fingers into the hair at the base of his neck, gently pulling. "You have no idea how much I've missed you," I whisper.

We both pull back, and my nose brushes against his.

He tilts his lips upward, giving me a loving grin. "Guess what," he says.

"What?" I ask, sounding curious.

"You won't be going home alone tonight. My research is done, and you won't believe what I discover—"

I kiss him before he can finish his sentence. To some, a month isn't a lot of time. The old Ayra would have thought that thirty sunrises and sets didn't mean a lot, but damn, this was rough. I grew used to being around Ryne, falling asleep beside him, and waking up in his arms. He'll never understand how much I missed him.

Our lips part, and warm goose bumps spread over my shoulder blades. Giddiness fills my core, and I smile widely as I look at him. "I can't wait to hear about it."

Kiki meows, greeting Ryne, but we both know who she's looking for. Maren pops out of Ryne's pocket, his black eyes lighting up at the sight of me, but his ears arch in response to another meow from the cat at our feet. Without a care in the world, Maren climbs down Ryne's body and clings to Kiki's neck. The two of them begin to chatter. Kiki walks in circles, like she's trying to make eye contact with Maren, but he's too busy rolling in her fur.

"Those two are such an unlikely pair of best friends," Ryne laughs.

"Kind of like us?" I add in with a knowing smile.

Scooping me back into his arms, Ryne spins me around, and I chuckle as my stomach flutters from the acceleration. When he stops, I kiss him with nothing but love and passion.

Our touches never cease to surprise me. One kiss, one brush or graze, and I'm left lightheaded. My heart races, and my body feels ten times lighter. Don't get me started on what happens when our touch gets heated; that's the last thing I need happening right now.

"Okay, missy." Ryne pulls away, and I whimper in disappointment.

He places me back on my feet, holding on to me to ensure I'm stable and not dizzy from the spinning and his kiss.

"Would you like a tour of this dreadful place?" he asks with an excited grin, and I more than happily oblige.

"That would be wonderful."

I'm a big fan of dark colors, but damn, this place needs a splash of bright color. I hope Traquore keeps an eye on their wizards because I wouldn't be surprised if half of them weren't depressed.

Ryne lights up the corridors. Hells, he's the only light within these halls. I lean against his arm, listening to his voice and relishing his presence.

"Do you see that?" He points down the hall. "That is the window I shattered with a Disk of Unyielding."

"You destroyed the only aspect of color in this place?" I tease.

Ryne pushes against me, and I end up with my chest against his. His hands rest on my lower back, and he looks down at me with nothing but love in his eyes.

"You light up the darkness. I wonder how my life would have differed if I had known you prior to the games. Maybe I would have aced all my classes."

"Probably not," I chuckle under my breath.

He tickles me in response, starting at my hips and moving toward my stomach. I squirm under his touch, my chuckling turning to desperate laughter in a matter of seconds.

"Ryne—please!" I say, out of breath, but he doesn't relent.

"Oh, and if I heard that laugh. Don't get me started," he murmurs in my ear before sucking my lobe. "Maybe I'll hear you scream my name another way before we leave—"

"Ryne?" A familiar voice interrupts us, accompanied by a high-pitched squawk and a flutter of wings.

Ryne and I look down the corridor at the same time, and the sight leaves me baffled.

"Machiis?" Ryne starts before walking toward him. "What are you doing here?" he asks before pulling him into a hug.

I look up at the miniature hawk-like creature, then back down at Kiki, unsure what to do with myself.

Ryne and Machiis start to chat, and I decide to join them because if Machiis is who he was months ago, his familiar would be nowhere near him, and he did promise that he would work on himself. He was cruel at Fraydora, but nowhere near as malicious as Cadie, and he deserves a second chance.

His dark eyes meet mine, and he smiles at the sight of me. "Ms. Brightheart."

My body doesn't respond how I would have expected it to. Prior to today, my muscles would tense and ready themselves to go on the defensive. Needle-like goose bumps would poke my skin, and I would generally feel cold. But not today.

"You look well," I say with a genuine smile.

And he does. His complexion is clear, his hair is neat and less unruly, and his irises are no longer dull. Whatever he did during these last few months saved him. I'd be willing to bet that this was the Machiis Ryne grew to adore.

"The Alps will do that to you," he says while resting his hand on the back of his neck. "Took a page out of this one's book." He points to Ryne. "I took the last couple of months to travel and self-reflect."

"And what did you discover?" Ryne asks.

"I was a total prick."

Ryne and I both chuckle at his realization.

"Granted, you're always a prick."

Machiis punches Ryne in the arm, and I laugh harder.

"Shut it, Gwydion."

I observe the two of them, happy that Ryne has his old friend back.

The gem in my ring glistens, and Machiis stops chuckling. "Is that what I think it is?"

He steps forward. I look into his eyes and smile when I notice he's grinning. "May I?" he asks.

I give him my hand, and he examines the ring, tilting it and watching the gem catch the light. I side-eye Ryne with an amused expression.

"Nice job, Gwydion," he praises Ryne for his choice of jewelry.

"Thank you, it belonged to my mother."

"Whom I have yet to meet," I add, sounding slightly irritated.

"Oh, they're going to adore you," Machiis tells me.

"They will," Ryne affirms. "They're returning this month to meet Ayra if you want to stop by and say hi to them."

"I would love nothing more, but first—" Machiis takes my hand in his and guides me down the hall. "Ms. Brightheart has a speech to provide."

"How could I forget?" I sigh and roll my eyes.

Kiki scampers along by my side with Maren riding her back like a horse. Ryne catches up, and with a loving look, he takes my other hand and squeezes it in reassurance.

Summoning all my confidence, I let Machiis and Ryne lead the way to the Grand Hall. Before I'm ready, we arrive, and I'm standing to the side as Headmaster Borrick and Headmistress Illana finish their welcome speeches.

"It is my utmost pleasure to introduce the winner from last

year's games, Ms. Ayra Brightheart." Illana's voice is sweet, reminding me of all the years I relied on her guidance.

I step on the stage, and clapping follows. I walk into her arms and hug her. Closing my eyes, I smile and sigh out of nerves. Illana places her hands on my shoulders and holds me at arm's length. She glances down at my finger and smiles wider.

"I see we have a lot to catch up on," she whispers before nodding toward the podium.

"We do," I say before she walks away.

I look toward Borrick, and he offers me an approving nod. I bow my head before looking out into the crowd.

A sea of witches and wizards are paired off and ready for the first game. I look at each of them, recognizing the hum of excitement in the air. They have no idea what challenges lie ahead, but that doesn't deter them. They're ready, just like when I was in position last year.

"Hello, everyone," I start, trying to settle the remnants of my nerves. "My name is Ayra Brightheart, and as you may know, I was the victor of The Academy Games last year. I've been where you are, so I won't sugarcoat it. You will change over this next week. The person you once knew will evolve and shape into someone else entirely. Each game will force you to think beyond what you're used to. It's important to be ready to adapt to the challenges and expect the unexpected."

Scanning the crowd, I notice that each pair of eyes holds a glimmer of anticipation. I wonder how the pairing ceremony went and if anyone reacted the way I did when Ryne and I were paired together. To think I once dreaded his company. The thought makes me laugh to myself.

"And trust me on this: listen to the voice, or voices, inside your head. They may sometimes be annoying, but they only want to help you."

My voices have yet to return, and while I can say that I don't miss them, I do rather like the nickname they bestowed upon me.

Interesting witch.

I glance over at Ryne, and with a smile, I finish my speech. "And remember, be *interesting* and have fun."

AFTERWORD

I'm sure it's pretty clear that I'm a raging perfectionist, just like Ayra. I was raised to believe that if I made a mistake, I was a failure. I was afraid that if I failed, I would be a disappointment.

I still have this belief system, but I'm aware of it and I'm trying to rewire my brain. It's taking a lot of work, and some days are better than others but I'm trying my best, and in the end that's all I can do.

Perfection doesn't exist, Ryne said so himself: "I wish she knew that no matter how hard she tries, she'll never reach the goal she's working toward. Not because she's not brilliant or motivated enough but because with each win she obtains, her standards get higher, at a certain point the air becomes thin, and she won't be able to breathe anymore. The weight of perfection will crush her."

Don't let the weight of perfection crush you. And don't forget, it's okay to fuck up. It's okay to throw your hands in the air and yell "Fuck it!" And then let it go.

Be strong my fellow perfectionists, and let's raise chaos.

Acknowledgments

To my husband, Anthony, thank you for always supporting me. I wouldn't be where I am today without you.

To my family, I'm sorry if I get annoying when I talk about my books a lot. Thank you for putting up with it and for supporting me.

To my fellow perfectionists, I see you, and if you need permission to let go, here it is.

My Distracted Inklings, thank you for all your support. I'm so happy and proud to be a part of this community.

The ladies of the Writer's Guild, I'm so glad we all met and that we have one another for support. I would be lost without our friendship and banter. I can't wait to see you all again soon!

To a certain author project that failed early last year. Not every step back is a step back. The Academy Games wouldn't be what it is today without you.

And last but not least, a big thank you to my readers. Your words of kindness and support mean the world to me. I write to share the worlds in my head, and I hope you enjoy them.

About the Author

Amber Paige is an indie author focusing on fluffy, HEA's, and spicy novels. She's a big mood reader and writer, but once something captures her attention, she hyper-focuses on it. She mainly writes fiction, romance, and fantasy but isn't afraid to drive into another genre if it calls to her. She writes from her laptop, either in bed or on the couch, with a cat by her side. When she's not overanalyzing commas or letting her imposter syndrome get the best of her, you can find her playing video games, watching too much TV, reading, writing, or hanging out with her husband and three cats.

Join my News Letter
Amber Paige's Merch Store

Symbol of Hope

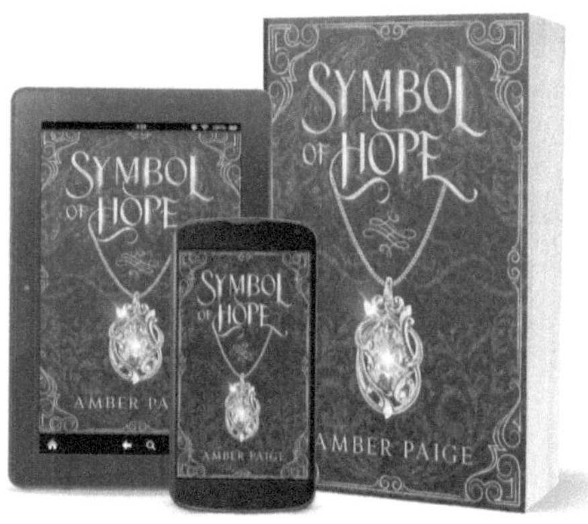

I didn't know my true identity until I was twelve. When the King of Altana arrived and told me I was his daughter.

In one day, my life was flipped upside down, twisted and formed into a tangled ball. Traumatic doesn't even begin to describe that moment in time.

The one thing I look back on is my best friend and the promise he made me. Adrian gifted me a necklace, vowing he would rescue me one day when we're older. Hope is a funny thing, I carried it around for years. Waiting for the day my knight in shining armor would whisk me away.

That's not how life works though.

Ten years pass. I've accepted my destiny to become the first female heir crowned to rule Altana. Sure, my stepmother and stepsister hate me. But who doesn't have daily challenges? My life settles into place, that is until the universe turns my world upside down again.

A horrific attack, a proposition to wed, a dashing Prince and his mysterious bodyguard now stroll the castle halls. The past keeps haunting me, along with old and new trauma.

Will I ever see my mother and best friend again? Will my world ever stop crumbling under my

feet?

Adventure, romance, and mystery knocks on my door.

Should I answer the call?

Available on Amazon and Kindle Unlimited.

ALSO BY AMBER PAIGE

Forever Crushed (The Forever Series: 1)

Long- term crushes are hard...

Gwen Roman has spent most of her life being overlooked. It never really bothered her all that much. Until she sees Ash Waylen, the guy she's had a crush on since the tenth grade. The moment he acknowledges her presence and says her name, that damn crush weaves its way back into her heart. So much for a stellar GPA this semester.

After his girlfriend shattered his trust and broke his heart, Ash Waylen plans to spend his junior year of college nursing his wounds and avoiding the opposite sex. The last thing he expects is to run into

Gwen Roman and have her tugging on heartstrings he thought his ex-girlfriend took when he broke up with her.

Gwen was always the shy girl who followed Chrissy and Zack Willows around in high school, her head always buried in a book. She never caught his attention before, but this time, it's different.

In an act of self-preservation, Ash averts his gaze knowing only trouble will follow him if he pursues the one thing he wants.

While Ash tries to resist temptation, Gwen might just throw caution to the wind and go after what she wants for the first time in her life.

Available on Amazon and Kindle Unlimited.